May 2023

DEVIL'S KISS

Happy reading!

Michelle
Bennington

DEVIL'S KISS

A SMALL BATCH MYSTERY

MICHELLE BENNINGTON

LEVEL
BEST BOOKS

First published by Level Best Books 2022

This novel is entirely a work of fiction. The names, characters and incidents portrayed in it are the work of the author's imagination. Any resemblance to actual persons, living or dead, events or localities is entirely coincidental.

Michelle Bennington asserts the moral right to be identified as the author of this work.

Author Photo Credit: Michelle Bennington

First edition

ISBN: 978-1-68512-112-9

Cover art by Level Best Designs

This book was professionally typeset on Reedsy.
Find out more at reedsy.com

To Brack, my moon and stars. My hero. Your support has been my bedrock in this and in all things. I love you always.

Chapter One

Sweaty, tired, and mad as a wasp, I flopped down in my favorite booth along the back wall of Tangled Up in Brew. I opened my laptop and furiously typed my official resignation from the English Department at the University of the Bluegrass.

I explained, in the most professional language, they could take their job and shove it. In short, I could no longer afford to work for the university. I'd served two years as an adjunct instructor with no prospect of full-time employment or benefits. In the past year, a third of my classes had been canceled, reducing my pay. Yet, in spite of this, the department expected me to operate like a full-time instructor.

Today had been the final blow. I'd had to attend a mandatory faculty meeting in preparation for the fall semester. However, my parking permit had expired. Since I hadn't been paid yet, I swallowed my twenty-seven-year-old pride and borrowed money from my grandma to renew the permit. I was too late and my sweet lime green Ford Fiesta had been towed away.

I sucked down one pint of Guinness and ordered another. In spite of my extra twenty pounds of flesh, I stuffed down my anger with chunks of gooey chocolate cake. I stabbed the keys, Sincerely, Rook Campbell.

My ex-husband, Porter Campbell, known as "Cam," slid into the seat across from me with a bottle of Kentucky Spice, a locally-crafted citrus-ginger soda. He pressed his back against the wall and stretched his legs along the seat. We'd been divorced for eighteen months after a five-year marriage.

My jaw fell open. The last time I'd seen Cam, he was shaggy, thin, and pale, but he'd made a miraculous transformation in the past few months. I snapped my mouth shut. Mercy, he looked good—the deep gray eyes and square jaw were the same. But now he had tan skin, sandy blond hair, close-cropped and highlighted, and muscles. He even smelled better, spicy and sweet like vanilla chai. Something stirred, as the Victorians would say, in my "crinkum-crankum." I was annoyed with him for still having an effect on me and annoyed with myself for my own weakness. I guessed my crinkum was a lot more crankum than it used to be.

I hit "send" on my resignation letter and shut the laptop.

"Hey, Rook." He sipped from his soda. He looked like a magazine model, as if he should be perched on a mountain range, staring at a sunrise. His gaze floated over me. "Lookin' good."

Yeah, right. After lugging my computer bag filled with a laptop and books up Nyquist Street in the intense August heat, I more likely looked and smelled like a wet dog. Self-consciously, I ran my finger under my eyes, coming away with evidence of smudged eyeliner. Perfect.

He tapped the side of his mouth. "Enjoying the cake?" His lips edged into a smile.

I wiped my mouth. Chocolate sauce. "You're looking pretty good yourself."

"Been working out." He sneered playfully and curled his arms like a pro-wrestler, his biceps bulging from under his tight-fitting T-shirt. "Been going to Planet Fitness with Jimmy."

"I see that. How is Jimmy? Haven't seen him in a long time."

"Good. Same as ever."

"He still single?"

"Of course." He sipped his drink. "Married to the job."

I glanced at Jacie, Cam's current flame and a part of why we divorced. She watched us intently from behind the bar. A diamond glinted on her left hand as she dried glasses. She was beach bunny bright with ringlets of shining blonde hair, a gym-sculpted body, tanned skin, and perfectly applied makeup. She was universally pretty. I envied her completely but refused to show it. I didn't want to be the sort of girl who fought over a man—however much it hurt to be the rejected one.

My insecurity mounting, I pulled the clip out of my hair, running my fingers through it. "So, you're engaged now?" Grabbing a chunk of hair, I studied the dark strands for dead ends. There were plenty. I needed a trim. I twisted and reclipped my hair into a messy ponytail.

He picked at the label on the bottle and shrugged one shoulder. "Yeah, I guess."

I chuckled. "You guess? You either are or you're not. The block of ice on her finger says you are. When were you going to tell me?"

Confusion mottled his features. He didn't owe me any explanations, but we'd split mostly amicably and were still friends. Our bond hadn't magically disappeared when we signed the divorce papers. Friends told each other when they were getting married.

"I wasn't sure how to handle telling you. I didn't think you'd want to know."

I choked down the rising emotions with Guinness as I bounced my leg under the table. I hadn't expected this reaction from myself. "Well... Congratulations." I hoped rather than believed I sounded sincere. "Anyway... " My skin felt too tight on my bones.

He glanced around the bar. "Why'd you want to see me?"

I sighed. *Here we go. Party time.* "I'm out of work."

"Oh. Wow." He frowned. "What happened? I thought you were teaching..."

I told him my situation. "I quit. Today." I rubbed my face, the dried sweat gritty against my hand.

"Without having another job in place first?"

His accusatory tone ratcheted my tension and my shame. We were gearing up for a fight.

"I knooooow." I traced my finger over a set of initials carved into the table. "I don't need lectures." I wondered if DM + BB were still together.

"I'm not—"

"Cam, I'm bone-tired of sacrificing so much for nothing, and being broke all the time. Meanwhile, my student loans keep compounding interest. My payments don't even touch the interest, forget about the principal. I've been applying for full-time teaching work for over a year and haven't received a single interview."

He nodded, peeling the paper from his bottle. "What about teaching high school?"

"It's not that easy. Kentucky schools require degrees in teaching, not only English, unless I substitute, but that's unstable work, too." My voice reached a fevered pitch. "And I can't go back to school, even if I wanted to—which I don't—because I can't afford to take out more loans."

His brows arched.

"I'm sorry." I stared into my Guinness. "I don't mean to take it out on you. I'm just…" Defeated, I propped my face in my hands and sighed. "Frustrated." And ashamed.

He wadded the piece of label he'd pulled off the bottle and flicked it at Jacie behind the bar. "Park illegally again?"

"Kind of. My tag was one day expired. I borrowed money from Prim to take care of it, but the permit office opens late and closes early in the summer." I rolled my eyes and dropped my head to the table.

"That stinks."

"I feel like such a failure." I groaned. "I've worked so hard…"

"Hey, look at me."

I lifted my face, resting my chin on my folded arms.

He put his hand on my arm. "You'll find a job soon. Something you love. You're super smart, and talented. It's only a matter of time."

I sat back, pulling away as if repelled by niceness. If he continued, I'd start crying. Which was unacceptable. Borrowing money from Cam would make life with myself difficult enough without thinking I'd extracted the money with tears.

"Anyway," I sighed. "I hoped you might…" I fiddled with the napkin in my lap, folding it over and over. "Maybe if you could lend me a little money. Just until…" I shrugged.

"How much?"

"I need only a little to get me through. Until I find another job. I'll pay you back. I hate to ask, but I didn't have anywhere else to go and I can't ask Prim again."

4

"Rook. How much do you need?"

I blinked. He wasn't fighting me. I'd expected cursing and dredging up past insults and hurts. "Um, at least three, four hundred, but whatever you can spare…"

"Hold on." He patted my hand and scooted out of the booth.

Jacie hovered nearby, sweeping. She stopped to watch him walk through the swinging door leading to the kitchen and office.

Cam soon returned with a thick envelope and threw it on the table.

Jacie slowed her sweeping, craning her neck to watch us.

A rush of shame and guilt burned my cheeks as I slipped the envelope into my computer bag without counting it. "Really? Just like that?"

He tucked his hands into his pockets and rocked back on his heels. "I know what it cost you to come here and ask. You paid more in pride than what's in that envelope."

I couldn't look at him. "Thank you. I'll pay you back as soon as I get a new job. It may take a while…" I bit into my bottom lip to quell the surging emotions.

"I know you're good for it. I'll get it when I get it."

Jacie glared at us, sweeping with short, angry strokes.

I packed my stuff. "I hate to beg and run, but it looks like storm Jacie is brewing." I managed a faint smile, polished off the last of my Guinness, and scooted out of the booth.

He shrugged one shoulder. "She'll be all right."

"I need to go."

"And don't worry about the cake and beer. It's on the house."

"Thank you," I whispered, squeezing his arm. Cam was solid as brick.

"Hey, uh…" He rubbed the back of his neck. "If you need work…you know, only temporary…you can work here. I always need help Thursday through Saturday."

My head swimming in Guinness, I laughed loudly, causing people to look at us. "Are you high?"

"I'm only saying…" He tucked his thumbs in his back pockets and shrugged.

"Hm…Let me see…" I pretended to think. "The ex-wife and the fiancée working in the same bar. Sounds like you're trying to start your own reality show."

He laughed. "Jacie could deal with it for a little while. It wouldn't be forever. Think about it."

"Thanks for the offer, but I'm going to decline. For everyone's safety and sanity." I pulled my phone from my purse. "Now, I'm going outside to call an Uber and go get my car."

"You want me to take you?"

I glanced at Jacie. "I'm not sure that's such a great idea."

He waved away my comment. "C'mon. You're not paying for an Uber. Let's go so I can get back before the dinner rush." He pulled his keys out of his pocket and led the way through the back of the bar. "Hey, Jacie, I'll be back in a bit. I'm taking Rook to get her car."

Her mouth dropped open, her blue eyes shooting daggers.

I followed him out the back door to the alley to his dusty, silver double cab pickup. He opened the door for me. In spite of being parked in the shade, the cab was stuffy and hot. Dust covered the dashboard and mud and hay littered the floorboard. I inhaled deep. I'd always loved the way his truck smelled like spicy cologne, leather, sweat, and earth.

Cam started the truck, and I rolled down my window while aiming the A/C vents in my direction. We meandered through downtown Lexington, a city named only months after the Revolutionary War began, back when Kentucky belonged to Virginia. Now glassy modern structures dotted the cityscape alongside the array of historical buildings in decaying neighborhoods. We talked about our families and our daily activities. For a moment, it felt like old times, when we were dating and in the early days of the marriage before everything fell apart. Regret, tempered with bittersweet nostalgia, settled over me.

He said, "What's wrong? You seem sad or something. If you're worried about the money…"

"Nothing's wrong. I'm fine." Cooled off, I rolled up my window.

"Rook," His voice was now soft and tender. "Look at me."

I hated being deep in my feelings and people wanting me to look at them.

It was the surest way to make me cry. I was already too much of a damsel in distress for my comfort.

"What?" I looked at him, discreetly jabbing my car key into the palm of my hand, using the pain to numb my feelings.

He guided the steering wheel with one wrist hooked on the wheel, the sun gilding his profile. "You take as long as you need. Seriously. I wish I could do more." He sighed and looked straight ahead. "I guess that's always been our story, huh?" He sighed. "Too little, too late."

I changed topics, rubbing the chill from my arms. "Are you excited about the wedding?"

"Sure. If it doesn't kill me first." He turned down the A/C. "She wants a huge wedding at a fancy church in Louisville and a honeymoon in Cancun."

"You hate the beach." Jealousy scratched at my ribs. He'd never taken me to the beach, though I'd begged to honeymoon in Florida. Clearly, he loved Jacie more than he'd ever loved me. That stung. I looked out my window. "Sounds expensive."

"It is. And we're still paying on the ring. But...she wanted a certain ring."

Guilt warred with my jealousy. "Dang it, Cam. I had no idea. I can't take your money now." Reaching in my bag, I extracted the envelope and lay it on the seat between us. "Here. Take it back." I shoved it toward him.

He pushed the envelope back at me. "No. You take it. I want you to have it."

"No, really. I wouldn't feel right about it."

He stopped at a red light by the Thai Café on Third Street. He tossed the envelope into my lap. "Rook. You're going to take the money. No arguments. Jacie'll waste it on wedding flowers and food that'll all be thrown away at the end of the day."

We rode in silence for the rest of the trip to the towing company. Of course, it was closed.

Chapter Two

Cam and I coasted along the gravel drive toward my grandma Prim's yellow farmhouse. I'd moved in with her at age eleven, after my mother's murder.

A white porch wrapped around the house, ending with a screened-in porch at the back. The house and an empty barn stood on two acres in Rothdale, a bedroom community about ten miles northwest of Lexington. Comprised now of mostly overgrown pastures, Prim and Pappy had once tended a flourishing farm. When Pappy passed away, Prim was forced to sell off all the livestock and let the land grow wild, except for a small personal garden.

The acid flared in my stomach. I didn't fear my grandma's anger as much as her disappointment. Since she was the one stable influence in my life, I'd rather be horse-whipped than upset her.

Cam's cell rang for the fifth time during our twenty-minute trip. "You'd better answer." I jumped out. "Jacie's going to be mad as a wet hen."

He silenced the phone and clapped it down on the dashboard. "I'll call her back in a minute."

"Thanks for the ride. And the money."

"Any time. Tell Prim I said 'hi' and I'll visit with her next time." He flashed a golden smile. "Tell her I sure do miss her cooking."

"Oh, lord." I rolled my eyes. "If I tell her that, she'll be in a flutter for the rest of the evening."

He winked at me and I shut the door.

Bryan Bishop's black '65 Mustang roared into the drive next door. We waved at each other and called out a greeting from our respective yards.

I stepped inside the screened porch, nudging aside a pair of muddy boots and a stack of dirty flower pots. Prim had been gardening again—in spite of all my warnings about heatstroke.

Standing at the door, I stared at the worn doormat covered with ladybugs and daises and listened to the wind chimes clink lazily in the corner while I tried to find the best way to break the bad news.

Prim opened the door. "Honey, what're you doing standing there like you're simple? Get inside, you goose." She pushed her rhinestone-rimmed, cat-eye glasses up on her nose with the back of her hand.

If ever a person's appearance matched their name, Primrose Vertrees's certainly did. My maternal grandma was petite, with limbs as thin as cornstalks and gray hair in a long wavy bob, which she pinned at the sides with rhinestone barrettes selected to match her outfit. Always dressed to receive, today she wore a pink cardigan, gray pants, and a white shirt under an apron.

The warm kitchen smelled of cucumbers, onion, vinegar, and spices. Empty Mason jars and lids, along with jars crammed full of relish, pickles, and dressed cucumbers, littered the countertops. A large canning pot steamed on the stove.

I kicked off my sandals by the door, wiggling my numb, red toes, and dumped my computer bag and purse on the floor by the baker's rack.

"Was that Cam's truck out there?"

"Yep. He says 'hi.'" I poured myself a glass of iced tea.

"Why's he bringing you home?" She rinsed dirt off a pile of cucumbers.

Flushed with humiliation and shame, I explained everything.

She shook her head, slicing a cucumber in quarters. "Nm-nm. You've got to get a grip on your temper, child." She stuffed the cucumber spears into a jar. "Your daddy had the same problem."

Ouch. That stung. I bit the inside of my jaw and grabbed a moon pie from the pantry. "I'll start looking for a job tonight after supper. Cam offered me a part-time job, if I get too desperate." Already knee-deep in shame, I refused to mention the money I'd borrowed from him.

The next morning, I stared out the window over the kitchen sink, waiting for my coffee to work its magic. Buried under her straw hat and one of Pappy's old flannel shirts, Prim watered her hydrangeas. I shook my head. She'd been complaining of backaches, but she continued messing with her flowers. Stubborn as an old mule. Batrene came out of her house to water her ferns. They greeted each other then, after a few minutes, Prim wandered next door, where they sat together on the porch in a pair of white rockers, rocking and talking. I was witnessing a meeting of two elite members of the Old Lady Network, which was an underground network of Rothdale's doyennes responsible for marriages, charitable events of all manner and size, and general gossip. Additionally, many a career got its start with the OLN. Those two were up to something.

With a breakfast of toast and blackberry jam, I fired up my laptop at the kitchen table and pored over every job search site in existence. Despite my master's degree and teaching experience, my prospects were bleak. I found only full-time office jobs which required two plus years' experience in the field or were way out of my range of experience and education. With a heavy sigh, I buried my face in my hands.

Prim limped into the house, moving stiffly and smoothing her hair.

"How's your back?"

"A little better." She shuffled around, pouring her tea and taking Advil.

"Maybe you shouldn't be out in your garden today."

"Batrene invited us to dinner tonight." She moved to the living room, kicked back in her recliner, and flipped on *General Hospital*. "I'm bringing the corn pudding."

I was suspicious. "It wouldn't have anything to do with my situation, would it?"

"We need to be there at six."

Prim opened Batrene's door and sang out, "How-do" while I followed with a hot dish of corn pudding. Maxine, a silky white Maltese, came running, yapping her greeting.

Batrene exited the kitchen, wiping her hands on a dishtowel. "Hello there.

Y'all come on in. I'm finishing the mashed potatoes and biscuits."

A purple floral polyester shirt with black polyester pants hugged her rotund body. A tight perm kinked her short, sandy brown hair—a style she'd maintained for as long as I'd known her. "Rook. Why, hello, darling." She tucked her chin, doubling it, and opened her arms for the obligatory hug.

She smelled of violets underpinned with onions and fried food. After kissing my cheek with sticky pink lips, she pulled back to admire me. "You're so grown up." She patted my cheeks. "And pretty with your long black hair and those dark-brown eyes. Like your momma. God rest her. You're the spit of her."

Maxine jumped on my leg, panting. I handed off the corn pudding to Batrene and picked up the dog, making kissy noises at her pink tongue darting to deliver wet kisses to my nose.

Too excited to be held, she wriggled from my embrace and scampered off after Batrene, who said, "Y'all come in and get a drink. We're waiting on Bryan. He's running late tonight."

Delightful scents of garlic, onions, and a variety of herbs filled the air. I'd completed a P90X video in preparation for the meal I planned to eat tonight, and my stomach grumbled impatiently.

Within the hour, Bryan, whom I'd nicknamed BB in childhood, arrived home and supper commenced in a noisy round of chatter and filling plates with fried pork chops, mashed potatoes, green beans, garden fresh tomatoes, corn pudding, and homemade biscuits.

Prim and Batrene were discussing Batrene's recent health issues while Bryan and I made small talk about the new season of *Game of Thrones*. We were both hoping to see more dragons, though we disagreed on who would win on the Iron Throne.

Our conversation was interrupted when Batrene reached over and patted Bryan's knee. "He takes such good care of me. Don't know what I would have done without my precious boy after his daddy died."

He flushed and nodded. "Until I have to change your diapers. Then we'll have to reevaluate the situation."

We all laughed.

"You're a mess." Batrene cut her pork chop. "So, Rook, what's been going on with you."

She knew good and well what was going on with me. She was teeing me up. I repeated my story. Once again, little Rook was in trouble. Once again, she needed a bailout.

"What?" Bryan smoothed his chestnut beard. "Why didn't you say something?"

Shrugging one shoulder, I poked at a green bean. "I don't know."

"We're hiring at the distillery. In the marketing department. One of the women there is moving away to New Orleans with her fiancé." He salted and peppered his tomatoes. "I can put in a word for you."

"Isn't that interesting?" But the knowing glint in Prim's eyes betrayed her as the puppet master.

I tore off a chunk of biscuit and popped it in my mouth. The soft, buttery bread melted into pure pleasure. "But I'm not qualified. My degree's in English."

He gulped half of his tea. "This is an entry-level thing. The owner cares less about credentials and more about people who're creative, innovative, and teachable."

"That exists for real? I thought that was some Google fairy tale."

"Of course, your connection on the inside helps." He waggled his brows. "What'd you teach?"

"Multi-media composition and rhetoric. How to write web content as well as traditional essays. I also taught public speaking within the context of our class projects."

"Sounds to me like you'll fit right in. You're a writer. You're a consumer with a lifetime of advertisements force-fed to you in every conceivable format." He broke open a biscuit and slathered it in butter. "You understand digital media. You may not be Zuckerberg, but you're smart and resourceful. Those qualities go a long way." He bit into the biscuit, speaking as he chewed. "You'd be perfect." He took another bite. Then he dug in his back pocket for his wallet. He extracted a business card and handed it to me. "Send your resume and cover letter to my email, and I'll make sure Pierce sees it. I know he wants to hire quickly because the team's working on a big event for September."

Gratitude, relief, and a dash of humiliation washed over me as I read the card. "Thank you so much, BB. Really. I appreciate this more than I can say."

"Don't mention it, Rookie." He clapped me on the shoulder. "Family takes care of each other."

Chapter Three

In a whirlwind week, I'd applied, interviewed, and landed the job. Though it was an entry-level marketing job writing copy and assisting with events, it paid more than I'd made at the university and included a benefits package complete with health insurance, 401K, three weeks' vacation, and a paid gym membership.

The drive to the Four Wild Horses Distillery for my first day of work was nothing short of glorious. A faint mist covered the grounds of the surrounding horse farms, hugging the ankles of the grazing horses. Lining the roads were rock fences built hundreds of years ago. I lowered the window, not caring about my hair, to take in the scent of fresh earth, clover, and honeysuckle and cranked up Bob Dylan.

Upon reaching the distillery, I coasted down the long tree-lined drive that opened into the distillery complex. The scent of mash bill—a little sharp, a little sweet—the unmistakable aroma of fermented rye, corn, wheat, and barley hung in the air.

The main building with the administrative offices and the visitors' center was the newest and most ornate buildings. They were styled like horse stables of gray stone with green tin roofs, complete with short spires across the top. On the side of the main building hung a giant bourbon barrel lid burned with the company logo: four horses, running and rearing, surrounded by a ring of laurel branches. A small café, gazebo, patio, and flower garden decorated the space behind the buildings. Beyond the flower garden, a walking path wound down to a pond ringed by a walkway dotted with willow trees and benches. In a valley beyond the main parking lot stood the heart of the distillery. The main rickhouse was constructed of old red brick and dated back to the late 1700s. The other rickhouses and production buildings were little more than tall metal rectangles, thoroughly modern and thoroughly without charm.

The reception area was gently lit with sunlight and copper pendant lights shaped similar to pestles and reminiscent of stills in the distillery room. The walls were exposed red brick with polished, dark wood floors, and plush leather sofa and chairs in a traditional style. I'd brought a book to read, but as a bit of a history buff, I was far more interested in the historical drawings and photos detailing the history of the distillery's development.

My boss, Pierce Simpson, was a short, wiry man with electric blue eyes, silver hair, and a golfer's tan; he walked and talked as if time itself was ending. Though he doubled my age, I struggled to keep up with him. He shook my hand with a firm grip. "First, I'll introduce you to the marketing team."

My strappy heels cut into my pinky toes as we sped down the hall to the back of the building artistic and dramatic pictures from the bourbon-making process lined the wall: the mash bill, which a picture of corn, rye, barley, and wheat grains; there were pictures of the giant fermenter bins full of the frothy brew-head, images of bourbon barrels, and the cooperage firing the barrels, the distillery logo, the rickhouses, the rickrollers, a photo of family past and present who owned the distillery, and a large picture of the current distillery team. I was a little disappointed we flew by the images too quickly for me to digest what I was seeing.

We passed several people in the hall in various degrees of urgency. Pierce stopped one girl. "Hey, Jenny, how's your palate feeling today?"

"Pretty good. Haven't had my coffee yet."

"Can you go over to the lab and test that new batch they're working on?"

"Sure thing. I'll head over now." The lithe blonde spun around and headed away from us.

Pierce explained that sometimes office staff had to help out with the sampling of the product to ensure quality taste.

We entered the marketing pit, a large room decorated much like the reception area with the large windows, exposed brick walls, exposed pipes in the ceiling, and the copper distiller-shaped pendant lights. There were about six cubicles in one half of the room. Only three of the cubicles were occupied. A long table and whiteboard covered with writing commanded the other side of the room.

My team lead, Lennon Ashfield, approached with a smile and his hand out. "You must be Rook Campbell. Very nice to meet you."

Lennon's cheeks and nose were sharp. His dark brows pitched over dark eyes, and his full, sensual lips gave him a brooding Byronic quality, a silver-screen allure. His white button-down shirt and khakis highlighted a body with the lean elegance of a swimmer in his physical prime. I thrilled at his firm handshake and his cologne fresh as clean, sun-dried laundry. Under his penetrating gaze, I was certain he could see my white and red dotted bra and panties through my flouncy gray skirt and black silk blouse.

"Please, call me Len. Welcome to the team. We're glad you're here." An impish glimmer filled his eyes. "We'll take great care of you. A couple people are out with meetings, but I'll introduce you to the rest of our promotions and sales staff."

I shook hands with Marla with lavender hair, who was sleek in a black sundress, and with bearded Jeff in a plaid shirt and skinny jeans. I was surprised by the mix of clothing styles that seemed to range from garage grunge band to business casual. I breathed an internal sigh of relief to know there was no official dress code and, as a result, I wouldn't have to buy a new wardrobe.

Len dropped his hands in his pockets and slouched with a relaxed air. "There are four of us in sales. We meet with the distributors, bars, shops, and such to get our product distributed. But we sometimes help pitch events to different sponsors and so forth. My job is the best job in the whole place. All I have to do is take people to dinner and give them bourbon to drink." Len and Pierce shared a laugh. I smiled affably. Len continued, "You and the other two would carry out the details of setting up events, keeping up with the social media, and anything else needed for promoting the brand."

Pierce added, "That's right. We are definitely a team here. Since we aren't as big as some of the other distilleries we all kind of jump in to help each other however we can."

I nodded, showing my approval of the team-player approach. "Got it."

"Which means," Len crossed his arms over his chest. "You will need to understand the distillery and the product inside-out. You might even need to fill in on giving tours occasionally or serving samples at events."

I nodded as the stress cranked tight at the roots of my hair as I thought about the pressure of learning so much information.

Pierce must've read the fear in my deer-in-headlights-eyes (a look common to my face when feeling overwhelmed). He attempted to reassure me. "We'll give you plenty of time to learn everything. We won't throw you to the wolves just yet."

We all laughed and the roots of my hair relaxed.

A petite, blonde woman rushed in. "Pierce. We've got a problem. Mr. Dermotte is here from the construction company and he says there's a problem with the permit."

Pierce smiled at me. "There's always something. We're getting ready to expand the distillery and build some new rickhouses. Our sales team is so good at building excitement for our brand, we have to keep making more barrels and we're running out of room to store 'em. Ain't that right, Len?" He clapped Len on the shoulder.

"That's right." Len laughed.

"Sounds like a good problem to have." I laughed along.

Pierce walked backward. "Len take Rook to the conference room. Have her watch all those videos." Then he said to me. "When you're done come to my office and we'll take a tour of the distillery." He didn't wait for a response. He spun around and headed out the door.

I was then shuffled off to the conference room to watch the obligatory anti-theft and anti-sexual harassment videos. As the new person, my antennae were primed, searching the atmosphere to get a feel for the ebb and flow of the energy and the thing that made this place unique. It seemed to be both relaxed, but in high, positive spirits. No pun intended. However, other than the décor and the product, the administrative side of the distillery seemed to function in much the same way as any office I'd ever encountered.

After the videos, I made my way to Pierce's office at the end of the hall for a tour of the distillery he'd promised. Pierce's door was cracked. My hand poised to knock, I heard Bryan's gravelly voice.

"I've been working on the books from last quarter and found more discrepancies." Papers rustled. "From what I can tell, this has been going on since the first quarter of this year."

After a brief pause, Bryan spoke again. "Here and here, too. I found this last week and this the other day. It's really concerning, so I'm going to go further back to see exactly when this began."

"Wow," Pierce said. "Thanks, Bryan. I'll look at these in more detail after lunch. I'm sure there's a simple explanation."

A petite woman carrying several manila folders approached Pierce's office, her honey-blonde curls and assets bouncing with her brisk steps. She was the same woman that had come into the sales pit earlier.

I moved away from the door, pretending to look at my phone instead of eavesdropping.

Her mouth stretched into a wide cheerleader grin, revealing wrinkles far deeper than her thirty-some years warranted. "Hey there. You must be the new girl." She held out her tiny, tanned hand. "Sorry I didn't get to meet you earlier. We had a little fire to put out. I'm Holly Parker. The administrative assistant here."

Her loud, powdery perfume wound like a boa constrictor around my throat. I smiled through the urge to cough. "Hi. I'm Rook Campbell. Nice to meet you."

"Rook?" Her penciled brows arched over her hazel eyes. "What an unusual name."

I didn't feel like explaining my name. "Yeah, I get that a lot."

She beamed, revealing unnaturally white teeth. "Well, we're super glad you're here. We always need more ladies around. Bourbon is such a boy's club." She rolled her eyes, touching my arm.

I'd spent my entire childhood navigating the fragile political system of female relationships in middle school and high school. I knew her type. An angel to your face, a viper to your back. I played along. "We ladies have to

18

stick together, don't we?"

Holly wrinkled her nose with fake laughter. "That's right. Girl power!" She raised a little bejeweled fist in the air.

A middle-aged Black man wearing a yellow polo shirt and carrying a mug and a paper sauntered our way. "Looks like Pierce is Mr. Popular today." He had thick glasses and a thin mustache. A small paunch hung over his beltline.

When Yellow Shirt reached us, Holly laid a hand on his arm. "Rook, this here is Mr. Trouble with a capital T."

He laughed and offered his hand. "Clarence Ford. How are you doing?"

We shook hands while Holly added, "Clarence is our accounts receivable-payable specialist as well as our supplier relations agent. He's responsible for getting all of the various grains we use in the bourbon and his family owns The Flying Eagle cooperage, where we get our barrels and such."

Running a cooperage and making the bourbon barrels was an art and craft in and of itself. It took a lot of skill to form the staves and fit them in the rims and to fire the wood for just the right level of char used in flavoring the bourbon. Surprised, I asked, "You didn't want to go into the family business?"

"My sister and I both wanted to be bookkeepers. She graduated first and got to the job before me." He laughed. "I didn't like the idea of working the production line, so I went outside the family business and landed here."

Bryan and Pierce came out of his office, agreeing to meet after lunch. Bryan jotted a note inside his red folder, nodding, and closed it.

When Pierce saw Holly, Clarence, and me standing outside his door, he clapped his hands. "Hey-o, looks like the party's out here. Holly, Clarence, y'all come on in." He checked his watch. "I've got another meeting in about thirty minutes, so we need to make it quick." Holly and Clarence filed into the office. Pierce turned to me. "Hey, Rook, I'm sorry I can't do the tour. Get with Len and see if he'll show you around. If he can't, then you and I'll get together this afternoon. Promise."

Holly and Clarence added, "Nice to meet you, Rook."

I repaid the politeness and joined Bryan. He sighed and tipped his head side to side, stretching his neck.

"Everything okay?"

"Today's crazy. Closing out a month is always a pain."

His office was a small space filled with cherry wood furniture, a filing cabinet across the room, and a window to the right of the desk. His college degree and an artistic photo of bourbon barrel stacks hung on the wall.

He threw the red folder on his desk and settled into his chair, grabbing his computer bag. He rifled through it. "You want to go to the Golden Dragon for lunch to celebrate your first day?" Extracting a thumb drive with the company logo on it, he plugged it into the port on his PC. "My treat." He smiled at me.

I perked. "If you're buying, I'm eating."

"Meet me here at noon. If you're late, you lose."

"Guess I'd better hurry to finish the tour of the grounds."

I rushed down the hall, my pinky toes squealing, to find Len in his cubicle. He swiveled and raked his dark gaze up my body in a way that made me feel both appreciated and awkward.

"Hey, Len, Pierce told me to ask you to give me a tour of the distillery. If you have time."

"I'd love to." His voice was as silky and creamy as dark chocolate mousse. And I had a heckuva sweet tooth.

We started with the visitors' center. The interior consisted of wall-to-wall polished wood. I met the workers there and scanned the wide variety of memorabilia, foodstuffs, and beverages with the Four Wild Horses logo. Then we passed the café, met the servers, while I received a history lesson about the distillery and the Conway family who founded it in the late 1800s.

"I saved the best for last. The production house and rickhouses." He opened the door for me and as I stepped through, I was hit with the sweet yeasty scent of the fermenters. The six giant drums held about twenty thousand gallons of brew topped with a frothy head that bubbled and steamed.

"Bourbon has to be at least fifty-one percent corn. After that, each distillery adds various blends of wheat, rye, and barley to create their own recipes.

20

We have a few different recipes, but we prefer a sweeter mash which uses fresh yeast. We're different in that respect, though many other distilleries are beginning to take up the sweet mash approach. Most distilleries use the sour mash which is where the yeast is fermented to make beer first, it's cooled and then distilled to make the bourbon." He introduced me to the workers. I shook hands with men and women in jeans and T-shirts.

My brain was going numb. The adrenaline and excitement I'd had about the new job early in the morning were beginning to wear off, along with my coffee high. I struggled to hold on to the information and the names and faces being thrown at me.

He smiled. "But don't worry. You'll get an information packet that will help with all this." I relaxed a little as he motioned toward a door. "Let's go this way to the distillery room."

As we walked, Len explained that the brew from the fermenters was funneled through large pipes as he pointed at the ceiling. "As it travels the solids are strained and it ends up in here." He opened the door for me and I stepped through into the distillery wing where towering pipes stretched two stories from floor to ceiling. The pipes pumped liquid into large copper stills where the alcohol was purified with intense heat and turned to vapor. That vapor was then collected and recondensed into a pure, strong alcohol. In the center of this production was a smaller still filled with white liquid that flowed into another clear container. Inside this box was a spinning wheel.

Len clapped his hand on the clear box. "This here is what we call white dog. It's about 140 proof. This is the alcohol before it's put in the barrels and aged into bourbon. You need a taste of this." He pulled a plastic sampler cup from the top of the box and poured a shot of white dog.

It smelled and tasted like buttered popcorn jelly beans or butterscotch and the alcohol was so strong it practically evaporated against my palate as soon as it hit my tongue. A soothing warm sensation trailed down my throat. "That's really good."

"Right?" He beamed. "We have the best white dog in the nation, hands down. Distributors are practically beating down my door to get it." He sniggered then he turned to look at the gleaming copper stills. "So once everything is distilled, we put it in barrels with about a three or four char level. The cooperage burns the oak staves inside and that burned wood helps to flavor the bourbon as the sugars in the bourbon react to the char and wood. It's also how the clear white dog turns into that pretty caramel color." He walked toward an exit door. "We'll go this way to the rickhouse."

We passed windows that looked in on a lab and a bottling space where bottles flowed along a conveyor belt. He escorted me into each room to introduce me to the workers there. The supervisors explained their jobs in the briefest terms and offered to help in any way they could, if I needed it. My mind was buzzing with names and faces and information and my stomach was grumbling for lunch. I laughed through the growing mental fog. "I will probably be back a lot to ask questions."

Len guided me through the exit door at the end of the hall. "It's always exciting to come out to see the hustle and bustle of the rickhouses," Len said as we crossed the parking lot in the glaring August sun. "I hope I don't offend you, but can I ask about the origin of your name?"

"I was born with black hair and my grandma and mom loved to play the card game Rook."

He chuckled. "Way more interesting than having hippie parents who loved John Lennon." He checked his watch. "How about we do only this rickhouse since it's the oldest with the most history. Basically, if you've seen this one, you've seen the others."

My stomach begged for lunch, my feet were angry, and I'd already broken into a sweat. "Fine by me."

He opened the door for me, and I stepped inside, where the air smelled sharp, sweet, and woodsy. Rows and rows of oak barrels lay on their side, stacked wall to wall, floor to ceiling. Workers bustled to blaring classic rock as they pulled down barrels in the center aisles and unloaded them for the rick riders to lock them into place.

"We're a pretty small operation compared to places like Heaven Hill or Maker's Mark. We have three rickhouses total, with plans to build a fourth. This one is the oldest, dating back to about eighteen-seventy. Built after the last building burned down in eighteen sixty-four, when Confederate troops set it on fire to keep it out of the hands of the Union. The other rickhouses were built about fifty years ago." He pointed at the ceiling. "The oldest and rarest bourbons are stored at the top because heat rises. The hotter, drier air aids the aging process. The lower levels house the newer bourbons. Those at the top have been aging for fifteen to twenty-five years. Each bottle from those barrels is worth upward of a thousand dollars and more."

"Wow." The thought of spending more than thirty dollars on a fifth of bourbon made my head spin. "But why?"

"So, these spaces aren't temperature controlled. They live in whatever temperature nature delivers to them. And Kentucky is perfect for bourbon because we get a wide range of hot and cold."

I chuckled and nodded, all-too-aware of the erratic Kentucky weather. "That's true. If you don't like the weather, wait ten minutes."

He laughed. "That's right. So the heat expands the wood, causing it to soak up the bourbon and the cold compresses the wood, squeezing out the alcohol." He opened and closed his hands to illustrate his point. "That of course helps with the flavoring. But the heat creates evaporation, what we call the angel's share. And the wood retains some of the alcohol, called the devil's cut. And the longer the alcohol sits in those conditions, the less bourbon we're left with. But we're still taxed the same. So, long story short, that's why the older bourbons are rarer and more expensive."

I looked up at the rows of barrels as my eyes widened at learning something new. "Oh, I see. That makes sense."

He picked up an empty bottle with a black label, thin Gothic script read Devil's Kiss in a swirl of red and gold flames and a devil's tongue. "Our Devil's Kiss is one of those rare brews. It's a sweeter bourbon whiskey. The mash bill is corn and wheat, with notes of vanilla, honey, cinnamon, and the slightest kiss of ghost pepper. Because of those flavors, we have to call it bourbon whiskey because, legally, bourbon can't have added flavors. Which is also why, legally, bourbon barrels can only be used once. So flavors don't mix."

I laughed. "Wow. That's serious business. But Devil's Kiss sounds delicious."

"It is. I've had it many times. One of the perks of being in sales." He winked.

"I wish I could afford a bottle."

He chuckled, replacing the bottle. "It's a small batch about ten years old. We've only made fifty barrels. Once it's gone, it's gone. Thus, the price tag."

"How many bottles can you get from one of those barrels?"

"Each barrel holds fifty-three gallons. There are five fifths in a gallon..." He squinted. "Around two thousand six hundred fifths."

Math had never been my strong subject, but I soon figured out one barrel would pay off all my student loans and buy me a decent house in Rothdale. I'd probably have a little extra to take a nice vacation. I was annoyed.

An average-sized man in jeans, T-shirt, and gloves came, rolling a barrel toward us. "'Scuse me." He stopped, turned the barrel, and rolled it into a rack with a grunt.

"That looks like a tough job," I said to Len.

"Yep. The barrel alone is over a hundred pounds. Add the bourbon and the barrels are about five hundred pounds. But getting those barrels in just right so the bung is at the top..." He touched a round spot like a belly button in the center of a barrel. "It's a special skill. Takes the new guys a while to learn. But it keeps us from losing valuable product."

"Let's get out of the rick rollers' way." He guided me out of the center aisle and navigated me down the walkway along the wall. "Come on over to the desk, and I'll introduce you to the supervisor, my brother-in-law, Randall."

We were cut off by a short, swarthy man in his forties who jumped out of a delivery truck and stormed inside. He had a pointy, stubbled jaw and hooked nose. He wore a black T-shirt with the company logo in white on the back. He was unkempt with an untucked shirt and pants bagging around the ankles of his steel-toe boots. With a paper in hand, he pointed at a bald man. "I want to talk to you. This is BS."

Len touched my elbow, guiding me toward the door. "Maybe this isn't the best time. We'll try later." He checked his watch. "Besides, it's almost lunchtime. Don't you have a date with Bryan?"

We stepped into the brutal sun. I squinted at him, blocking the sunlight with a hand at my brow. "We aren't dating. Bryan's more like a brother."

Len smiled at me. "Good to know."

After the tour, I stopped by Bryan's office to meet him for lunch, but Pierce and Clarence were in his office. It didn't sound like a happy conversation.

Clarence said, "Bryan, you're paranoid. Looking for nonexistent problems."

Bryan said, "For the past three months, these problems have existed. I've been reviewing the records and I've uncovered some things."

"What is it you think you've found, anyway?"

"Like I told y'all last week, one thing is we're using The Flying Eagle cooperage for our barrels, though they have a poorer quality, always botch our orders, and charge hefty delivery fees."

"Stop right there." Clarence's voice rumbled deep and stormy. "You're talking about my family now."

"I mean no offense to you or your family, but the Farleigh-Jackson cooperage has better quality barrels and lower delivery fees. I talked to another distiller who uses them, and they say their orders are always perfect and on time."

"Wow," Pierce said. "We should probably reevaluate…"

Clarence said, "There's no way—"

Pierce said, "What else do you have, Bryan?"

Bryan said, "Well, there's the matter of the inventory. We're showing—"

A cell phone rang.

Pierce answered and told the caller to hold. "Bryan, let's talk about this after lunch. I'll tell Holly to clear my schedule for the rest of the afternoon. We'll get to the bottom of this."

Pierce left, talking on the phone, Clarence stormed out, mumbling to himself. A moment later, Bryan came out, closing his door. He wrapped his arm around my shoulders. "Let's go to lunch. I'll drive."

As he unlocked the car, the swarthy guy from the rickhouse stormed forward, shouting, "Hey, you! Bishop! Stop right there."

Bryan groaned, muttering, "Geez-Louise, what now?" He glanced at me and chuckled in his raspy voice. "Don't get the wrong idea about this place. It's not usually like this. I swear." Then he said to the guy, "Hey, Dewey. What's up?"

Up close, Dewey resembled a troll with his beaked nose, pointy chin, and wide mouth full of sharp teeth. He reeked of stale cigarettes.

Dewey waved the paper in his hand. "This is what's up. You shorted my paycheck, man. I should've received twice this mileage."

"No. We checked the odometer, and it didn't match what you recorded. If you want to discuss it—"

"You calling me a liar? I've made every delivery on my schedule."

"I'm not calling you anything, Dewey. Let's talk about this after lunch."

"Naw," Dewey spit. "We're going to talk about it right now."

"All right." Bryan handed me the keys. "Rook, start the car, get the A/C on."

I jumped in the passenger seat; the leather interior burned the back of my legs. I leaned over, started the car, and cracked the windows.

Bryan said, "Dewey, the records didn't match. We can't pay you for mileage you didn't clock. Randall covered for you this time with Pierce, but if it happens again, you'll likely be fired."

Nodding, Dewey poked his tongue into his bottom lip, looking off in the distance. He pointed his nicotine-stained finger. "This ain't over, you hear?"

As Dewey stomped away, Bryan climbed into the car.

I fanned myself with a yellow paper I'd discovered on the floorboard. "That guy sure was mad at you."

Bryan sniffed, throwing the car into reverse. "I reckon he'll have to get in line today."

I opened the paper in my hands. *Dead men don't snitch.* The letters were square and rigid. "What's this?"

He glanced at the paper and grabbed it. "Oh, nothing. Some stupid… Nothing you need to worry about." He tucked it under his sun visor.

"I don't know, BB. I believe I should put worrying at the top of my list today."

Chapter Four

After lunch, Bryan and I returned to the distillery. He opened the car door and stopped. He looked straight ahead. "Rook, if anything ever happens to me, will you take care of my mom?"

My lunch transformed to stone in my belly. "Of course. Why would anything happen to you? Are you sick? In some kind of trouble?"

He smiled. "Nah. Just thinking. I'd better go prepare for this meeting with Pierce. Wish me luck, Rookie."

"You've got this, BB." I playfully punched his arm as we entered the building. But the strange conversation lingered and a shadow of unease followed me.

I passed Clarence in the hall, a hand tucked in his pocket. He seemed rigid. "Hey, Clarence."

He gave a sharp dip of his chin by way of greeting, apparently too focused for pleasantries.

After cleaning my cubicle and organizing my supplies, I switched on my computer, ready to create all my passwords and figure out the software I'd be using. Since I had little experience with Photoshop and Canva, I predicted lots of YouTube tutorials in my future. Nevertheless, I had no doubt I was going to be way happier here than I'd ever been as an underappreciated, overworked, underpaid adjunct instructor at the university.

Around three, I took a break, intent on grabbing a cup of coffee from the break room, while trying to ignore the siren song of the Milky Way Midnights in the vending machine.

I was pouring vanilla creamer into my coffee when a man's scream echoed from the other end of the building. "Help! Help!"

I shoved the coffee carafe into its holder and stepped into the hall.

Pierce stood in the hall outside Bryan's office. His face bright red, he shouted, "It's Bryan."

I bolted toward Pierce and the gathering crowd.

"What's wrong?" I puffed, pushing my way inside the room.

Bryan lay splayed on the floor among scattered sheets of paper. Vomit pooled near the garbage can where he'd missed. His tumbler lay on the floor to his left; the contents had spilled, forming a darker green spot on the carpet. His desk chair was rolled away from his desk.

"Oh, my God! What happened?" I rushed forward and dropped to my knees beside him. "What happened?"

"I dialed nine-one-one. I don't know. I came to get him for our meeting because he was late. I found him like this. Maybe he had a heart attack?" Pierce rambled.

I placed my shaking fingers to his neck. No pulse. I watched his chest. I still couldn't detect a beat. I lowered my ear to his mouth. No breath. Nothing. "What happened? Did anyone see anything? Hear anything?"

By now, the entire admin staff had gathered in the doorway, rubbernecking.

"No. I came in to get him for a meeting and found him like this."

I slapped Bryan's cheeks and shook him. "Bryan! Bryan! Please…" No response. Panic flooded my veins, clouding my thoughts.

"Someone go wait by the door to direct the paramedics."

Holly said, "I'll go."

I searched the faces, all still strange to me. "Does anyone know CPR?" I had taken CPR classes a long time ago when I first became a teacher. I hoped I still remembered; it was his only shot.

"I do." Len pushed through the crowd.

"You pump, I'll breathe."

I pinched Bryan's short nose, covered his mouth with mine, and pushed my breath into his lungs, willing him to breathe.

Len planted his hands in the center of Bryan's chest and pumped with his whole body.

I issued another breath, then put my ear to Bryan's mouth again. Over and over we breathed, pumped, and listened until the sirens cried out in the parking lot below.

The paramedics clomped up the stairs carrying a gurney topped with equipment bags, shouting for people to step aside. They nudged me out of the way, and I scooted over by Bryan's desk chair. The dark spot of liquid from his tumbler had crept toward the desk. Near the desk lay a pen and a few green needles that looked similar to rosemary sprigs or short spruce needles. There weren't many. Bryan must have tracked them in on his shoes. But how? Batrene didn't grow anything like that around her house. There were some evergreen trees around the distillery. Maybe he picked it up here. But these needles didn't look like pine or spruce. I studied them, fear changing to cold, dark dread, weighing like lead in my blood.

My mind slipped into the past. I was a kid again at my parents' house, searching the darkness, through pine trees, standing at the window, icy to the touch. Movement in the yard below, a figure splayed on the ground. A woman in a bathrobe. No face. I shuddered, cold.

The paramedics set to work on Bryan, chattering in an incomprehensible jargon. They cut open Bryan's shirt and slapped the adhesive ECG electrodes on his chest. One paramedic fiddled with knobs and buttons, looking at the screen. I kept hoping to hear a rhythmic beep or see a jumping line. But there was nothing. The monitor guy told his friend to administer a gobbledygook drug. They shot him full of something. Still no beeps, no jumping lines. Tears stung my eyes. This was not happening. I was not really seeing any of this.

Len knelt beside me and touched my arm. "Rook? Are you all right?"

I blinked at him as though I didn't even recognize him. Nothing looked familiar to me. I spoke to anyone who would listen. "Is Bryan okay? Is he alive?"

"It'll be okay." Len squeezed my hand. "They're doing all they can."

A paramedic pulled out some paddles from his bag and there was more jargon and fiddling of knobs. Then he clapped those paddles on Bryan's chest. His body seized and jolted, but then fell unresponsive. Again and again, they used the paddles and administered the drugs, but still, the line on the heart monitor remained steady and flat. Intense pressure built in my head like a wrecking ball was about to blow through the inside of my skull.

The paramedics sat back on their heels and looked down at the floor.

And I knew. Bryan, my best friend who had been like a brother to me, the guy I'd grown up with, was gone. Just gone. I couldn't move, or cry, or scream. I wasn't even sure my spirit was still inside my body. I watched images of one of the paramedics stand and talk to Pierce while another talked on his phone. Co-workers hugged and cried. But all I could hear was the thrumming of blood in my ears. Then I couldn't breathe and gasped for air. Len tried to comfort me but I threw him away and crawled toward Bryan.

I grabbed his cooling hand and melted onto the floor beside him.

Chapter Five

Somehow I ended up in the parking lot. I was losing my grip on time. Just as I had done when my momma died. And I tried to force my brain to grab hold of the present and reality as I watched the Franklin County Corner roll into the parking lot. I leaned against a tree since my body was too weak to stand on its own.

Deputy Jimmy Duvall, Cam's friend, approached me. I hadn't noticed the sheriff's department had arrived "Can we talk?"

"What time is it?"

He seemed surprised by the question. "Uh…" He glanced at his watch. "Little before three."

"Okay." I nodded. I mentally repeated the number three, pictured a clock dial in my mind, and glanced at the sun—anything to anchor myself to the reality and the moment. My brain darted for answers, for something to do, some action I could take to make everything better, to put the world in its proper order, and to keep myself grounded. Action was grounding. Thinking was not. "Batrene. I need to tell Batrene. My phone. It's in my purse in my office." I started for the office building.

"Whoa." Jimmy grabbed my elbow.

I stared at him without seeing him, seeing only my warped reflection in his mirrored sunglasses.

"Rook, please come over here and talk to me." He guided me to a bench by the visitor's center.

I sat on the bench, watching the other deputy, LaDonna Price, in the parking lot direct everyone else out of the way of vehicles. A shy girl in high school, she'd developed a commanding presence as an adult law officer.

Most huddled under the shade trees like a bunch of flies on a drop of honey. The ambulance sped away, wailing. I buried my face in my hands and rocked back and forth as nausea rippled through my gut. Blood thudded in my neck. The thick stench of stale cigarettes from the nearby ashtray triggered flashes of a man, digging in the moonlight, the woman in the bathrobe.

There was a touch of tenderness in his voice. "Rook? You okay?"

Leaning over on my knees, I stared at my hands. "I'm fine." My voice crumbled. "Bryan's not. But I am."

"It's good to see you again, though I hate that it's under these circumstances."

I wiped my tears. "Me, too." I toyed with my ring of antique silver swirls embracing a round turquoise stone. It had been my mom's.

"I'm sorry about Bryan. I'd only met him once at yours and Cam's wedding, but he seemed like a good guy."

"He was." My voice sounded far away and thin. "Is…"

Poor Batrene. She was going to be devastated. I dropped my face into my hands. Bryan and I had grown up together. He'd taken me under his wing when I had no one else but Prim. He sat with me on the bus and never minded me tagging along with him and his friends. We supported each other through high school heartbreaks and dramas and spent our summer evenings playing horseshoes and chatting in the backyard under the stars. He was more than my surrogate brother. He was my best friend. I couldn't imagine my life without him.

Jimmy said, "Can I get you something to drink?"

I shook my head, dazed. "No." The intense heat further drained my ability to form thoughts or feelings. *This isn't happening. Please, God, this can't be happening. Not BB. Not my BB.* Tears filled my eyes and choked my ability to speak. I squeaked, "I couldn't help him. I tried. I was too late." I couldn't help my mom either. But then at eleven years old, I hadn't even realized she was in trouble.

He hung his glasses from his shirt. "Why don't you walk me through what happened today."

"I don't know." The tears dried into numbness. "This is my first day. Bryan helped me get the job." I drifted outside of myself. Why was it so hard to form a thought? "He seemed fine. He had meetings. We went to lunch. Then..." I stared at the drive as if the ambulance would bring Bryan back. "Is he okay?"

"I don't know yet." He drew his pen and notepad from his breast pocket. "You said you went to lunch?"

I tucked a strand of hair behind my ear. "To celebrate my new job."

"Where did you go?"

"The Golden Dragon." We'd been happy, talking about our favorite shows, laughing at Batrene finding a spider in her shoe.

"What did you all eat?"

"We both had the buffet."

"Have you felt ill or anything since eating there?"

I shook my head. I was only eleven when the police and attorneys questioned me about my mom's murder. Since then, I'd read and watched everything involving true crime and forensics, living with the hope of remembering more about my mother's death, proving the sheriff wrong, and exonerating my father. Though Jimmy was a friend, having him question me in his official capacity, wearing the uniform, was unnerving. It all seemed like it was happening to someone else.

"Did he say anything about feeling ill after lunch?"

"No."

"What does Bryan do here?"

"Accounting."

"Would you say it's a pretty stressful job?"

Flashes of his meetings with Clarence and Pierce and his run-in with Dewey crossed my mind. "Yeah, I guess it can be. Certainly seemed like it today. He said closing out a month is tough."

"How long has he worked here?"

"About five years."

"If memory serves, he's your neighbor, right?"

I nodded, looking at my red polished toes. I needed to get to Batrene.

I'd made a promise. The numbness had taken root and winnowed into my limbs. She would need someone.

"So you know him well?"

"Of course. He's one of my best friends."

"Has he been complaining of any health issues?"

"No. He was healthy as a horse. And strong. He was a big guy, loved his food, but he played sports, worked out. I've seen him toss hay bales, one after the other, like they were rag dolls."

"Even seemingly healthy people can have—"

"No." I stared at him. "If Bryan had any sort of major health problem, he would've told me and his mother. If he didn't tell me, then I know his mother wouldn't have been able to keep such information quiet."

"Okay. Okay." He made a few notes. The official tone crept into his voice. "Walk me through everything the best you can. Did anything stand out to you? Was he acting funny or did he say anything about feeling unwell?"

"No. He was having a rough day, though. There were a few problems with the accounts and with a couple of coworkers."

"When you saw him on the floor, was anyone else doing anything?"

It was hard to recall exactly, everything had been chaotic. "Not really. Pierce was screaming. Everyone else was standing around. I checked for a heartbeat and breath. I couldn't find either one. I told someone to wait for the medics then I asked if anyone knew CPR."

"You know CPR?"

"I was trained a long time ago. I did the best I could."

His tone was understanding. "I have no doubt."

"Len helped me. I tried. Bryan wouldn't wake up. I kept hoping..."

"It's okay." He patted my shoulder. "The important thing is you acted fast and you tried." He asked a bunch of questions that seemed to be a variation of everything else he'd already asked.

When was this going to end? My coworkers mingled under the shade trees, people hugging each other, dabbing their eyes and noses. Pierce spoke with Deputy Ladonna Price. Holly and Len stood close together, talking.

A brown and white SUV with the sheriff's department logo on the door pulled diagonally across the handicapped parking spots in front of me.

Sheriff Harlan "Bulldog" Goodman jumped out of the SUV and approached Ladonna. His head was as square and thick as a cinder block. His brown uniform hat sat low on his head, shadowing his face. His thick russet mustache only accented his perpetual frown. Since Kentucky had unlimited terms for sheriffs, he'd been in office for as long as I could remember. For several years, his campaigns boasted a determination to single-handedly "take back the streets" from the meth makers and dealers and make our community safe again. Epic fail. The meth and pharmers were flourishing in Kentucky. Though to be fair, it wasn't entirely his fault when there was only one deputy for every 2,500 citizens and criminals were creative and adept at their trade. However, I had a bigger reason for hating the man. He'd not only arrested my dad for murdering my mom but had had a direct influence on the prosecutors and judges to ensure my dad's conviction for a crime he hadn't committed.

Goodman sauntered toward us. "Miss Daniels."

"It's still Campbell."

Goodman's amber eyes glinted. He ignored the correction.

Jimmy jumped in. "Sheriff, I've been taking Miss Campbell's statement. She performed CPR on Mr. Bishop."

Goodman hooked his thumbs in the belt under his paunch. "It seems we can close this case, Deputy. Just received word. Mr. Bishop is dead. Heart attack."

"What?" I searched Jimmy's face as everything vital in me fell to the ground and rolled away, leaving my empty body to clamor for a straw of reality. I didn't know what to do: scream, cry, run. I sat there, gasping for breath in the whirlwind of emotion. *Impossible. This is not happening.* Dizzy, I scanned the parking lot, unable to recognize anything or anyone around me.

Jimmy said, "Rook? Rook? You all right?"

His voice sounded far away. I might've nodded.

A small voice in the back of my mind screamed through the whirlwind. *No. This isn't right.* Jimmy and Goodman talked to each other.

Something clicked. The fog lifted and my thoughts fell into place. This whole scene was wrong. I stood. "No!"

They looked at me with the steady gaze of law enforcement professionals. "Bryan did not die of a heart attack."

Goodman said. "What makes you so sure?"

"He was a big boy and he had a stressful job. There's no denying that. But he was healthy. We were best friends. He would've told me if there were any health problems. He was strong. He didn't do drugs. He drank very little. It wasn't a heart attack."

"Please, do enlighten me, Miss Daniels." His words were tactful, polite, and professional but underscored with malice in his cold, dead eyes. "What, in your expert opinion, do you believe happened?"

"I'm saying Bryan was in good health."

Jimmy said, "You don't think he died of natural causes?"

My heart raced, but the shrieking in my gut was impossible to ignore. I refused to allow Goodman's challenging gaze to silence me. "I think he was murdered."

For a split second, we all froze, as if enacting a modern-day *tableau vivant*.

Goodman exchanged a look with Jimmy. "Murder? You do have a vivid imagination, Miss Daniels."

"Campbell."

He was trying to get under my skin, unsettle me by using my maiden name, my father's name. Goodman had been upset with me ever since I told him he bungled the investigation of my mother's murder case. He'd said I was like my daddy. And he'd meant it as an insult.

"It's not my imagination." Anger like a herd of wild mustangs tore through me. My hands itched to claw the smirk off his face.

But Prim's voice echoed in my head, *Control your anger, child.*

Glaring at Goodman, I sucked in a deep breath and released it. "I know you have difficulty assessing the facts in murder cases, causing innocent people to suffer, but maybe this time you'll get it right. If you'll listen."

He spread his legs wide in a power stance and crossed his arms over his chest. "And what are the facts?"

"First, my maiden name was Daniels. I've been Campbell for over five years." My temper brought clarity to my thinking. "Before Bryan and I went to lunch, he was in his office talking to the owner, Pierce, and Clarence, the accounts receivable/payable guy. Clarence seemed upset."

"About what?" Jimmy asked.

"Don't know exactly. I'm not an accountant, and I didn't get to see the papers they were talking about."

Jimmy said, "Do you know where those papers are now?"

I shrugged. "I guess they're in Bryan's office. He was carrying around a red folder today. Maybe the papers are in there." I brushed a tendril of hair out of my face. "When we went to lunch, he said some people were about to be upset with him because he'd found problems with the books."

"What problems?" Jimmy wrote in his notepad.

"I don't know. He didn't specify. And then there was Dewey."

"Who's Dewey?"

"A driver. There was a discrepancy with his pay. He confronted Bryan about it as we were getting in the car. Something about not getting paid for the mileage he'd claimed. Bryan told him he claimed more than he'd actually driven. Then Dewey said…" I pointed my finger and did my best impersonation of the angry driver. "'This ain't over.'"

Goodman's eyelids grew heavy with real or pretend boredom. "I fail to see how that points to murder."

"I'm not surprised." I assumed my own power stance. "It points to murder because there are people with possible motives for wanting him dead." I remembered the paper in the car. "Oh! And there's something else. I found a letter in his car that said 'Dead men don't snitch.'"

Goodman cocked his head and squinted. There was a reptilian flicker of interest. "We'll look into it." Though he continued to glare at me, he said to Jimmy, "We can't give anyone any reason to say we aren't doing our jobs, can we, Duvall?"

Jimmy licked his lips and shifted his weight onto his back foot. "No, sir."

Goodman faced Jimmy. "Carry on. Finish with Miss Daniels' statement." The sheriff shouted for Deputy Ladonna.

Deputy Ladonna jogged over to us, holding her belt.

"I'm going to the hospital. I'll have the medical examiner meet me there. You get the techs over here to process for a possible murder. Then you and Duvall start interviewing everyone here. Get Rogers and Fiske over here to get them to help with the interviews. Start with two men named Dewey and Clarence. Get the photographer and artist over here and y'all do a grid search of Mr. Bishop's office."

"Yessir." She gave a sharp nod, pulled her phone out, and placed a call while walking away, toward Pierce.

Goodman scanned the distillery grounds. "I'm going to need you to hang around town for a while, Miss Daniels. We may need to talk to you again." He walked away.

I looked at Jimmy. "You believe me, don't you?"

He hemmed.

"You don't. Nice." I flipped my hair off my shoulder, wishing for my hair clip.

"No, no. It's not that. It's just…" He licked the corner of his bottom lip, where a faint scar trailed from the lip to the chin. "Why didn't you tell me about the run-ins and letter earlier?"

"I wasn't trying to hide anything from you, Jimmy. I was upset. I couldn't think straight."

He shook his head and looked out across the parking lot. "It doesn't look good, Rook."

"Fair enough. Will you promise this investigation will be done right? I don't trust Bulldog."

Jimmy narrowed his eyes and readied his mouth to speak. He glanced over his shoulder at Goodman. "Let's finish this statement so you can get out of here. You must be worn out."

I hadn't realized how tired I was until Jimmy had spoken the words into existence. Suddenly, I felt both heavy and hollow. He finished taking my statement, where I had to repeat everything I'd just told him about Clarence, Dewey, and the note.

When we finished, he pulled out a business card and wrote on the back. "This is my cell number. Rook, if you think of anything else, or if you need anything, I'll make time for you. Okay?" He handed me the card. "We'll catch up soon." He patted my arm, winked at me, then strutted toward the rest of the office staff like he was crossing a football field.

By the time I'd joined my coworkers, word of Bryan's death had made the rounds. Some people shook their heads with sadness. A few people quietly dabbed at tears. Deputy Ladonna and Jimmy were talking to people at separate points in the parking lot.

I stood with the marketing team, waiting for the all-clear to retrieve my belongings and go home.

Len's fresh, laundry-clean cologne now mingled with the scent of his sweaty skin. "I'm sorry about Bryan. It's so unexpected. Are you okay?"

Nodding, I scanned the crowd, watching faces and reactions as if that alone might tell me who'd wanted Bryan dead.

"I know you two were close. If there's anything I can do..."

Biting my lower lip, I shook my head. "No, thanks." In true Scarlett O'Hara fashion, I'd have to think about my feelings when I could stand it better. Right now, I thought only about getting to Batrene. I'd made a promise to Bryan that I'd care for her in his absence. Chills pimpled my skin. Our earlier conversation now struck me as prophetic.

Deputy Ladonna released Holly, and Holly wandered our way to stand by Len. She dabbed at her eyes. But they seemed pretty dry already. "Y'all, this is awful, isn't it?" She hugged herself. Her voice quaked with emotion. "I can't believe this. I'd seen him only a few hours earlier. Then suddenly..." She blew her nose. "I wonder what happened. He seemed healthy enough to me."

"Yeah. It's a crazy day." This was my first day on the job, but I felt as though I'd been here a decade.

Len said, "Do the police or paramedics have any ideas about what happened?"

"They believe it might have been a heart attack or something, but I have my doubts."

"Why?" Mild defensiveness rose in Len's voice.

"I don't know. All I know is Bryan was healthy. I have difficulty believing it was natural causes."

He blinked. "I suppose…" He blew out a breath.

"I don't know…" I rubbed my forehead. Maybe I was crazy for thinking he'd been murdered. Maybe something had been wrong with Bryan I didn't know about. "Maybe I'm imagining things."

His eyes lit with humor. They looked like yummy pools of espresso, dark, inviting, warm. "Must be the heat."

Holly's tears stopped. She scoffed. "Are you serious? Are you talking about…" She lowered her voice to a whisper. "Murder?"

I shrugged. "Who knows?" The bile rose in my stomach as Bryan's body, zippered in a black bag, was rolled across the parking lot toward the ambulance.

She said, "It doesn't make any sense. Why would someone want Bryan dead?"

The paramedics shut the doors.

"I was wondering the same thing. And I aim to find out."

Chapter Six

Prim and I hovered at our kitchen window as the deputies' patrol car backed out of Batrene's driveway.

Prim tsked. "Poor Batrene. I know what she's going through."

I looked at her profile. Growing up, I'd been more involved in my own problems, I hadn't devoted enough attention to what Prim must've endured. We'd carried on—at least outwardly. My mother was dead, but her daughter was dead. Murdered. And the real killer hadn't been caught. And she'd had to finish raising me. How on earth had she managed it?

"She'll never be the same." Her voice was soft and deep with sadness. Prim moved away from the sink and started pulling food out of the fridge and the cabinets. She dumped the ground beef into a pan and added minced onions.

"Should we go over there now to offer our sympathies?"

"Not yet. She'll need to be alone for a few minutes. I'll make this Shepherd's pie and we'll go have dinner with her. I need you to chop some potatoes to boil." She moved stiffly and slowly. She rubbed her back with one hand as she stirred with the other.

"What's wrong with your back?"

"I hurt it earlier today out in the garden."

"What happened?"

She told me of how she'd bent over to pick up a basket of beans she'd picked. Her legs gave out and she fell to her knees. "Get me the frozen veggie mix." Prim shifted from foot to foot. Her face hung long, sallow, and there were heavy purple bags around her eyes. Her puckered face indicated pain and fatigue.

I handed her the pack of veggies. "Why don't you have a rest? Let me do this." I tried to wedge myself between her and the stove, but she held her ground and nudged me with her bony elbow.

"No. I'm fine." She put the bag of frozen veggies on her back. "Go on. Git."

"All right," I sighed. "Be stubborn then." I chopped the potatoes while she finished browning the meat. "Did you at least set a doctor appointment today?"

"Yes. I can see them next Wednesday." She set aside the bag of veggies and switched off the burner.

She slid the grease tin forward from the corner of the counter. She liked to keep her meat grease for cooking. Gripping the pan in both hands, she attempted to do what she'd done a thousand times before. She twisted and lifted the pan to pour the grease into the tin.

Instead, all at once, she cried out and dropped the pan with a loud crash against the countertop and dropped to her knees as if her legs had been kicked out from under her. As I lunged to catch her, hot grease splashed on me, searing my face and arms like tiny hot coals. The tin flipped over and oozed hot grease over the counter, the cabinets, and the floor.

I tried to help her to stand, but she shouted through her tears. "I can't stand. I can't."

My mind raced, trying to decide how to help her. She couldn't stand, and I couldn't lift her to carry her. "I'm going to lay you down, okay?"

She howled as I eased her to the floor and helped her lay in a fetal position. She whimpered like a baby while I dialed 911.

After a late night in the emergency room and cleaning the mess in the kitchen, I dragged myself out of bed at six the next morning, wishing I could stay home with Prim. Not only to help her, but also because work was the last place I'd seen Bryan alive. Yet, it was only my second day at the distillery. I desperately needed the money, more so after last night's ambulance ride and ER visit. And I didn't want to give my new employer any reason to question my work ethic and whether or not hiring me had been a mistake. After all, I was on a ninety-day probation period, where I could be fired for any reason.

Adulting really stunk sometimes.

Though I preferred natural makeup, I applied the under-eye concealer heavily, sprayed dry shampoo on my unwashed hair, and pinned it into a messy bun. In my robe, I sat on the end of my bed, staring into my closet, trying decide what to wear. My attention drifted first to the picture collage on my wall. Bryan and me at a tailgate party. Prim in a lawn chair at the lake. Cam holding up a fish he'd caught. An old picture of my mom and dad holding me as an infant. All the people who'd mattered most to me. How many did I still have? Bryan, gone. Mom, gone. Prim, here for now. Dad, in jail. Cam…limbo. Everything I loved was slowly slipping from my grasp.

I snapped out of my reverie and made myself busy with selecting an outfit to wear, settling on a navy belted shirt dress and nude ballet flats.

As I turned, I noticed the pile of dirty clothes from yesterday. Something was stuck to my skirt. I bent over, picking up the skirt. Little green sprigs were stuck to the cloth. They were like the green needles on Bryan's office floor. They must've stuck to my skirt when I scooted out of the way to let the paramedics through. I picked them off and placed them on top of my dresser.

I dressed quickly and rushed downstairs to make a breakfast of toast with jam and coffee. Prim staggered from the stairs into the kitchen. She wore a thin cotton gown covered with pink flowers and a pink cotton robe to match. She shuffled, zombie-like, across the linoleum. Her hairline was damp.

"Why are you out of bed?" I asked.

Her mouth hung heavy, impeding her ability to form words clearly. "I'll make breakfast. What do you want?"

"Prim, you should rest. I'm only having toast. My stomach feels bad, anyway."

"I rested already." Her eyes pressed out lethargic blinks. She put her bony hand to her head. "Those pills the doctor gave me. I don't like them."

"Yeah, they're going to make you really tired. They're strong. You can't drive or operate any dangerous equipment. It's best to take it easy. Work on your crochet, watch your stories on the TV."

She slumped into a chair at the kitchen table.

"I'll get your coffee. You want something to eat?" I grabbed a mug from the cabinet and filled it with coffee. "I can whip up some eggs for you before I leave."

"No. I'm not hungry right now. I'll get a little something later."

I added a touch of cream and two teaspoons of sugar, according to her preference. "How's your back?"

She swayed in her seat. She still wore the identification bracelet from the emergency room. "Okay, I guess. I can't feel much of anything right now."

I set the mug on the table and knelt in front of her. "Now, Prim, you promise me you'll take it easy today. Okay? We don't want to land in the emergency room again. Do we?"

She sipped her coffee. "I'll be alright."

"Promise."

"Okay," she snipped. "Go on with you."

She wasn't going to make the promise, likely because she intended to break it as soon as I left. I pulled a paper and an orange prescription bottle from the center of the table. "You need to do the stretches the doctors gave you." Images and explanations of the recommended exercises covered the paper. I slid it over to her. "Here's the sheet." I shook the pill bottle. "And here are your pills. Take these. You'll take more when you go to bed tonight."

She shook her head. "Okay. Okay. Go on to work now. Quit fussing over me."

I didn't want to press my luck with her, so I stood and grabbed my toast from the toaster, scraping a thin layer of butter over the half-burnt bread. "I hate leaving you alone."

She slurped her coffee. "I'll be fine."

I bit off a corner of toast, pondering what to do about Prim. I couldn't afford an in-home care person. Normally, I'd ask Batrene for the favor, but she was dealing with her own grief. That reminded me. "You and I need to visit Batrene tonight when I get home since we didn't get to do it last night."

"Absolutely. I'll have to make her—" She stood, pushing herself up with both thin arms and a deep grunt.

I interrupted. "Prim, please don't do a bunch of cooking."

She shooed me. "You need to get to work or you're going to be late."

"I'm going to have to get someone in here to keep you company." But who? It needed to be someone we both knew and trusted. Someone who wouldn't be at work until later. It hit me: Cam. I hated to do it, but I didn't see I had any choice. I dug my phone out of my purse and dialed Cam.

He answered with a sleepy, "Hm?"

"I'm sorry to wake you…"

He spoke through a yawn. "What's wrong?"

"Prim and I were at the emergency room until around one this morning. She had a fall last night."

He perked. "She okay?"

"Yeah, she's fine, I guess. She's been having back trouble. And the doctor gave her strict instructions to do her stretches, ice her back, take her painkillers, and rest. I just got this job. I can't afford to miss any work to stay home with her."

"I don't need to be watched like a child," Prim shouted.

"Will you please check in on her this afternoon before you go to work?"

His end of the line was quiet, except for the deep, rhythmic breath of one on the brink of sleep. I imagined him lying in bed, eyes closed, phone pressed to his ear.

I kept talking, as if he needed more convincing. "I really hate to ask and inconvenience you. You've already done so much. I can't afford to pay anyone, and you're the only person I could think of who might be available to help."

Prim squawked behind me. "I said I don't need a babysitter. I can take care of myself."

"Yeah, I'll do it." Cam chuckled sleepily.

"Thank you. Tons. I owe you big time."

"Sounds like I'll have my work cut out for me."

"Big time."

Prim slapped the table with her dainty hand. "You tell him to stay at home. I don't want him over here."

45

I said, "She doesn't really mean that."

"Oh, yes, I do."

"I'll be over in a few hours. Will she be okay until then?" he asked.

"Yeah. And you don't have to stay for a long time. Just peek in on her. I should be home around five-thirty."

"Sounds good," he said in a sexy, half-sleepy voice. "I'll have her tame as a kitten by the time you get home."

"I won't tolerate…" Prim grumbled, limping angrily from the room.

"Yeah, right." I laughed. "Good luck."

Chapter Seven

Cam was still with Prim when I arrived home; they were in the living room shouting answers at *The Family Feud*. I set my stuff on the kitchen table and joined them. Prim was stretched out in her recliner, crocheting. She wore a purple blouse and gray pants. Purple rhinestone clips glittered in her hair, and her cheeks and lips were rouged pink as peonies. I smiled. She only wore rouge and lipstick at church, weddings, funerals, and other such special occasions. Cam's visit was apparently special enough.

Cam lounged on the couch, munching on popcorn, in worn blue jeans and a tight red T-shirt, his socked feet propped on the coffee table. "Hey there. We're watching *Family Feud*. Prim's leaving me in the dust."

"She's pretty good. How long have you been here?" I smiled, crossing my arms and leaning on the doorjamb.

He lowered the volume on a car commercial. "Since about ten or eleven this morning."

The same tender, gooey feeling that accompanied images of baby animals beset me. "Oh, Cam. You didn't have to spend that long. I only wanted someone to peek in on her. You probably need to be at work, don't you?"

"Jacie and Mike are watching the place for me until I get there. I figured Prim needed me around here today." He put the bowl on the table and stood, brushing his hands on his jeans. "But since you're here, I can leave." He grabbed his ball cap off the couch. "Hey, Prim, I'll see you tomorrow, okay?" He stepped over and kissed Prim on the cheek, and she patted his taut, tanned arm, kissing him back.

"Bye, dear." She left a pink lip stain on his cheek. "Same time tomorrow?"

"Of course. I'd never miss a date with my favorite girl."

She laughed and slapped his arm. "You're a mess. Get out of here, you rascal."

I almost laughed. "Prim, I don't—"

Cam cut me off with a serious look and pointed toward the kitchen. "Walk me out?"

We stepped into the kitchen. He sat in a chair at the end of the table closest to the door, wiping the lipstick from his face. He wiggled his feet into his tennis shoes, looking at me, he whispered, "She needs someone here. She can't stay alone."

"It's that bad?"

He nodded, tying the laces. "Yep. This morning, I caught her trying to get in the car. Said she was going to the grocery. She was stoned out of her mind on her meds." He picked up his other shoe. "Luckily I got here when I did, or there's no telling what might've happened." He stuffed his foot into the shoe and bent over to tie it.

"Dear Lord." I covered my mouth. About a thousand horrific images of all the worst things that might've happened flashed through my mind, and the weight of our wonderful fortune pressed on me. "Thank heavens you were here."

He stood and pulled up his jeans. "I'm happy to do it." He averted his gaze and smoothed his hand over his short hair spiked in a thousand directions. I liked the tousled, bedhead look on him. "I'll come every day and watch her for you, okay? At least until she gets off these painkillers."

"I can't ask you to do that. She could be on them for the next ten years." The inevitable pushed on my mind. I'd have to hire in-home care. Sooner rather than later. Would insurance cover that? "Maybe if you could watch her until I can afford in-home care. Or at least until Batrene feels better."

"Yeah, Prim told me about Bryan. I'm sorry to hear about him. He was a great guy."

Pressure built in my throat and head. I still hadn't cried. Come to think of it, I hadn't been able to cry since my mom died. Since then, I'd closed down and gone numb. Anytime something awful happened, I became heavy, tired, and numb. "Thanks. He was really special. A brother, one of my best friends."

"What happened?"

I told him everything I knew. And everything I suspected.

"Wow. You think he was murdered?"

I nodded. "I'm hoping to find some kind of proof to give to Jimmy."

"Jimmy's a good deputy. If it is a murder, he'll prove it." Cam wrapped one arm around me and pulled me into a side-hug. "C'mere. You have enough to worry about. Let me help with Prim, okay? For as long as you need me." He kissed my temple.

"Between work and this, you're going to be exhausted."

He shrugged. "I'll nap when she does. Like parents do with babies."

We exchanged a smile. "I can't thank you enough…"

Cam clasped my hand and gave it a squeeze. "It's what friends are for."

"What about Jacie? She's going to be ticked at you helping out your ex-wife and spending your time over here."

He was silent for a moment. A dimple formed in his cheek and his eyes crinkled at the corners.

He was still holding my hand. He stroked my knuckle with his thumb, hardened and callused with work, his touch calming, reassuring. "She'll understand."

I started to disagree.

"When do you leave for work in the mornings?"

"About eight."

"I'll see you in the morning."

After changing into a comfortable pair of shorts, a T-shirt, and tennis shoes, I began preparing a tuna casserole to take to Batrene's. My cell phone rang. It was Millie, my best friend.

We'd known each other our entire lives. Growing up, we'd been practically inseparable since our first day in kindergarten. She'd moved to Lexington several years ago to establish her massage/yoga center, so seeing each other and talking to each other daily dropped to about once a week phone calls, daily Facebook interactions, and monthly visits.

She didn't need to say "Hello." She launched into her side of the conversation. "I heard about Bryan. I'm so sorry. Mom told me a few minutes ago." Millie's mom was recently inducted into the Old Lady Network.

"Thank you." I opened a can of tuna and drained the liquid.

"How's Batrene doing?"

"Fairly well. I haven't seen her yet. We were planning on going last night, but Prim fell and we ended up in the ER." I dumped the tuna into a bowl. "I'm making a tuna casserole now. We're going to take it over and visit a bit."

"Omigosh. What happened to Prim?"

I told her about Prim's troubles while opening another can of tuna and a can of cream of mushroom soup.

"Do you know what happened to Bryan?" Millie asked.

I grabbed a bag of frozen peas from the freezer and dumped them into the bowl. "I don't know. The sheriff believes it was probably natural causes. Maybe a heart attack. But...I don't know."

"You mean, you think it wasn't natural?"

I stabbed at a clump of frozen peas. "I know Bryan was a big guy, but he wasn't that big or unhealthy. And he was young."

"It's not impossible either, though."

I sighed. "I guess. It's..." I pulled a box of Velveeta out of the fridge and an onion out of the bin in the pantry. "Something isn't right. I can't explain it. A gut feeling, I guess."

"Detectives have to go on facts, though."

"I know. I think someone wanted to hurt him."

She sighed. "Please don't take this the wrong way—"

"I know what you're going to say. You're going to say I watch too many crime shows and read too many mysteries. I have an overactive imagination. And though my mom was murdered, not everyone who dies is murdered."

"Right."

"I know." I peeled the skin off the onion. "But I'm telling you something

50

isn't right. Bryan had discovered an accounting discrepancy and died a few hours later."

"Really? What was the discrepancy?"

"I don't know." I sliced the onion, with a loud clack, clack, clack of the knife against the cutting board, rivulets of tears on my cheeks.

"You okay?"

"Yeah, cutting onion. Anyway, there's this guy from the docks who was really angry about his paycheck and confronted Bryan."

"Do you think he did it?" Millie sounded eager, getting sucked into the story.

"I don't know."

"Wait..." She paused. "But what would the dock worker have to do with the accounting issue? Aren't those two separate things?"

"They are very different. I don't know how they'd be connected, or how I'd find out without getting in the sheriff's way." I stirred in the minced onion, poured the mixture into a casserole dish, and slid it into the preheated oven.

Millie said, "I wouldn't get on Goodman's bad side, Rook. You see what happened to your dad."

"I'm not sure the man has a good side." I cleaned the countertop.

Chapter Eight

Though Batrene only lived about twenty yards from our house, the tuna dish was hot and I didn't want to risk Prim falling. Since the pills made her loopy, we drove.

We knocked on Batrene's door. Maxine yapped inside. Batrene opened the door, wearing a black shirt over a black skirt. Her glasses sat atop her unkempt hair. She had large drooping eyes, and she pressed a handkerchief over her mouth and nose. She broke into tears as soon as she saw us.

"We brought you a casserole, if you can manage to eat." I shoved the dish forward, grabbing up Maxine, who scrambled to climb my legs.

Batrene accepted the dish. "That's so nice. Thank you, sweetie. Please, come in, come in."

We followed her into the beige living room as she crossed the dark hall and disappeared into the kitchen. She spoke as she moved dishes around. "People have been bringing me stuff all day. I'll never eat it all before it spoils. You'll need to take some of this food back with you."

She returned to us, arms held wide. "I'm happy to see you two." She pulled Prim against her enormous bosom and hugged her. "You're both so kind and sweet. I'm blessed to have friends like you." She pulled back, studying Prim, then said gravely, "How you doing, honey? I saw the ambulance last night. Are you all right? I prayed and prayed for you all last night."

Prim rubbed her hand over Batrene's back. "I was down on my back. I'm better now, though. Don't you worry about me. Your own worries are way bigger than mine. How are you doing?"

"I'll make it, I reckon, the same as anyone. One day at a time. But I don't know how." She reached for me. "Come here, child."

I placed Maxine on the couch and Batrene clutched me tight.

She broke into sobs, her tears wetting my shoulder. She pulled away. "Oh, look at me, blubbering like an old fool." She dabbed her eyes and blew her nose. "I've been out at the Tanbark Funeral Home to pick out his casket and make arrangements. It's awful. I don't know how I'll survive it."

"But you will. As I did," Prim said. "You cry as much as you need to."

I squeezed Batrene's hand.

We all sat on the couch, Prim and me sandwiching Batrene. We each held one of her hands. Maxine sat in my lap, panting.

The tightness in my throat and the pressure of unspent emotion in my head and chest hurt, but I couldn't seem to release the tears. "I'm sorry, Batrene. Everyone who met him loved him." I idly stroked Maxine's silky white fur.

Batrene nodded, tears spilling. "He was such a good boy." She patted my hand. Her rings cut uncomfortably into my flesh. "Sweet girl. You were like a sister to him, you know."

I nodded. "I do. And he was like a brother to me. I truly loved him."

Her bottom lip pushed into the top and quivered. Tears fell and she wiped them. "I know you did. And he loved you."

Prim patted her arm and they fell into discussions of the funeral arrangements and consoling each other over having to outlive their own children.

I'd never been one to handle grief with wallowing. I needed something to do, something to keep my hands and mind busy. "Would you mind if I help pick out his suit?"

"Sure, child. Go right ahead."

I passed down the dark hall to the last door on the left. I hadn't been in Bryan's room since last summer, when he wanted help picking out an outfit for his first date with his ex-girlfriend, Sheila.

I flipped on the light. Other than the bed cover with the blue, red, and green geometric design, the room hadn't changed much. The rumpled bed appeared as though he'd recently risen from sleep. Posters of the U of B Thoroughbreds college basketball team and the Dallas Cowboys football team hung over the head of the bed. Nightstands flanked each side of the bed.

Hanging by the window was a collage of pictures: his prom night, pictures of his parents when they were younger, and his stint as best man at his cousin's wedding. A picture of him and Sheila. And the picture of us, in high school, sitting on a wagon of hay bales during a homecoming party hayride. I didn't remember being that young. I'd never felt as young as I looked in that picture.

A large bookshelf loaded with books stood on the other side of the window. Most of the books were biographies about musicians and sports figures. There were a few accounting and business management books. His fiction books consisted of a collection of Stephen King, Jim Butcher, Tolkien, and George R. R. Martin. A shame he didn't live to complete his Martin collection. The spines of all the paperbacks were weathered. He'd read these all more than once. A dusty acoustic guitar occupied the corner by the bookshelf. The last time he played for me was in the spring. Out in the backyard near a fire. It had been cold that night. I wore his fleece jacket and sang badly whatever words I could remember to whatever notes he could remember. Mostly we talked and drank beer.

The desk stood at the end of the bed. Above the desk hung a bulletin board covered with a mess of pictures, papers, and memorabilia pinned to it: a blue ribbon prize for some unknown highlight, reminders, and bills. A whole life pinned to the board like little butterflies. There, behind a business card, he'd pinned a small orange fish I'd fashioned out of clay in summer camp. I'd been eleven and had made it for him because he loved fishing, spending most of his summers at a nearby creek. I couldn't believe he'd kept it all these years. This silly chunk of clay. I rubbed my aching forehead.

A clutter of books, papers, envelopes, bills, pens, and paperclips topped the desk. He couldn't be accused of neatness. I flipped through a few of the papers. He'd been helping Batrene pay her medical bills and managing all the accounts for her. She'd probably still need help with those things. At the bottom of the pile, a desk calendar spread over most of the desk with business cards and notes tucked in a corner tab. I pushed papers aside and saw where on Friday, he'd written *Meeting Dr. Thompson, 9A—Mom*. I hoped Batrene wasn't ill.

I scanned the other papers and didn't see anything of any interest or possible connection to his death. I moved on to his closet, opening the double doors. A wide variety of sports accessories, primarily related to golf—bags, shoes, shoe boxes, gloves, balls, tees, and clothes—crammed the closet. The far end of the closet was packed with his suits. I selected a navy suit, white shirt, and pale blue tie and lay those on the bed. I also found his favorite jersey—a replica of Billy Reynolds #43 from the Thoroughbreds. He'd been a superstar several years ago and was the brother of Deputy Ladonna Price. Though he'd long gone on to the NBA, fans in Kentucky still hailed him as one of the greatest point guards the Thoroughbreds had ever known.

Nevertheless, it was Bryan's favorite shirt. He wore it every time the Thoroughbreds played. It'd be nice to place this in the casket with him. At least, I'd offer that as an option to Batrene.

I inspected it. When I tried to remove the shirt, it snagged on what appeared to be a large manila envelope affixed to the crossbar with binder clips. I pulled the shirt off and removed the envelope.

Aghast, I flopped onto the bed, holding the envelope. People didn't go around pinning envelopes inside their clothes. Bryan must've been afraid of something or someone.

I opened the envelope. Inside were a letter and a thumb drive. I opened the letter. His tangled scrawl said:

Dear Mom,

I've always tried to make you proud and do the right thing. I love you and I'll do my best to take care of you. I hope I'm only being paranoid, but if anything happens to me, the reason is on the thumb drive. In case you haven't found it yet, my last will and testament is in my desk. I bequeath all my earthly possessions to you to dispense as you see fit.

Love always,

Bryan

I rolled the black thumb drive over between my fingers, wondering what it contained. Further, what had happened to make him resort to such precautions?

Batrene said, "What are you doing?"

I'd been deep in my thoughts, so her sudden appearance frightened me. I clapped my hand over my heart. "Heavens to Betsy you gave me a fright."

Prim peeked around Batrene's wide shoulders.

"I'm sorry, sugar." Her gaze drifted to my hand. "What's that?" Batrene stepped into the room, frowning.

I closed my fist over the thumb drive. "Batrene, we need to talk."

Chapter Nine

We sat at the table, drinking iced tea and eating a condolence peach cobbler with sympathy ice cream.

"I don't know what the police have told you..." I lowered my spoon and sat back.

Batrene shrugged, chewing her cobbler. "The sheriff told me Bryan died at work. He said it might've been a heart attack, but he's going to investigate to be sure. I'm sure it's only a precaution."

"That's all he said?" I exchanged a glance with Prim. "Batrene, did Bryan ever have any serious health problems?"

"Nothing out of the ordinary. He had the flu a few times, chickenpox, and mumps as a child. The normal sort of thing."

"He never complained of heart issues? Pain in the chest, shortness of breath? Or did he have sleep apnea or high blood pressure? Anything at all that might indicate heart problems?"

She was silent for a moment. "No. Nothing I'm aware of. He's always been healthy as a horse. I mean, he was a big boy, stout, but he worked hard." Her forehead creased. "Of course, we have heart problems in our family. My granddaddy died of a heart attack, and my dad had double bypass surgery, though ultimately a stroke got him."

"Is it possible Bryan died of a heart attack?"

Prim said, "What's this all about? Why do you keep asking her that?"

I sighed and rubbed my face. "I don't know how to talk about this..."

Maxine trotted to her silver monogrammed food bowl. She gobbled the wet food loudly, her collar tags jingling with her movements.

"I don't want to alarm you, but you deserve to know. I was hoping the sheriff would've told you everything."

Batrene frowned. "Told me what?"

"I'm not convinced Bryan's death was natural."

Prim and Batrene's brows shot up. Their voices rose a couple pitches. "What?"

"I was there. Something wasn't right about the scene. I don't think he died of a heart attack. I believe he might've been…" I swallowed, looking between the two women, who were turning gray and sitting still as pointers on prey. I cleared my throat. "Murdered."

The older women gasped and looked at each other then fell back in their chairs.

"I can't believe it, but it makes sense." Batrene sat quiet for a moment. She slammed her dimpled fist on the table. "I knew it. I knew my boy didn't die of any heart attack. When the sheriff told me that, it didn't feel right." Her face reddened. "But I thought he ought to know since he's a professional and all. He lied to me."

I put my hand out as if to push down her rising anger. "Hold on. I'm the last person to defend Sheriff Goodman. Hateful man. And yes, he should've told you everything. He believes Bryan died of natural causes. When I told him Bryan didn't die of natural causes, his underwear bunched in a knot. Part of it, I'm sure, is resentment toward me and his determination to prove me wrong. Since he doesn't believe the murder theory, he probably didn't want to upset you unnecessarily without being certain."

"He still should've told me everything. I'm calling the station in the morning and giving him what for."

"You're right. I don't blame you. And you should do exactly that." I imagined Batrene chewing out Goodman and delighted inwardly. I bit my lip to suppress my smile.

A deep line formed between Prim's brows. "Rook, are you sure? That's a heavy accusation."

"No, I'm not sure." I told them my suspicions regarding the discrepancies he'd discovered and the run-ins with Clarence and Dewey.

"Dewey Stiggers?" Batrene's voice seemed loaded with accusation. "That boy has always been nothing but trouble. His daddy used to run around with your daddy. No offense, Rook."

I wasn't offended. How could I be? My dad inhabited a prison cell as we spoke. I lifted my hands in surrender. "Can't be offended with the truth. I have no illusions about my father."

Batrene snarled. "I'd bet my eye teeth Dewey has got something to do with this."

"But would he really kill Bryan over a paycheck dispute? Seems like a trifling thing to kill someone over," Prim said.

"People have been killed for far less." Batrene pulled her arms over her ample frame. "Wouldn't surprise me a bit. How did he do it? Did he..." Her lip quivered and her voice broke. "How did he hurt my baby?"

I hemmed. I didn't want to tell her, but she deserved to know. "Bryan didn't have any wounds I could see. Maybe poison? There was a spilled drink on the floor. And vomit. And there were other symptoms that could've been associated with poisoning."

Prim leaned on the table. "That doesn't sound like enough evidence to go around accusing people of murder. Isn't there anything else?"

I touched the envelope. "This. He left this letter. Batrene, you should see this." I slid the envelope toward her.

She opened it, read silently, and burst into fresh tears, holding the letter to her heart. "Oh, my heart. My sweet boy."

"He clearly thought he was in trouble. I'm going to find out what's on this thumb drive. His letter said it has evidence to prove something might've happened to him. Does he have a computer here?"

Batrene said, "It should be in his room. Didn't you see it when you were in there?"

"I don't remember." I frowned and jumped to my feet. "I'll go check." I searched his room. Nothing. I returned to the kitchen. "It's not there. Did he take it to work?"

Batrene shrugged. "He must have."

"Do you have any other computer here?"

Batrene snorted. "No. Lord, I wouldn't know what to do with one." She swelled with emotion. A sob broke out and she squeaked through her tears. "Bryan managed all the business stuff for me. The bills, the insurance. I don't have a head for business. I don't know what I'll do without him." She swiped her eyes with a napkin.

"Rook, you shouldn't have upset Batrene like this." Prim touched Batrene's arm. "It'll be okay. We'll help you the best we can."

"I'm not trying to upset her. I'm sorry, Batrene."

"You didn't upset me, child." Batrene blew her nose. "You gave me what I asked for. I'm mad, though. Mad the sheriff didn't tell me all this. Mad Bryan didn't tell me any of this. Why wouldn't they tell me anything?"

I had a bad habit of letting my mouth speed ahead of my brain. "I don't know what happened, but I'm going to find out."

Prim said, "What are you going to do? You could get in trouble if you don't turn over what you found to the sheriff."

"I don't trust the sheriff as far as I can throw him. After I look at what's on here, I'm going to take the letter and thumb drive to Jimmy Duvall. I trust he'll do right by us."

As soon as Prim and I arrived home, Prim medicated her pain and went to bed. I picked up my book *Mindhunter: Inside the FBI's Elite Serial Crime Unit* by John E. Douglas while noshing a moon pie and Kentucky Spice. I'd worry about counting calories again tomorrow. After all, in the immortal words of Scarlett O'Hara, "tomorrow was another day."

Staring at my closed laptop on the coffee table, I began to regret my impulsive promise to find out what happened to Bryan. Of course, as an old friend, I wanted to know what happened to him. I wanted justice for him and for the people who loved him. I shouldn't have made such a promise to Batrene, though. I watched mystery shows, police procedurals, and forensic shows. I read true crimes, forensics books, and mystery novels. I wasn't completely ignorant to how crimes were solved, but I was in no way a professional crime solver.

Of course, I wanted to help, but I was scared. Scared of messing up the investigation. Scared of disappointing Batrene and Bryan. Scared of overstepping and getting myself in trouble with the sheriff. Or maybe getting myself killed. Because, if Bryan was murdered, then the killer was very likely still at the distillery.

Turning the thumb drive around and around in my hand, I wondered if I was prepared to deal with its contents.

A huge Bryan-shaped hole burned right through my heart. This was exactly the sort of thing we would've ruminated over while sitting on the back porch, drinking a cold beer. I would've asked for his advice and he would've offered wisdom beyond his years. I rubbed my forehead trying to imagine what those words would be now.

I was a former English Composition Instructor. I had a master's in English. Other than books, I had zero training in police procedure or in forensics research. That didn't prevent me from opening my big mouth and telling Batrene I'd find out the truth. That was as good as a promise. I had to follow through now. I wasn't like my dad. I told the truth and I kept my promises, even if I regretted biting off more than I could chew.

But if I discovered who took Bryan from me, I could bring peace to Batrene and myself. I knew the burden of carrying an unsolved murder, to always feel chained to ghosts and wander through the fog of doubts, questions, and the unknown. Always seeking the closure that never seemed to come. I couldn't live with that again. Maybe I could help provide closure and ease a little of the burden.

I reached for my laptop, flipped it on, and inserted the thumb drive. I opened another moon pie. I was in this now—for better or worse.

Chapter Ten

I woke up the next morning on the couch with *The Golden Girls* theme song playing and the scent of coffee permeating the house. Prim grunted under her slow progress down the stairs. I kicked off the afghan and hurried to the stairs to watch her descent, to ensure she made it safely to the ground floor. She'd already showered and dressed, wearing her navy pants, a white shirt, and a lavender sweater. She'd touched her cheeks and lips with pink. She felt for the next step with her little pink house shoes.

"You're dressed already? You really shouldn't be doing that without my help."

"Quit telling me what I should and shouldn't do." She side-stepped down the stairs, holding onto the banister.

I chuckled. "I'll think about it. How's your back?"

"Hurts. What do you want for breakfast?"

"You need help?" I started up the stairs.

"Get back. I've got this."

I held up my hands and stepped back, but I hung close. "Okay. I'm going to make breakfast. What do you want?"

"I'm not hungry." She made the final step and shuffled into the kitchen to fix her coffee.

I pulled out a chair at the table for her and hovered close. I grabbed her elbow and helped her in spite of her grumbling.

I placed a plate of buttered toast and a jar of apple butter in front of her. "Here. Toast and coffee. You need to eat with that medicine. Your pills are on this napkin."

"Don't you need to get ready for work?"

"Going right now." I jogged up the stairs with my coffee mug and jumped in the shower.

By the time I'd dressed for work and fixed my hair and makeup, Prim had relocated to her recliner. She nibbled at her toast and laughed at one of Rose Nylund's St. Olaf stories.

My laptop stood open on the coffee table. I saved the information from the thumb drive to my computer. I'd have to look at the information later, though I was in way over my head with the information I'd discovered. There had been several files containing account ledgers, inventory spreadsheets, receipts, and invoices. Anything beyond practical math, like balancing checkbooks and figuring out recipe measurements and square footage, made my head spin.

As I slipped the thumb drive into my red capris pocket, I remembered Bryan had plugged a thumb drive into his computer at work yesterday. Likely, the one in my pocket had been filled earlier and contained only partial information. After all, if he'd been researching the accounts for potentially illegal discrepancies, then the rest of the materials would be on the thumb drive in his work computer. It had likely been taken into evidence already, along with his computer and laptop, so I'd have to satisfy myself with only partial information to guide my investigation.

Prim said, "Are you really going to try to find out who killed Bryan?"

I pushed up the sleeves on my navy and white-striped boatneck shirt. "I said I would. I'm going to stand by that."

"You're messing with a dangerous game, child." She stared me down over the rim of her rhinestone glasses. "If someone hurt Bryan, they're probably still hanging around. And they wouldn't care to get you out of the way, too."

"I know. I've considered that already. Remember, I have an advantage the police don't. I'm inside the office. I might be able to get a read on something important to help find the killer faster."

A knock sounded at the back door. "Cam's here."

I kissed her head, feeling the skull under her thin, clammy skin. "Don't worry about me. I want to find enough evidence so the sheriff can't possibly deny he was murdered. I'll be fine." I wiped my nude rose lipstick from her skin and winked at her. "Don't give Cam any trouble today."

I dashed through the kitchen to open the door.

Cam's tousled hair, unshaven face, and rumpled clothes gave him the appearance of a horse that'd been ridden hard and put away wet. His heavy, bloodshot eyes screamed for more sleep.

He presented a grease-soaked bag. "Donut? They're from Irene's."

"Ohhh. Irene's." I stepped aside to let him enter. "I'll definitely take one if you have a raspberry and cream Danish in there."

"I'm not new to this." Like a genie with a snap of his fingers, one of Irene's delectable raspberry and cream-filled donuts appeared. "Just for you," he smirked.

I accepted the gift, bit into the piece of sugary, fried heaven, and wiggled a little dance. "There's coffee over there if you want it. Help yourself." I nodded in the direction of the coffeepot. "You look like you need it."

He pulled a mug out of the cabinet and poured a cup of coffee, stirring in a bit of cream. "I do. I didn't get much sleep last night."

"Everything okay?" I hoped he'd forgo any stories detailing a romantic evening between him and Jacie.

"Yeah, it's been one of those nights. We got in a fight about how much she's spending on the wedding. She's having difficulty with the fact I'm not Bill Gates."

"I get paid in a couple weeks. I'll give you at least half of what I owe you."

"It's not that," he sipped his coffee and propped his backside against the counter. "It's all of it."

"Is there anything I can do to help?"

He chuckled. "You got any plans for a cheap wedding lying around somewhere?"

I laughed. "She could have the wedding we had. It was cheap."

He laughed. "Dirt cheap. But it was the best time. Dawn on the Natural Bridge at Red River Gorge."

"And canoeing. Remember when you tipped the canoe?"

He laughed. "I wasn't the one who tipped the canoe. You—"

"No, no. You tried to stand."

"You weren't paddling right."

I rolled my eyes, smiling. "Whatever. I know the truth." I popped the last bite of donut into my mouth. I'd deal with the regret later. "And it was crazy cold. Middle of October, soaked to the bone."

"But then," he reached in the bag for a glazed donut, "we got to dry off in front of the fire while sipping Irish coffee. And ..." His gaze grew distant. His faint smile bespoke a pleasant memory. He shook off the past. "Well..." He screwed up his mouth and swallowed his words with a sip of coffee. "Anyway, I think we had the perfect wedding. Secluded and quiet, tucked away in the woods, just us. I still think about those days. Don't you?"

My skin crawled with awkwardness, like I was wearing a twisted bra. Admittedly, I did think of those days. Sometimes with sweet nostalgia. Sometimes with resentment.

He looked at his boots. "But that was a long time ago." He smiled at me, sadly.

This was getting weird and uncomfortable. We were friends, in spite of our problems. In the spirit of said friendship, I made myself say, "Relax. Everything will work out fine between you and Jacie. You'll have a beautiful wedding and a romantic honeymoon, I'm sure." I grabbed my purse and keys. "Hate to rush off, but work beckons." I doubled back for the *Mind Hunter* book with hopes of reading at lunch. "Prim's already had her medicine. Thanks for everything. I owe you big time." And I had no idea how I'd ever pay him back.

During my drive to work, I developed my plan of attack for finding evidence proving Bryan had been murdered.

I passed Bryan's office as I headed toward the marketing pit. The lights were out and the police tape had been removed. I peeked inside and flipped on the light. I glanced around and slipped inside unseen and eased the door shut.

Bryan's office was simple, small, and utilitarian: a filing cabinet near the window, two chairs in front of his small desk, a computer, and a bookshelf with a lower cabinet. The bookshelf had only books, binders, and a printer.

His cup had been removed from the floor, though the carpet was still dark with the spill and the vomit. In fact, the office smelled of a strange blend of vomit and a faint but bitter herbal scent, perhaps a cleaning agent.

Starting with the filing cabinet, only one of the four drawers had anything in it. I thumbed the manila tabs with printed labels: invoices, receipts, tax forms, credit memos, payroll—the usual stuff one might expect an accountant to have. I flipped through the payroll folder. Copies of old reports. Nothing here stood out to me.

Next, I searched the desk. The papers that had been there Monday were gone. I sat in Bryan's desk chair, feeling like an intruder. I reminded myself I was doing this for him. I recalled him sitting here, looking at his papers, working away on the last day I saw him. I opened all his desk drawers. Nothing of any importance. I twisted around and opened the cabinet.

The door opened. "Young lady, what're you doing in here?"

I almost jumped out of my skin. I spun around. Clarence Ford. "I might ask you the same."

He crossed his arms over his thin chest, his gold watch glittering in the office light. "As the bookkeeper, there are files and documents I need access to."

"As Bryan's good friend, I came to retrieve his personal belongings for his mama."

He inhaled sharply, pressing his lips into a tight line. He glanced at his shoes. "I'm truly sorry about Bryan." His voice was soothing, deep, and rich. "We had our differences, but I'm sorry about his death. I guess the stress got to him."

Now was my chance to start digging to see what I could discover.

"What sort of differences?"

The half-wink of his eye betrayed his suspicion. "We didn't always agree on certain business matters, but I liked him as a man."

Maybe Clarence had seen or heard something around the office. He had to have known about the issues with Dewey.

"I heard Dewey was mad at him. Is he the sort of person who'd threaten Bryan and act on those threats?"

He shrugged a shoulder. "Dewey's a hothead. He's had run-ins with practically everyone. He's always throwing threats around. I wouldn't pay much heed to him. All bark, no bite."

"You don't think he'd act on any of his threats?"

"I don't really know the guy. I guess anything is possible." He rubbed his nose. "I mean, everybody has their breaking point. Right?"

"Can you recall anyone who had problems with Bryan?"

He tilted his head. "You think someone hurt him?"

"Not necessarily. I don't know. Like you said, anything is possible. It might explain why he died so young and suddenly." I wasn't getting anywhere with Clarence, and there wasn't anything of import I could find in Bryan's office anyway. There might be evidence in Clarence's office, though. I stood. "Anyway, there's nothing here to take back to his mama." I headed for the door. "Thanks for your time."

Clarence said, "I will say this..."

I turned.

"Seems Holly had a run-in with Bryan once. He caught her using petty cash for her personal purchases and also charging non-business-related items to the company credit card."

Bingo! "That's pretty serious."

He sniffed. "Not really. Holly's kind of a ditz."

Not true. Holly was sharper than she let on, but I didn't want to interrupt him since he was giving me a bit of information.

"Bryan finally got through to her that she'd been wrong, so she paid everything back. She's been fine since then." He tucked his hands in his pockets and rocked on his heels. "I'll tell you something else. If Bryan had been nosing around in the wrong man's business, he should've known when to stop." His tone implied a threat. His poker face shifted. He squinted and blinked. He knew something; it radiated from his eyes a moment before his poker face slipped back into place. "Because nosy folks get themselves in a world of hurt."

Chapter Eleven

I headed toward my office, panic setting in. Clarence hadn't said anything particularly incriminating, but there had been something threatening in his looks, in the way he spoke that rang my alarm bells and frightened me. Of course, vocal tone wouldn't stand up in court, so I had to find actual evidence.

Now I had three potential suspects for my list: Dewey, Clarence, and Holly, albeit tentatively. Dewey and Clarence held the top spots. Though Holly may have misused the petty cash, and though I didn't trust her sticky sweet veneer, I was convinced Clarence threw her name into the mix to deflect attention from himself.

I nearly ran smack into Len as he exited the break room. He grabbed his coffee cup with both hands to steady it.

"Sorry," I said. "I was…"

He lifted the cup to his lips, his dark, beautiful eyes glimmering with humor. "No worries." His kissable lips spread into a bright smile. One dark brow lifted. He reminded me of one of the pretty boys on Prim's soap operas, complete with the blue button-down and khakis. He sure smelled pretty, too—fresh and mossy, like a spring running through a shady field on the side of a mountain.

"Come on back and let me show you the campaign we're working on and what I'll need you to do today." He guided me toward the marketing pit. "Best way to get training is by jumping right in. I'm sure you can handle it."

I didn't want to drop my current chase, but I still had to work, so I followed him. I pulled a chair over to sit beside him in his cubicle.

He switched on his computer and pulled out pamphlets and fliers. "We're currently working on the Bourbon, Bands, and BBQ Festival. This is the first time we've put together an event this big. We're partnering with the other distilleries. There will be live music, food trucks, and, of course, BBQ vendors. We'll also have local arts and crafts vendors." He pulled up an image of Rothdale's main street on the computer. "The plan is to close Main Street and put vendors and tents here." He pointed at the screen, moving his finger along the image. "And food trucks all along both sides of the street here, and here…" He pointed at the courthouse in the center, where both sides of the street converged. "In the center, in front of the courthouse, we're going to erect a stage for the bands."

"Wow. Sounds like a big deal."

"It is. Huge. An all-day event. We're also going to have a kiddie playland, bouncy castles, games, and a small petting zoo over here."

I leaned in closer. It didn't escape my notice how close we were. Our knees were touching.

"Hey, you two," said a perky female voice behind us.

Holly bounced in, wearing a floral skirt with teal, lime, and gray and a lime green blouse which didn't do her any favors. In fact, it only enhanced her acne-scarred skin and thick-caked makeup. She smiled, batting her mascara-clumped eyelashes. "Don't you two look cozy?" There was a tightness to her dimpled, high-glossed smile.

I fought the urge to hold my nose and cough against her heavy woodsy perfume. And, apparently, she'd bathed in it. The strength and volume of the perfume assaulted the senses. Already, my sinuses were swelling, and a deep throb rose from the depths, spiderwebbing over my entire head.

Len said, "Snug as a couple fleas on a hound dog."

I chuckled because such an idiom completely jarred with his suave image.

Her eyes widened a bit, giving her the air of a crazy clown. "How fantastic." She turned to me. "Are you enjoying the job so far?" Her penciled brows arched.

"Yes. I'm really happy to be here. It's slim pickings out there."

Len said, "I know I'm glad to have you here. I'm sure you'll be a valuable asset to our team."

Holly batted her eyelashes again and pursed her glossy lips with a sharp inhale. "Len, when you get a second, I need to talk to you."

"Sure. No problem. I'm almost finished here."

She spun and flounced from the room. His gaze lingered a half-second longer on her backside than it should've in a work environment.

I wanted to get on with the work so I could proceed with my investigation. "What do you want me to do?"

"We could really use help gathering other sponsors and vendors to fund this thing. Lots of cold calling, I fear."

My stomach churned. I'd rather have my foot run over by a spiked wheel than make phone calls to strangers to ask for money. I sighed. "Alrighty then."

He must've read my disappointment. "You won't always be stuck with the grunt work. It's where the greatest need is right now, though." He smiled, his gaze lingering over my face, and pulled a folder from a shelf. "Here's a call list."

"Guess I'd better get cracking." I sat at my desk in my cubicle and began making phone calls.

Len left his office to speak with Holly.

After a few calls, my mind turned over to my suspect list. I wondered how many of my colleagues were on Facebook or Twitter. Social media would be an excellent way to find out more about people, to get a hint at their character and how they lived. I glanced over my shoulder. I didn't like sitting with my back to the door.

In a small window, I opened Facebook and started with Dewey Stiggers, since Batrene believed he was the most likely culprit. His page was an open book. It always amazed me how many people didn't secure their privacy. He'd last posted a year ago and his wall contained only three pictures. In one, decked out in hunting gear, he stood by the carcass of an eight-point buck. In another, he straddled a motorcycle. And in the last, he leaned against an orange Dodge Daytona. I checked Twitter. Nothing. I gathered he was private, perhaps to the point of paranoia. He liked guns and machinery, typical symbols of toughness and a masculinity deeply embedded in machismo culture. Many men used guns and cars as props to bolster their self-esteem and self-image. These traits, combined with the temper I'd already witnessed, spoke of a man who was volatile, violent, and insecure. A powder-keg combination.

Next, I tried Clarence because he held a high rank on my list. His Facebook page was secured, so I could only access a few pictures. There was one of him with an older man and a middle-aged woman, presumably his father and sister. The older man was in the middle, his arms around his children. They smiled like a loving family, but the body language was contradictory. The father stood closer to the sister, with more distance between him and Clarence, almost as if they were afraid to touch. Though Clarence smiled, the sentiment didn't quite reach his eyes. An underpinning of sadness weighed the corners of his mouth.

Maybe there were troubles between father and son. Their relationship might be more strained than that of the father and daughter. If so, Clarence might feel a need to prove himself to his father. He would push harder for success and the resulting material trappings—as evidenced by the other pics of Clarence at Lexington's elite Paradiso golf course and in a private box at the famous Keeneland horse racing track, where all the men, including Clarence, were wearing the exclusive Keeneland Club pins. He might need to maintain a certain image to impress others in order to feel important and successful.

Recalling the conversation I'd overheard, he was upset Bryan didn't want to use The Flying Eagle cooperage anymore. Clarence's family's business. Maybe Clarence secured the deal between Four Wild Horses and the cooperage to impress his father. If the deal went under, then a deep rift might develop in the delicate father-son relationship. Would that be enough to incite Clarence to murder? It didn't seem like a strong enough motive. I had to find another way of ferreting out anything he might be trying to hide. If I could just get into his office...

Someone entered the marketing pit. I closed the search window and turned to see who had passed by. Marla. She didn't seem to have noticed what I'd been doing. After ensuring the all-clear, I reopened the window. I checked Twitter. Clarence didn't appear to have a Twitter account. Not surprising, since Twitter tended to a younger crowd.

Lastly, I tried Holly. Her Facebook page was an open book. She had no privacy restrictions in place and posted many times a day. In fact, her last post consisted of a selfie taken that morning in the car *#feelingfine #nofilter*. The cover photo was the obligatory romantic suburbanite pic of her husband, her two kids, and herself all dressed in white, walking on the beach. Her profile image showed her in a café, wearing a silly hat and sunglasses, sipping a giant margarita. Memes with a religious bent; funny, snark-laden memes; cute animal pics; and selfies littered her feed. And there were many selfies. Lots and lots of selfies, many of the annoying duck-lipped variety, some filtered, some not. She also seemed to love taking pictures. There were a ton of pictures of her family, food, pets, vacation, house. On and on the pictures went. It would take a long time to look through them and get a good impression of her character.

I sensed someone entering the room behind me, so I minimized the window on my computer, then waited.

"Hey," Len said.

Panicked, I closed the window completely and reached for the phone and my phone list.

He leaned on my cubicle wall. "How's the list going?"

Flushed and flustered, I fumbled around. "Oh-uh…well…"

"Any trouble? Any questions?"

"No, um…" I tucked a lock of hair behind my ear. "I'm good." I smiled. "Really good."

After another mind-numbing hour of cold-calling people and being hung up on and snipped at, I remembered I needed to call Jimmy. The time on my phone said ten. Time to recaffeinate.

Len popped over the top of the cubicle partition. "How's it going? Everything okay?"

"Sure." I smiled at him. "Everything's fine."

He stepped around beside me. He spoke with enthusiasm. "Great. I know it can be a hassle making these calls, but it's the most important job here right now. Have you had anyone register?" He relaxed against the partition.

"One 'yes,' three 'maybes,' two 'I'll call you back,' two 'hang ups,' and three irritated rants." I sang, "And a partridge in a pear tree."

He laughed. "The important thing is to not take the rejection personally."

"I'll try, but I may be traumatized before it's all over."

His dark eyes lit with mirth. "Don't tell your boyfriend I was the one to traumatize you."

"I don't have a boyfriend."

He blinked, surprised. He smoothed a hand over his hair and grinned. "Well, in that case, there's always lunch to heal the trauma." His gaze lingered on my face, dipping to my lips and up again. The smile faded briefly before popping back into place. "Would you like to go to lunch?"

"Oh…" I screwed up my face. I'd actually planned to return to social media to search Holly's profile. "I'd like to, but I can't today. I have plans. Maybe another time?"

"Sure. No problem."

"I'm going to take a quick break, then I'll jump back in the saddle."

When the marketing pit emptied out for lunch, I ate Cheez-its and drank a Diet Dr. Pepper I'd snagged from the vending machine. My *Mind Hunter* book beckoned me, but the lure of Facebook was stronger. I wanted to know more about my co-worker, Holly. I discovered she was athletic, passive-aggressive, vain, insecure, attention-seeking, and humble-bragging and loved the high life. There were lots of pics of 5Ks and gym shots, where she posted about running through pain or running farther than before. Another post stated "I woke from a nap, no makeup, at dinner with hubby, and guys are still hitting on me. Seriously?"

I rolled my eyes. *Phuleease!*

There were other selfies where she had reportedly rolled out of bed in the morning with *#morningfresh #nomakeup #filterfree*. However, the images were obviously staged to show her as a beautiful angel. Her audience appeared to have fallen for it with lots of Likes, Hearts, and comments along the lines of "Stunning," "Beautiful," or "Hawt." The hashtags indicated an

Instagram or Twitter presence. I checked both platforms, but a quick scroll told me it was more of the same. I went back to Facebook.

There were lots of pics of expensive vacations. A fancy Tudor-style house surrounded by shrubs. Spas. A white Lexus. A gold SUV. Charlotte Tilbury makeup. Hair styled at the elite The Maxx in Lexington. Gourmet food. Was there anything this woman didn't take a picture of? Her daughters were involved in child pageants, dance, and gymnastics. None of those things were cheap. There were lots of beach and boat pics of her posing seductively in a bikini, glamorous selfies. There were several pics of her children in soccer and baseball uniforms and ballet tutus. There were a few of her husband and even fewer of her with her husband. Those of the family were designed to give the impression of the perfect family. Yet, there were a great many more pictures of herself, where she had carefully crafted an image of a free and independent woman. Her profile sat on the verge of signaling she was single and available.

There were also a lot of vague, passive-aggressive posts begging for attention, also known as vague-booking. Posts such as "I can't anymore…" or "I'm so sad right now…" or "Please send prayers…" She'd actually posted a picture of herself crying. My stomach knotted with disgust at the attention-seeking porn.

I sat back and stared at the computer, taking in what I'd learned about Holly. Clarence had said she'd been misusing petty cash. Her pictures proved she clearly enjoyed spending money. Perhaps she carried a lot of debt or had a compulsive shopping problem. But that didn't amount to murder, unless she was embezzling a great deal of money from the distillery. Yet, she was only the administrative assistant. She didn't handle the books. So, how could the discrepancies Bryan uncovered relate to her? In spite of her character flaws and questionable spending habits, I didn't see a motive for murder. Yet.

I checked the time. People would be returning from lunch soon, so I needed to conclude my social media search. But I was curious about one more thing. In the search window, I typed Len's name. His page wasn't secured, but he didn't seem to use it much. His profile was a picture of him, shirtless, slick with oil, hair wind tousled. He had a nice body, firm pecs, and six-pack abs. Deeply tanned, he stood in a boat on a river, smiling, with mirrored sunglasses. The room seemed to be getting warmer. His cover picture was of him and a few friends on top of a mountain. Searching deeper, I found most of the pictures were him with friends at sporting events, hiking, or concerts. Occasionally, he posted a thought about a book or a movie. Overall, his page gave the impression of an intelligent man, well-liked, relaxed, secure. Best of all, I saw no indication of a girlfriend or wife.

Chapter Twelve

The rest of the workday dragged by. Five o'clock had never looked so good to me. My brain buzzed numbly from working the phone all day. Before leaving, I stopped by the restroom. A cleaning woman scrubbed the toilet in the next stall. An idea sparked. I returned to my desk and pretended to work.

Len, with his computer bag on his shoulder, sighed and stretched. "Quitting time."

I imagined the suntanned torso from the Facebook picture and averted my gaze to my computer again.

"This has been a looong day. Aren't you leaving?"

"I have a few more things to finish before I leave."

"Dedication. I like it." He smiled and winked then left the room.

I hid my car keys in my computer bag and waited in the break room. When one of the cleaning crew came in, a middle-aged woman with dyed red hair, I smiled. "Guess I need to get home. Have a good night." I pretended to leave then circled back to the break room and found the red-headed woman wiping the table.

"I'm sorry to bother you." I rolled my eyes and acted dim. "I'm such a ditz. I've locked myself out of my office. Would you care to let me in?"

"Sure, hon. Which one is yours?"

I led the way to Clarence's office.

Red-hair unlocked the door. "You can leave it open and we'll lock up when we're done vacuuming."

I thanked her and she left.

The office was small, with a shaded window behind the desk laden with files and papers.

On the wall to the right stood a bookshelf stacked with papers, binders, books, and files, flanked by a filing cabinet. No laptop on the bookshelf or in any of the filing cabinets drawers. I searched the desk. No computer. I slid behind the desk chair to open the drawers on the left. The smaller drawers at the top had nothing, but, upon opening the larger drawer at the bottom, I discovered behind the hanging files, a plastic bag with a flat, rectangular object inside.

Removing the package from the drawer, I extracted a computer bag which looked quite similar to Bryan's. I unzipped the bag to reveal a silver-lidded laptop with a U of B Thoroughbreds sticker on it. Bryan's computer. I searched all the pockets and recesses but still didn't find the other thumb drive.

However, at the bottom of the laptop bag, under the panel, was a yellow legal-sized sheet folded several times. It read: *Nosy men die.* The writing was distinctive, square, and rigid. It looked like the writing on the other letter I'd found in his car.

My mouth dropped open. This was a definite threat. The child-like handwriting in black ink was as chilling as the message itself. I shuddered. Since Bryan had never said anything to me about this, I assumed he hadn't mentioned it to Batrene, either. He wouldn't have wanted her to worry. Besides, if she'd known of the threats, she would've told me the night Prim and I ate dinner with her. However, maybe Bryan didn't take the threat seriously.

Also, the phrasing *Nosy men die* resembled something Clarence had said earlier. He'd said, "Nosy folks get themselves in a world of hurt." Though not verbatim, the statements were similar and conveyed the same sentiment. Had Clarence written the threatening letters?

I returned the computer to the bag. This needed to get into Jimmy's hands immediately. Since I'd been a teacher, my computer bag was wide enough to carry not only a laptop but a few books, too. I stuffed Bryan's computer bag inside mine.

Standing to leave, I noticed a thin strip of red peeking from under the large desk calendar. I shifted the calendar. Bryan's red folder. I stuffed that into my computer bag too and started for the door, looking around a final time to ensure everything was in its place. I switched off the lights and started down the hall. As I rounded the corner, I bumped into Holly.

We both gasped. She smiled. "You scared the hide off me." Suspicion filled her eyes though she continued to smile. "What are you doing here so late? Len must be pushing you really hard."

"Not at all…" I smiled. "Finishing up now. On my way out."

She glanced at my computer bag. "Uh-huh."

"I can't believe you're here this late." I tried to distract her.

"I work a lot of late evenings. Especially around the end of the month. I help with sending out invoices and such." She frowned and stepped around me, heading toward Clarence's office. "Oh, goodness. Look at that. Clarence's door is wide open." She closed the door and looked askance at me.

"I guess the cleaning crew forgot to close it."

"Uh-huh," she said, flatly.

I gave my perkiest smile. "Gotta run. See you tomorrow." I hightailed it out of the building before Holly could ask any more questions.

I flew from the distillery, calling Cam on my cell. When he answered, I heard *Wheel of Fortune* in the background. He was still with Prim. "Can you watch her a little bit longer? I need to run an errand real quick."

"How much longer? I need to get to the bar."

"Fifteen, twenty minutes? I swear, I'll be as fast as possible."

He hesitated. "Okay, I guess. Hurry, though."

I phoned Jimmy. "Where are you?"

"At the gym."

"Can you meet me at my house when you're done?"

"Sure. What's up? You sound…hectic."

"I'm fine. I'm in a hurry. I'll see you soon." I hung up and swung into the library on my way. I dug the red folder out of my computer bag and ran inside to make copies of the contents.

Back in my car, I opened Bryan's computer. Maybe I could transfer the files to myself. Password protected. Dang it. Just like him. Ever since he had his bike stolen when we were kids, he locked everything, even his gym bag. Like anyone would want his sweaty socks. And he was too smart to make the password easy to guess. I'd have to make do with the papers I'd copied. I stuffed it back in my bag and raced home.

Jimmy arrived as I prepared dinner. Prim sat at the kitchen working a crossword in her pants and blouse. I stood barefoot at the counter in an old Beatles T-shirt and running shorts while the bacon sizzled and I sliced tomatoes for BLTs.

He came in the back doorway, wearing a black Metallica T-shirt and khaki cargo shorts, smelling shower-fresh. He removed his sunglasses and hooked them on the neck of his shirt. "Evening, ladies."

Prim brightened. "Jimmy Duvall. I haven't seen you in a dog's age. Where've you been keeping yourself?"

"Under rocks and 'round trees."

Prim laughed. "Come give us a hug." She forced herself to stand.

"I'm awfully sweaty. I've been at the gym."

"Oh, I don't care about such things." She hugged him close in spite of the distance he tried to provide. "You'll stay for dinner."

"I'm not fit for supper. If I'd known—"

Prim looked through the bottom of her glasses at him. "Nonsense. You can. Rook, get Jimmy some tea." She patted the chair beside her at the table and sat.

I placed a glass of iced tea in front of him. "We're eating simple tonight. I hope you don't mind BLTs, macaroni salad, dressed cucumbers, and watermelon."

"Sounds great to me. Thank you." He gulped his tea.

I finished putting together the sandwiches while Prim began an excavation for information she'd no doubt put to good use in the OLN.

After supper, Prim fell asleep to *Entertainment Tonight* while Jimmy and I stepped out onto the back porch with our tea. I brought Bryan's computer bag and the thumb drive I'd found in his room.

The sun rested low in the sky, but we were still a few hours away from darkness. The scent of honeysuckle swept around us as the breeze toyed with the wind chimes.

We each claimed a rocking chair.

"Sorry you got roped into dinner. I'm sure you hadn't planned on that tonight. But I do appreciate you coming out. I couldn't come to you because I can't leave Prim alone." A strand of hair escaped my clip. I reclipped my ponytail.

"I'm glad you called. Been thinking about you. I had a nice time. Supper was good. Thank you."

"You made Prim's day. She doesn't get out to see people much anymore, so I know it's wearing on her."

"She's a sweet lady. I've always liked Prim." He paused then turned to business. "But I'm not here for a social call, am I? Is everything okay?"

"I'm convinced Bryan was murdered. I only suspected it before, but now I'm sure of it."

"What makes you think that?" He narrowed his hazel eyes, more brown than green, made prettier by long, dark lashes.

I pushed my rocker into motion. "Last night I was at his mother's house. She said he was in good health, in spite of the stressful job. Also, I found some stuff." I handed over the evidence. "This is Bryan's computer bag. In it you'll find one of the thumb drives, a red folder of documentation you might find helpful, his laptop, and another threatening letter."

"You've been busy. Where did you get all this?"

"That's not important. Though, you should know, there's another letter in his car, in the visor. I told you about it."

"Right. We retrieved it."

"Interestingly, both letters have the same writing. Also, the thumb drive contains files that should point to reasons for his murder."

"How would you know?"

"I looked at it, not knowing its contents. After opening it, I realized the files pertained to the distillery's accounts, so I decided to turn it over. There's something on here that will lead us to Bryan's killer, I know it."

"How can you be sure?"

"There have been weird happenings at the distillery. I told you about Bryan discovering discrepancies in the books and his run-in with Dewey. I've now found two notes meant to intimidate Bryan. And yesterday, after lunch, he asked me to look after his mom if anything should happen to him. Then today…" I tweaked the truth a bit. "I found Clarence in Bryan's office. Later, I found the computer bag and folder in Clarence's possession."

"How?"

I smiled, looking out across the yard. "Maybe it's best you don't know everything."

"Rook…" He shook his head and looked off across the street. "If you did anything illegal—"

"You'd have to prove it first."

"I hope you don't make me arrest you before this case is over."

"I'm trying to help."

He leaned over the arm of his rocker. "I understand that, but when you do things like this, you put me in a really tough spot between doing my official job as a sworn officer of the law and being your friend. You're forcing you to make really tough choices here."

"Say his mother found them and turned them in."

"Hell's fire, Rook. You're asking me to lie?"

"Look, you have the evidence now. Do what you want with it. Pay special attention to the red folder."

He sighed. I rocked my chair in silence.

After a few moments, he unzipped the bag and examined the contents. "Wow. This should all provide a few leads. Thank you, Rook. Even if you probably did something underhanded."

I sniffed a laugh. "I have a few suspects already."

"Oh, yeah? I wonder if your suspects match mine."

I leveled a side gaze at him. "You have suspects already?"

"Sure."

"Who?"

Humor lit his face. "Ah, see, as a law enforcement professional, I don't have to divulge information because it could compromise the case. However, you'd be doing your duty as a concerned citizen."

I laughed. "I see. Such a double standard. I'm the only one giving in this relationship."

He laughed. "It's the way of the world, I'm afraid."

I hung one leg over the rocker arm and folded the other leg beneath me. "Fine then. Batrene, Bryan's mom, favors Dewey Stiggers as the number one suspect. She doesn't think too highly of him. Says he's always been trouble. My favorite is Clarence Ford, the bookkeeper." I relayed the details of my conversation with Clarence earlier that day and the bad vibes I'd received from him. "He's involved in something shady, but I'm not completely sure what he's doing. It might involve Flying Eagle cooperage, his family's business. I suspect Bryan discovered something and was about to expose him, which seems like a good motive for murder."

"Is that all on your list?"

"Holly Parker is on my list too because she's proven herself shady in an incident of misusing of petty cash. She's kind of low on my list, though. Yes, she's shady. Yes, there's something off about her. But I can't yet find a strong motive for murder."

He stared at the horizon, rocking. "All good information. I'll definitely take that into consideration. And thank you for this evidence. I'm sure this will be a huge help."

"Anything to help find Bryan's killer."

After a brief pause, he said, "How are you doing?"

I shrugged, picking at a scab on my knee. "As well as can be expected, I guess. Bryan was like a brother. My best friend." My voice quavered. "My life is changed forever. That's why I have to help. I need to know who did this so I can have closure in a way I didn't have with my mother's case."

He frowned. "Your mother's case was solved."

"No. My father went to prison. Doesn't mean the case was solved. Y'all have the wrong person."

"How do you know?"

"Because the man I saw in the yard that night wasn't my father."

He winced, scratching his dimpled chin. "I mean no disrespect, but you were eleven when the murder happened and twelve when it all finally went to court. Memory and eyewitness testimony is highly unreliable. Especially from a child."

"I know what I saw."

"Who was it then?"

"I don't know. That's the problem. I can't remember his face."

"If your dad is innocent, he can appeal."

"He's trying, but with his record and background..." I shook my head, sipping my tea. "He's made a lot of important people in this town very angry. His chances are slim. Unless we can find the killer and prove Dad's innocence beyond all doubt."

"Have you found anything pointing to his innocence or to the identity of the murderer?"

"No. And, honestly, I haven't tried in a while. Life kind of ran over me."

He chuckled. "I understand that."

"Besides, my dad doesn't make it easy to help him. I haven't spoken to him in a year."

"It's hard with fathers sometimes." The flash of disappointment on his face indicated he'd had experience in the area of difficult fathers. He stood, digging his car keys out of his shorts. "I don't mean to rush off but ..."

I stood. "No, I understand. I need to get up early."

"Thanks for this great evidence. I promise I'll do my best."

"I know you will. And I'll see what else I can find and I'll keep you posted."

He hung the computer bag on his shoulder. "Whoa. Hold on. I don't mean for you to go on a digging expedition, Rook. Seriously, you shouldn't do anything to throw yourself in harm's way. If you happen to come across valuable information, that's great. Otherwise, you should step back and let us do our job." He squeezed my shoulder. "You've already done more than enough."

"No, I haven't. Someone at work killed my best friend. His mother is now unable to function without him. Worse, that person hasn't been caught yet, which means everyone else at the distillery is also in danger."

"I don't want to have to arrest you."

I smiled. "I'll stay out of your way, but I can't rest easy until Bryan's killer is arrested and locked away."

After Prim had gone to bed, I sat on the couch with a glass of iced tea and a slice of hummingbird cake Batrene had sent over from her condolences food stash. I flipped on *Forensic Files* for background noise while studying the copies I'd made from Bryan's red folder earlier.

There were dozens of pages. There were invoices and various reports: an aging report, a profit and loss statement, an itemized expense statement, and an income statement.

With all those numbers floating around, I didn't know what I was looking at. Most importantly, I didn't know what I was looking for. This was going to be tougher than I'd expected.

Chapter Thirteen

The next morning, I arrived early at the distillery to get a head start on the Bourbon, Bands, and BBQ Festival. After a few hours, I needed a break.

I stepped out of the restroom stall at the same time Lucia, the receptionist, exited hers. She had a smooth, heart-shaped face framed by a sleek black bob, which made it difficult to accurately estimate her age. I guessed she was at least forty-five.

"Hey, sweetie." Lucia washed her hands, her bright red nails flicking in and out of the suds. "I'm sorry about Bryan. I understand you were good friends."

"Thank you. We were very close." I washed my hands.

"Do you know his arrangements?"

"Visitation will be Saturday at noon at Tanbark Funeral Home with the service at Rothdale Presbyterian and the burial on Sunday at Rothdale Cemetery."

She shut off the water and extracted a paper towel from the dispenser. "I'll be sure to stop by visitation. I liked Bryan." She rubbed the paper over her fingers, the many jewels winking in the light.

I dried my hands. "His mother would like that."

"It really makes you think. He was young and healthy. And then..." She snapped her fingers. "Gone." She shook her head.

In my first week at the distillery, I'd already observed there were certain people who enjoyed gossiping and kept a finger on the pulse of the business politics. Lucia was one of those people. As such, she might have information or might have noticed something leading up to Bryan's death.

I tossed my damp paper towel. "I'm curious. Did Bryan get along with everyone here? Did everyone seem to like him?"

She pulled a tube of lipstick from her pants pocket and leaned toward the mirror. "For the most part."

"For the most part? Sounds like he might have had a problem with someone."

She filled her lips red, wiping the excess from the rim. "I believe Holly is the exception. She doesn't get along with most people." She pressed her lips together repeatedly and pulled another paper towel. "She's bossy. She can be a little much. It's no surprise a lot of people have difficulty with her." She blotted the color onto the paper towel.

"Did they butt heads recently?"

"About a month ago or so. They argued about petty cash. Apparently, Holly had used it for personal reasons and didn't have a receipt. I don't know what happened, exactly. I overheard them yelling at each other in her office one day. Actually, Holly did most of the yelling while Bryan tried to talk her down."

"But afterward everything was fine?"

"Seemed to be."

"What about Clarence? Did he get along with Bryan?"

"Mostly. There was some tension there. Clarence has been the bookkeeper here for a long time, and when Bryan was hired, Clarence became a little jealous." She checked her hair in the mirror, smoothing it with her fingers, her red nails darting in and out of her silky jet hair. "Bryan was younger, more educated, and essentially became Clarence's boss, which ticked him off. But what are you going to do?" She shrugged. "The company expanded, and we needed our own in-house accountant. Overall, they seemed to get along well enough." She checked her watch. "Guess I better get back to my desk."

I stopped at the break room to refill my coffee. Clarence still held the top of my suspect list. But Lucia's information about Holly gave a little more dimension to Holly's personality, character, and potential motives for wanting Bryan out of the way. But I couldn't understand her motives until I knew why they were fighting.

I returned to my desk and the call list.

Len arrived, handsome in his blue button-down, gray blazer, and khaki slacks. "Wow, look at you. Really grinding away. Here early this morning after working late last night."

"I didn't work that late."

"Holly said you were here at least until five-thirty."

Interesting. I wondered if she also mentioned the circumstances under which she'd discovered my late stay. I couldn't think of an organic way to broach the subject. "I wasn't aware I'd stayed that late." Nothing in his demeanor hinted of an awareness I'd been caught near Clarence's office.

"No apologies necessary." He set his stuff down in the cubicle beside mine. "I like a strong work ethic."

He handed me a slick, colored magazine with and image of the Four Wild Horses Distillery on the front. "Here's your study guide. Tells you everything you need to know about the distillery, the bourbon process, our special mashbills, char levels. Everything."

I accepted the guide and thumbed through it, glancing at the pictures. "Oh, awesome. I can't wait to get started." Which was the truth, though I could already see the amount of information was a little overwhelming.

"How far have you gotten on the call list?"

"About halfway through." I smoothed my cotton A-line skirt, white with big red poppies. "I'm hoping to finish it today."

"Great. You want to take a walk with me to the main rickhouse? I need to find out how much Devil's Kiss we have on hand for a small private tasting event for the Humane Society fundraiser this weekend."

We strolled toward the rickhouse as if we had all day. At nine in the morning, the katydids and humidity heralded another scorching day. The grass had become yellow and crispy. We needed rain. Bad. I was already overheating in my red cap-sleeved blouse.

He said, "I was wondering, are you...dating anyone?"

"No." I ran my hand over my long braid.

"Really? That's surprising."

"Until recently, I haven't had much time for dating. Academia has a way of sucking you in and consuming everything."

"Only if you let it."

Walking with my hands behind my back, I nodded and smiled at the cobblestone path leading to the rickhouse. "True enough. But when you love something, it's easy to lose sight."

The sun cast auburn highlights in his hair. "If you loved it, why'd you leave?"

"It's complicated."

Lifting a brow, he chuckled. "Cryptic answer."

I didn't feel like telling the story for the hundredth time. "Loving something doesn't mean it's good for you."

He looked at me, his gaze mixed with fascination and surprise. "I suppose that's true."

We stopped in front of the rickhouse.

He grabbed the handle but didn't open it. "Well, since you're not attached, maybe you'd like to go out with me? Tomorrow night perhaps?"

Taken aback, I hesitated, unsure how to answer. I was definitely interested. Based on his Facebook profile, he seemed interesting and fun to be around. Great qualities when paired with a great body and lips that beckoned kisses. It had been ages since I'd been on a date or had any male attention. Besides, I wasn't sure the company allowed coworkers to date.

"You've been silent too long. I guess you're not interested..."

I shook off my reverie, laughing. "That's not it. Are we allowed to..." I lowered my voice. "Go out together?"

"Look, how I see it is what the company doesn't know won't hurt it. I won't tell anyone. Will you?"

"Tell what?"

Now, plenty of folks would probably judge me for my lack of integrity, but I hadn't been with a man or had a date since Cam and I divorced. Strict diets of any kind were susceptible to the occasional temptation.

He beamed. "Great. It's a date. I'll pick you up at your place around six-thirty, and we'll go to The Castle. I'll make the reservations when we get back to the office."

"You can get reservations there on such short notice?"

A devilish grin crossed his lips. "No worries. I know the bar manager. He's a big fan of our bourbon. We'll get in." He winked.

How exciting! I'd never been to The Castle; it was too fancy for my budget. "Sounds fantastic." My spirits exploded into a flurry of butterflies. A date. The butterflies settled into my stomach. But Prim. I couldn't leave her alone. I'd think of something. The butterflies flittered apprehensively. I hadn't been on a date in seven years.

Chapter Fourteen

The rickhouse bustled with men rolling barrels and loading trucks. Men shouted directives over loud classic rock radio.

Len and I crossed the floor, dodging workers, to the standing desk in the corner. The wall to the right of the desk was covered with a bulletin board laden with papers pinned askew. The long wall held a whiteboard divided by names, store numbers, times, etc. A stocky bald man stood at the desk writing. He wore a black polo shirt with the company logo on the chest, a pair of long khaki cargo shorts, and steel-toe boots.

Len shouted, "Hey, Randall."

The bald man looked up and waved. He had a lump in his bottom lip. He spit brown juice into a soda bottle. My stomach protested. He tucked his pen behind his ear and shook hands with Len.

Len said, "Rook, this is my brother-in-law, Randall Tilkey."

Randall and I shook hands and exchanged a few pleasantries.

Len spoke with Randall about the inventory for Devil's Kiss while I scanned the dozens of columns and rows of barrels; the dust motes in the sunlight streaming in from the warehouse doors; and the barrels rolling up the ramps into the trucks. Dewey stood at the rear of his truck, leaning against the wall, packing dip into his bottom lip.

Dewey noticed me looking at him. He raked his gaze up and down me, sneered, and turned his back on me.

Randall showed us the corner where the bottles of Devil's Kiss were being held for the event. "We have five fifths reserved of Devil's Kiss. I've locked them in here." He entered the numbers on a combination lock on a safe.

"Doesn't sound like much," I said.

Len faced me. "Any time we release a new, limited edition bourbon, we have an exclusive tasting event. It's a catered affair with entertainment and such. We sell no more than fifty tickets…"

"For big money," Randall added. "Five hundred a ticket."

"Dollars?" I gawked at him. "Are you kidding me?" My mind ticked through about a dozen things I could spend that kind of money on. "I suspect I'm on the wrong side of the business."

Laughing, the men exchanged a pointed glance with each other.

"Isn't that the truth?" Randall said.

Len rubbed his hands together and asked Randall. "And do we have the tents and everything ready to go?"

"Yep." Randall shut the door and locked the safe. "Upstairs. We'll have everything pulled and set up on Saturday morning."

Len's phone rang. "Excuse me. I have to take this." He stepped outside.

Randall and I stood in silence for a moment while I worked out how I might ask him about Dewey.

Randall asked, "You liking it here so far?"

I fiddled with my ring, turning it round and round on my finger. "Yeah. It's great." I was no master of small talk. I struggled to grasp the tiniest thread to start a conversation about Bryan's murder.

"Yeah. It's a good company. Do you work in Len's department?"

Think, Rook. Think. "Sure do. I was wondering about Dewey…" Not the most graceful segue, but it would do.

"What's that?" He scratched his chest through the button-gap in his shirt.

"He seems like a hot-tempered sort."

Randall snorted. "Sure is. He'd fight a rattlesnake."

"Do you think he's prone to violence?"

"Probably. Why? You wanting to date him?" His eyes lit with a mixture of humor and curiosity.

I chuckled. "No. Definitely not my type."

"Who is your type? Len?" He winked.

My cheeks grew warm. I smiled awkwardly and shook my head.

He chuckled quietly. "All I'm saying is, it's been a while since he's dated anyone. I was beginning to wonder if he'd given up." He scratched his nose. A classic sign of lying, according to one of my criminal profiling books. What was he hiding?

Len came back, slipping his phone into his pants pocket. "Sorry about that." He nudged my arm. "We should probably be getting back to the office."

Randall said, "I almost forgot. Len, Vonda wanted me to tell you about next weekend. We're having a few people over. Going to have a little shindig for Caleb's birthday. We'll grill out and have cake. There'll be beer, of course. Maybe we'll play horseshoes or something. Real laid back."

"Sounds great. What should I get Caleb?"

Randall shrugged. "Whatever. The kid has everything." He waved his hand. "He's easy to please. Hey, Rook, you ought to come, too. I'm sure Vonda would like to meet you."

Len's lips tightened and knots formed in his jaw. His gaze locked on Randall with tension around the lids. Then he smiled at me, relaxing. "That's a great idea. But I can understand how it would probably freak you out to meet my family when we haven't even had our first date yet."

I understood the tension now. He probably felt put on the spot. "I'm down for whatever. I don't want to impose."

Len said, "Nah. It'll be fine."

Honestly, I hated the idea of hanging out with Len's family. I didn't know any of them. Len and I barely knew each other. But a voice in a far corner of my mind whispered that I might be able to get some information about Dewey in a less conspicuous way. In fact, Randall seemed like a "good ol' boy." Which meant he'd probably be half-drunk by noon and more pliable when I started to dig for information.

I said to Len, hesitantly, "If you wouldn't mind...I mean, it sounds fun. I like barbeques."

Chapter Fifteen

Cam met me in the kitchen in his sock feet when I arrived home. He greeted me with a whisper. "She's sleeping."

"How'd she do today?" I peeked into the living room, where Prim was stretched out in her recliner with an afghan pulled up to her chin.

"Okay, I guess. But she really needs to go to the doctor. She seems weaker every day."

"She has an appointment on Wednesday. I'm hoping she can hold on a few more days." I kicked my shoes off at the door and wiggled my toes.

We discussed the highlights of our respective days.

He said, "I'm looking forward to a day off tomorrow."

"How did you get lucky?"

"I decided I needed a day off. Plus, Mike, the new guy, needs some hours. I'm throwing a few his way."

"If it's too much to watch Prim…"

He waved me away. "Think nothing of it. It's peaceful here."

"And you're okay with watching Prim tomorrow?"

"Sure. I don't have any plans."

I poured us each a glass of iced tea. "Something kind of exciting happened to me today."

He grabbed his tennis shoes by the door and pulled out a chair at the kitchen table. "Oh, yeah?" He sat and stuffed his feet into his shoes.

"A coworker asked me out…on a date for tomorrow night." I placed a glass of tea beside him.

He sat up and looked at me, stunned. "Really? That's…" He slid his hands up and down his thighs. "Great. I'm happy for you." He gulped his tea. "You need me to watch Prim tomorrow night too?"

"Uh, well, I'll try Millie first. See if she can watch her for me. I can't make you stay here that long."

"I don't mind..." His phone rang and he answered. "Yep. All right. Okay. I'm on my way." He shot a look at me, indicating his annoyance with the interruption. His voice became increasingly impatient. "I'm coming right now. Okay. Fine." He sounded like a petulant teenager talking with a demanding mother. He ended the call and stood. "Jacie's all wound up. I've got to go."

I needed to find a sitter for Prim for tomorrow night before I started supper preparations. My heart sank. Had Bryan been alive, I would've called him and he would've sat with Prim. I missed him in so many ways. I dialed my bestie, Millie, who agreed, thankfully, to cover for me.

After supper and Prim had retired to bed, I sat with work materials: the study guide, which I still hadn't touched and the red folder copies. I began with the study guide and could only get through the About Us and the Mission Statement when the red folder copies and mystery around Bryan's death called out to me. I cast the study guide aside and picked up the papers from Bryan's files. I'd made no progress the night before. I'd been overwhelmed by the sheer volume of numbers. Tonight, I started with logic. Clarence was a bookkeeper. He was clearly up to no good because he'd taken Bryan's laptop and red folder. He likely held the other thumb drive, too. He took those things because he wanted to hide something. The main thing a bookkeeper would want to hide was fraud. Bryan must've discovered Clarence's involvement in fraudulent activity and was going to expose Clarence. That would certainly be grounds for murder for a person desperate to keep the crime quiet.

I opened my laptop and began with a ridiculous Google search: Types of bookkeeping fraud. It was silly, but it couldn't hurt. A long list of links appeared. Wow. Surely one of them would give me a lead to chase. I clicked on the first link and started reading.

The next morning, Prim was still asleep by the time I'd finished dressing. Cam would be here soon, and I didn't want him to be responsible for dressing her. I nudged her awake. "Prim? Are you okay?"

"Yeah," she said weakly. "I'm fine. So sleepy."

"Cam will be here soon. Let's get you dressed."

She cleared her throat. "All right," she mewled. "Help me."

I helped her sit up and she dropped her thin legs over the side of the bed, dangling a few inches from the floor.

"What do you want to wear today?" I stood by her closet door.

"I don't care. Pick something out for me."

That wasn't like Prim. "Are you okay?"

"I'm fine," she snipped. "Quit asking me that." She inched herself forward until her feet touched the floor. She wiggled her feet into her slippers and pushed herself to stand with a grunt. She pulled a pair of underwear and a bra out of her chest of drawers and carried them into the bathroom with her.

I focused on her closet. I picked out a blue paisley blouse, a gray cardigan, and navy pants. She flushed the toilet. Then the shower started.

When she finished her shower, she stepped out, wearing a robe, freshly powdered all over. She dropped the robe and stood there in her bra and underwear.

I held her shirt. As she slipped into it, I noticed a small knot under her arm.

"What's that?" I lifted her arm, examining the knot in her armpit. I touched it. "Does it hurt?"

"No. I didn't know anything was there. What is it?"

"I don't know. It looks kind of like a cyst of some kind."

She felt around and looked in the mirror. "I don't know. I'm sure it'll go away soon. It's probably a bug bite or something."

"Prim, that's not a bug bite. It's as big as a robin's egg. You need to talk to the doctor about that on Wednesday when you go."

"Okay. I will. I will. Get out of here and let me dress. Go on." She shooed me away like a fly at her picnic.

I jogged downstairs, made her a piece of toast, poured her coffee, and placed them at the kitchen table with her morning dose of pills. While I waited for Cam, I salted and peppered a beef round and dropped in a Crock-pot, covered it with baby carrots, chopped onions, and tiny red potatoes. I set the Crock-pot on low.

Still Cam hadn't yet arrived. Holding my keys, purse, and coffee, I waited for Cam, taking turns pacing and peeking out the window over the kitchen sink, worrying about Prim. I searched Google on my phone and discovered the knot could be a benign lipoma—a little collection of fatty tissue. The knot under Prim's arm resembled that. Maybe it was genetic.

Cam finally arrived, and I shot out the door, greeting him in the driveway. "Hey, Cam. Sorry, but I'm in a huge hurry. Prim's upstairs. Still getting dressed. She might need help getting down the stairs."

"Don't worry. I've got it." He waved.

I rolled down my window and honked at him, shouting, "Thank you, you're the man," as I backed out the drive.

He flexed his biceps.

Chapter Sixteen

I kept my head down and focused on my work between flirty conversations with Len and watching for suspicious behavior from coworkers, especially Clarence. I hadn't figured out exactly what he'd done, but was sure I'd find something in my research soon.

Then there was Holly. Based on what Lucia and Clarence had told me, I needed to take a closer look at her. My plan consisted of simply striking up a conversation to ferret out any information that might point to a motive in Bryan's murder.

I found Holly sitting at her desk, typing. Her office décor was *Southern Living* chic, complete with white peonies in a clear vase, pictures of her family on the bookshelf, and an apple pie-scented candle burning on her desk.

"Good morning, Holly."

"Hey." She glanced at me, unsmiling, and didn't stop typing. "What'cha need?"

A tray full of papers stood on the corner of her desk. A yellow legal pad lay on top of the stack. The same sort of paper that had been used for the threatening notes given to Bryan. I had an idea. I smiled again. "Can I have a sheet of paper? There's, uh, something HR told me. I need to jot it down real quick before I forget."

She eyed me as if I'd grown three heads. "Uh, sure."

"Thanks..." I pulled a piece of paper off the pad. Grabbing a pencil from her desk, I pretended to write on the page. Then I folded the paper and tucked it in the pocket of my capris. "Thanks! I appreciate your help." I lingered, trying to determine a way to bring the conversation around to Bryan.

"Is there something else?" She glanced from her computer screen.

"Actually, um…"

She widened her eyes, indicating her impatience.

"I wanted to tell you about Bryan's arrangements. Maybe you'd like to send out a company-wide notice for folks who might want to attend. Visitation begins at noon on Saturday at Tanbark Funeral Home, and the funeral is at noon on Sunday at Rothdale Cemetery."

Malice flickered through her eyes. She hadn't liked Bryan, and she didn't like me. But she tilted her head and the animus melted into a mask of piety. "I'll be sure to let everyone know. I'm sure Pierce will want to send flowers or something on behalf of the distillery."

"Oh, okay. I understand. But…" I paused, gathering the right words. "You and Bryan worked together for a long time, didn't you? At least five years."

"Working with someone doesn't make you family."

"True, but this seems like a fairly tight-knit group of colleagues, kind of a family atmosphere."

She leaned on her desk. "Yes, but there are some families who don't get along and aren't that close. I don't speak to my family anymore."

That was right. I recalled her Facebook page. Her husband and children were the only family present in the pictures. "True. I'm sorry. I never really knew my family. Except my grandmother."

"Family is often a source of disappointment. You're not missing much."

Wow. Harsh. Not entirely wrong, but the venom behind her words shocked me. But it explained why she crafted the image of a perfect family on her Facebook page. "I guess if this is your work family, Bryan would've been like your brother." I chuckled.

She scoffed and reached for a stack of papers, flipping through them. "More like my father."

I'd come too close to touching a nerve and shutting her down completely. "I'm sorry to hear that. I only knew him outside of work, and sometimes people act differently in their private lives than in the office."

98

"That's the truth." She set aside one stack of papers and skimmed the pile in front of her.

Not with Bryan. He was stable of mind and character. There were no mind games or hidden agendas with him. But one thing I learned from Holly's social media was she seemed to love sympathy and flattery and stroking those needs might open her up.

"I'm sorry if he picked on you."

Her jaw knotted. "All the time. I could never do anything right. He was always nosing in my business, telling me what to do. He acted like my father."

"That's tough." I wondered if we were entirely talking about Bryan.

She looked at me. "So, you see, I am sorry he died. I truly am. But we weren't very close, and I only go to funerals of people I'm close to."

"I understand. You seem like a good person and a hard worker." Oh, those lies were bitter in my mouth. I sweetened them with an equivocal statement. "I'm sorry Bryan didn't treat you as you truly deserved." I started to leave.

"Oh, by the way, you and Len have a good time tonight." Her mouth smiled, but her eyes shot daggers.

On my way down the hall, I passed Lucia in the reception area. Lucia had worked here for decades. She seemed to know all the dirt.

I swung by. "Hey, Lucia. Can I ask you a question?"

She smiled at me. "Of course, sugar."

"Does Holly ever talk about her family? Her parents, siblings?"

She thought for a moment. "Not for years. It's my understanding they don't get along."

"Why do you think that is?"

"Well…" The phone rang. She answered it and redirected the call. "What was I saying?" She picked her hair with her nails. "Oh, yes. From what I understand, she was quite the wild child. Wore her parents out with drugs, stealing money from them, and all sorts of rowdy behavior. I don't know for sure. But you hear things, you know."

"Of course."

"They've always fought and she says she disowned them, but I suspect it might be the other way around. Her sisters won't have anything to do with her, either. They took the parents' side."

"Sounds dysfunctional."

"Like a Jerry Springer show, sweetie."

"I hate to hear that. I was just curious. Something she'd said about family struck me as odd. Thanks." I rushed to my desk.

If what Lucia had said about Holly held even a fraction of truth, it was quite an indictment. She thought of Bryan as similar to her father. Someone who interfered in her fun, who bossed her around, and who expected her to follow the rules. Then, presumably, hatred for her father would transfer to Bryan. Though still vague, a motive for Holly to commit murder was closer to taking shape. There might've been something Bryan had said or done to trigger a deep-seated rage and incite her to murder? But what?

At my desk, I flattened the yellow paper. However cheesy and cliché, I'd seen the shading method on lots of mystery and forensic shows through the years. It didn't hurt to try.

Using a pencil, I shaded over the page. Like magic, the squared, blocked letters appeared *Dead men don't snitch*. Excitement and fear rushed through me. But why would this be in Holly's office? There were many reasons. She'd had a run-in over petty cash with Bryan, so she might've written the letters out of anger, maybe trying to scare him into quitting. Another possibility was the killer had planted the notepad in her office either to frame her or to deflect from themselves. That seemed over the top as well. Or, she might've been in the killer's office, taken it to use, and forgotten to give it back. Or the killer left it in a common area and Holly took it. Supplies traveled around offices all the time.

"Hey," Len said behind me. "What'cha working on?"

I jumped, flipping the paper over, hoping he hadn't seen anything.

He laughed. "Sorry. Didn't mean to scare you."

"Thinking about the layout for the big event. Can I talk to you?" I pointed at the hall. Making a mental note to give the paper to Jimmy as soon as possible, I stuffed it into my computer bag.

We stepped into the hall. I whispered, "Why did you tell Holly we're going out tonight?"

He rubbed the back of his neck. "Man, it slipped out. We were talking about plans for the night, and I was so looking forward to our date that…" He smiled sheepishly. "I'm sorry."

"What if she tells someone? Are we going to get in trouble? I just got hired." *Stupid, Rook.* How dumb to put myself in this situation all because I was a little lonely. Nevertheless, I couldn't stop recalling the picture of him on the boat, all shirtless, tanned, and ripped.

He patted my arm. "It'll be fine. I'll handle it. I'm sure we'll be okay. We're just hanging out."

I tucked a strand of hair behind my ear. "You're right."

He locked his index finger with my pinky and he lowered his voice. "I'll still see you tonight?" He flashed puppy-dog eyes.

"Yes. I'm not going to miss a chance to eat at The Castle."

After work, I rushed home to dress for my date. I dashed into the house and threw my purse and keys on the table. Cam was still there.

He came from the living room. "Hey, how was your day?"

"It was okay." I unplugged the Crock-Pot. "Did Prim have a good day?"

"Pretty good. She's been complaining of pain under her arms and, of course, her back still hurts. She didn't want to move around much today. She's asleep now."

"Okay…" I fidgeted with my ring, frowning. Either the pain was a recent development or Prim hadn't been honest with me this morning because she didn't want me to worry. She was sleeping more, too. Only a few more days and I could take her to the doctor, though the diagnosis scared me. "I'm going to jump in the shower. Thanks for watching her today."

"Happy to do it. I'll wait until you're finished. In case Prim wakes up and needs something."

I rushed upstairs, tucked my hair in a shower cap, and took a quick shower. I rolled my hair in hot rollers, shook out the curls, and applied my makeup darker for the evening. After trying on several dresses, all a wee bit too tight, I found a rosy pink georgette halter dress with a forgiving A-line skirt. I walked into a spritz of Samsara perfume and descended the stairs barefoot, carrying my nude heels and a small sparkly pink clutch purse.

Cam whistled. "Whoa! You look hot. You never looked like that for me."

I set my heels by the door and chuckled. "You never took me anywhere for me to dress fancy." I pulled my ID, credit card, and cash out of my purse and stuffed them in the clutch with my lipstick and perfume.

"Fair enough." Cam hovered nearby. "You smell good, too. Who's this guy you're going out with?"

"Len Ashfield. I work with him." I popped a couple breath mints in my mouth and dropped the rest in the clutch.

He scoffed a laugh. "You move fast. You've only been there a few days."

That rubbed me the wrong way. Probably because there was some truth to it. It had moved a little fast. "Am I not allowed to be happy? To have a good time?" I sat at the kitchen table and put on my heels, buckling the ankle straps.

"I'm not saying that. I hope you don't get in trouble dating someone at work."

"It's only one date. It'll be fine." I stood and fluffed my hair. I was already feeling guilty for leaving Prim. "Don't get in my head, okay? I want to have a good time, for the first time in many years."

Cam grabbed me, clutching my hands. His callused hands were dry and warm. Perfect.

He looked serious. "I hope this guy deserves you." There was a sadness in his voice.

"Cam..."

"Sometimes I think I didn't deserve you."

My insides went all warm and gooey. I touched his face. "You're sweet." I squeezed his hand. "You weren't that bad. Most of our time together was pretty good."

"It was, wasn't it?" He smiled.

"I could've been a lot better, too. I share a lot of the blame."

We hadn't been able to communicate. We'd never had money and fought constantly over our finances. Work kept us busy so we rarely saw each other. I'd grown emotionally connected to a guy in graduate school because I'd

102

spent more time with him than my own husband. Cam became attracted to Jacie. We lost our common ground and grew apart. The connection we'd once shared snapped like frayed ropes under the strain. He broke with Jacie and we tried to repair our marriage, but the fighting only increased. Then came the silence, more poisonous than the fighting. It'd settled between us like a stone wall. Then one night I came home from school and he'd moved out. I couldn't afford to live alone, so, confused and broken in spirit, heart, and finances, I moved back in with Prim.

"If this guy can't give you everything you want, you should drop him."

Balancing on my tiptoes, I kissed his stubbly cheek. "You need to shave." I winked at him. "I have to finish. Why don't you and Prim sit and eat?" Dropping his hands, I went to the living room to help Prim stand and gauge her pain. She denied she was in any pain, though it was written all over her face.

I brought her to the table and Cam helped me ease her into the chair. Yearning tenderness for him yawned inside me. I hadn't seen him quite like this before. The knife of regret twisted in my gut. Regret for what we could've had, for the lost potential. And regret, more than anything, that I couldn't have seen our troubles earlier and prevented our breakup. Maybe that was a fantasy.

My phone rang. It was Millie. My heart sank. Dreading what she'd have to say, I answered.

"I'm so sorry." Her voice trembled with fear and distress. "My car broke down. I'm out on Versailles Road."

I heard the roar of cars around her. "Oh no! Are you okay? You want me to come get you?"

"No, no. Jared's coming to get me. I've called a tow truck. But I'm not going to be able to make it tonight. I feel horrible. I know you were looking forward to this."

"No worries. I understand. Let me know if there's anything I can do." I ended the call.

Munching on a bit of roast beef, Cam said, "What's going on?"

"Millie can't make it. Guess I'll call Len and cancel the date."

Len arrived in a pearl white Impala. Of course. "There's Len now. Dang it." Disappointed, I watched him through the window over the sink, struggling to determine the best way to break the bad news to Len.

"Go on your date," Cam said.

"What?"

"Go on your date. I'll stay with Prim."

I almost jumped on the offer, but I hedged. "But...what about Jacie? She'll be irate. I can't do that to you."

"Don't worry. I'll explain it to her. She'll understand."

"I doubt it."

"Go on your date. Have fun."

I lowered my voice. "But you've already been with Prim all day. I can't leave you here—"

Prim said, "Don't talk about me like I'm not here." She gnawed on a carrot, half-dazed with sleep and drugs.

"We're only trying to figure some stuff out, Prim." I nudged Cam to step onto the screened porch.

As I closed the door, he said, "I don't mind staying. What's a few more hours?"

"Why are you doing this?"

"I want to help. That's all."

Relief and delight washed over me, marred with guilt and a touch of suspicion. I didn't want to do this to Cam, but I did want to go out. Since Len was already here, I hated to send him away. Besides, this was the first date I'd been on in ages, and Cam was already engaged and planning a wedding. Dang it, I deserved happiness too.

Len strode toward the porch, carrying a rose.

"Is this the season premiere of *The Bachelor*?" Cam muttered.

"Be nice," I warned.

Cam leaned over and whispered, "This guy's a goober."

I slapped his arm and muttered, "Stop. He's a nice guy." I greeted Len as he opened the screen door and stepped inside.

Len wore a slim-cut gray suit with a silver shirt open at the collar. His

104

black hair was combed back. His fresh cologne reminded me of hiking on a bright, crisp spring day.

"Apologies. I'm running a bit behind." He handed me a red rose.

"Oh, how sweet. I love roses. Thank you."

The men exchanged a competitive once-over. My nerves fired, like millions of little ants crawling under my skin. This was awkward. I launched into introductions. "Cam, this is Lennon Ashfield. He works in the marketing department with me. Len, this is Porter Campbell. Everyone calls him Cam. He's the owner of Tangled Up in Brew, a bar in Lexington."

Len's eyes darted. "Never heard of it. I'll check it out next time I'm in Lexington."

Cam looked at me as if he'd bitten into rotten catfish. They clasped hands briefly, shoulders rigid.

Cam crossed his arms over his chest, tucking his hands in his pits. "I'm her ex-husband."

Len's brows arched, and he looked between Cam and me. "Oh?" He chuckled nervously. "Okay. That's—"

I'd been trying to leave that bit out of the conversation for as long as possible, but since Cam had opened that particular can of worms, I added through gritted teeth, "Thank you, Cam. I was getting to that." I could've pinched a hole clean through his arm. "Cam's helping me watch my grandma. She hasn't been feeling well."

Len looked askance. "I see."

I laid a hand on Len's arm. "Would you care to wait in the car while I put this rose in water?"

"Sure." He went to his car as Cam and I entered the house.

I spun on Cam. "How could you do that to me?"

"I don't like him."

Glaring at him, I shook my head. Huffing, I pulled a mason jar from the cabinet, filled it with water, and jammed the rose in it. "You're jealous. But don't you dare ruin this for me only because you're jealous. You're already engaged. I have no one. You can't have your cake and eat it, too."

"What's that supposed to mean?"

"You can't have Jacie as your wife and keep me single because you're jealous."

"That's not what this is about." Cam motioned toward the kitchen window, where we watched Len sitting in his car, toying with knobs on the dashboard. "I'm telling you. This guy's a jerk."

"He's probably nervous."

"He's wearing skinny pants."

"Really? Skinny pants are your criteria for being a jerk?"

"His handshake was all limp and clammy. He never looked me in the eye. Not once. I'm telling you, don't trust this guy."

"You don't get a vote here. You lost all your votes when you left me."

Cam sighed and slouched into a chair at the kitchen table. "I don't want to fight. I'm trying to help. Trying to protect you."

"Guess what? You lost the right to that, too."

Cam held his hands up in surrender. "Look, I hope you have a wonderful time tonight. I hope I'm wrong. By all means, fall in love, get married, have twelve babies. Whatever. Just—"

Len honked the car horn.

Cam motioned toward the window and pinched his lips together as if to say, *See what I mean? Jerk.*

I kissed Prim's cheek and smoothed her hair. "I'm going on a date tonight. Cam will be here, okay? I'll only be gone a few hours. Promise."

She nodded. "You have a good time, hon."

"You feel okay?" I touched her head. Clammy. No fever.

"All right," she said, weakly, poking at her potatoes.

"I've got to go. Love you, Prim."

Chapter Seventeen

The Castle restaurant stood on a hill, off the road between Rothdale and Lexington, surrounded by tall pines. It was a modern-day castle built over a few decades, once owned by a millionaire and his wife until their divorce. Through the years, it changed owners several times until it finally became a hotel and restaurant that hosted many events throughout the year, including a popular annual Renaissance Festival.

We passed through the courtyard into the main entrance and were escorted to a dim corner lit with candles on the table and soft gold string lights above. A jazz quartet played at the front of the room near a fountain. We started with Old-Fashioneds aperitifs. He ordered the bourbon-glazed duck and I ordered the salmon. The prices were astonishing. I'd never eaten at a place this fancy. I felt awkward, like a mule among thoroughbreds.

Len didn't seem fazed. He sipped his wine. "Cam seems like an interesting guy."

I chuckled. "That's a word for it. You should know he and I are in no way…" I draped my napkin in my lap. "We're over. He's engaged."

He smiled a crooked, sexy smile. "It's all cool. I'm not worried about that."

Relieved, I relaxed and we started to get to know each other. Though I was enjoying my time with him, something seemed amiss. The energy with him was different, less comfortable than with Cam. Even on my first date with Cam, I'd been more relaxed. Cam made me laugh. At least when we first dated and during the early years of our marriage. I couldn't easily connect to Len's sense of humor. Also, our interests in music, books, television, and movies didn't align. I liked classic rock, he liked hip-hop and techno stuff.

I liked genre fiction, he liked avante garde literature and sci-fi. I liked *The Office*. He didn't watch sitcoms.

He leaned over his pan-seared duck, the candlelight washing his face in a golden light. "Have the police contacted you anymore since Monday?"

"No. Not yet. They probably will as their investigation continues."

"I was only curious. They've asked me to come in for a follow-up interview."

"Really?"

He nodded, cutting into the meat. "Seems to me the only reason they'd call people back for interviews is if they thought there was foul play. Do you suppose he was actually killed? I mean, it seems too wild to be true."

Shrugging one shoulder, I cut a piece of my bourbon-glazed salmon. "Crazier things have happened. It's not out of the realm of possibility."

Chewing, Len was silent for a moment. "It's surreal to think a murderer might be loose at the distillery. I mean, who would want to kill Bryan?"

"I don't know, but I hope the monster is discovered soon and then punished to the fullest extent of the law."

He sat back, looking at me. His curious mood shifted to something dark and obdurate. "Sure, of course. Me too." He emptied his wineglass and refilled it, topping off mine. Then he smiled. "Well, let's not dampen our good time." He smeared honey butter on a yeast roll. "Do you like to dance?"

"I do."

"We should go sometime. I like dancing at The Zone. Has three levels. Hip-hop, Techno, and Pop."

"That'd be great. I haven't been there yet."

We ate in silence for a few moments.

He said, "Who do you think it is? The distillery killer. If there is such a thing."

I'd never share my list of suspects with anyone but law enforcement. Besides, we were talking about the death of my best friend. My shoulders tightened, and I shifted in my seat. I tried to put him off with a noncommittal answer, hoping to redirect the topic. "I don't know. I haven't been there long enough." I smiled.

"I think it's probably Dewey. Or...let me think..." He chewed his food, brow furrowed, eyes darting.

"I thought you wanted to talk about lighter subjects."

He held up his hands in surrender. "You're right. You're right. I can't stop thinking about it since the police phoned, though. I'd hate to think they believed I'm a suspect."

"I doubt they do. Why would they?" I eyed him while sipping my wine.

He wiped his fingers on the napkin in his lap. "You're right. Cops make me nervous."

"They probably want to see what you know because they have a suspect in mind."

"You're right. Of course." He stabbed an asparagus spear. "I'm being paranoid for nothing."

I tried to change the subject again. "Do you like musicals? I saw *Les Miserables* in Lexington last November. It was amazing."

"I don't really do musicals."

Deflating a little, I drew deep on my wine.

After a few moments of silent eating, he said, "I'm kind of creeped out that a killer works with us, though. Aren't you? The rest of us might still be in danger."

He wasn't wrong. Likely, my snooping threw me directly in the killer's sights. After all, I'd seen enough *Forensic Files* to know those who dance close to the flame are in greatest danger of getting burned.

After dinner, Len and I climbed into a horse-drawn carriage for a stargazing tour along the trail behind The Castle. We settled in the carriage, Len's arm around me, his cologne enveloping me like sunshine.

I smiled at him. He leaned in and kissed me, a soft, melting kiss. I wanted more of this and my crinkum-crankum certainly agreed, but my ringing cell phone shut us both down.

I winced, silently communicating that I'd forgotten to silence my phone. As I drew the phone from my purse, I noticed Cam was calling. "I need to take this."

When I answered, Cam started speaking without a greeting. "Hey, Prim's in trouble. She's headed to the ER. I'm following the ambulance. We're going to St. Joe's Hospital."

Sirens wailed in the background. "Oh, no." I bolted to stand. The carriage pulled forward and I fell back. "Stop the carriage," I shouted. "Please. Emergency."

The carriage halted.

"I have to go. Right now. It's my grandma."

I jumped to the ground, no easy task in heels, before he stood. I ran toward the parking lot with little mincing steps, my toes screaming at me. I settled on tapping away with my heels, barely keeping pace with Len's long stride, which soon put him in front of me.

We slid into the car seats.

I said, "Can you please drop me by St. Joe's?"

"Sure. No problem." He threw the car in reverse and plowed down the dark lane, turning left onto the main highway leading to downtown Lexington.

Within fifteen minutes, he pulled into the emergency room parking lot. "Do you want me to come with you?"

"No. Thank you for the dinner. It was a lovely evening."

"How are you getting home?"

"I can probably get a ride from Cam, if I go home tonight. I'll have to see if they're going to keep Prim overnight."

As I exited the car, Len touched my leg, his hand resting on my knee, under my georgette skirt. He squeezed my leg. His hand was hot, smooth. "Okay. We'll try the carriage again another time."

His words weren't soaking in. I was too preoccupied with Prim. "Sounds great." He could've told me I was the size of a house with scaly chicken legs, and I would've said the same thing. I jumped out with a final "thank you" and sprinted toward the hospital, hoping I wasn't too late.

Chapter Eighteen

A nurse showed me to a curtained holding area in the ER. Prim was laid out, moaning, crying from pain. Cam stood by her side, cupping her fragile hand between his. His hands were thick and strong and could've crushed hers like a bunch of dry twigs.

When he saw me, we rushed into each other's arms, squeezing each other in a panicked embrace.

"What happened?" I stood by Prim and held her hand. "I'm here. I'm here."

Her lids fluttered open. She screamed, her voice hoarse, "Oh! It hurts. It hurts so bad." Tears slid down her face.

A hole opened in my chest. "I know. I know. I'm sorry." I brushed the hair from her face with my other hand.

"I don't know what happened. We were watching TV. She tried to get out of her recliner to get ready for bed and she…" Cam clapped his hands together to emphasize Prim's collapse, "fell to the floor like a sack of potatoes." His eyes bulged with fear. "Then she started screaming and screaming."

I pressed the tight spot in the center of my forehead. "Heaven above," I whispered. "I'm glad you were there."

"Me too." His jaw knotted.

"Have you seen a doctor yet?"

"No. We just now got back here."

An elfish male tech with bangs sweeping over one eye popped into the room. "I'm going to take her vitals and get her on an I.V. drip. Which of you is related to the patient?"

"Me," I said. "Will we see a doctor soon?"

He pulled out all his implements for starting the I.V. "Unfortunately, we do have a few people ahead of you with traumatic wounds. We need to get them stabilized and we'll be with you as soon as possible."

"But she's in so much pain. Can we at least deal with that first?"

"I'll see what I can do." His thin fingers worked nimbly to start the I.V. and complete his assessment of her vitals.

For at least an hour, nurses and techs popped in and out to complete the myriad of tasks that go into patient care.

Cam's phone rang. Withdrawing it from his jeans pocket, he looked at it. He sighed. "Jacie." He answered the phone. After a pause, he said, "I'm going to be late tonight." Another pause. "I'm at the hospital with Rook and her grandma." A longer pause. His face reddened. "Now listen…" He stood and walked out of the room. After about fifteen minutes, he came back with two cups of coffee and resumed his seat.

He handed me a Styrofoam cup. "You still cream only?"

"Yes." I accepted the cup and thanked him. I sipped the hot coffee, the precious elixir slipping downward, spreading warmth into my stomach and throughout my body. "I guess Jacie isn't happy you're here?"

He sniffed a laugh. "You got that right."

"You should go on. I'm sure Jacie needs you at home." I imprinted my name on the rim of my cup with my fingernail.

He leaned his elbows on his knees. "I'm sure not going home right now while she's all ticked off. I'll let her cool off a bit." There was a moment of silence. "How was your date?"

"Good. We went to The Castle."

"Wow. Fancy."

"It was." I stared at the blinking green heart on Prim's monitor.

His pinched lips and half-lidded eyes conveyed his doubt. He etched lines around the lip of the cup with his thumbnail. "Must make some pretty good money if he can afford such a costly place."

I looked at him. He watched the techs work, sipping his coffee. He made an interesting point. Len would make more than me because he'd worked there longer, but I couldn't imagine he made a huge amount more as merely a team lead. He lived alone. Paid his own bills. Drove a nice car. Wore nice clothes. I'd learned at dinner he also had a mountain of student loan debt. It did seem at odds. But maybe he came from a wealthy family.

My thoughts were interrupted by a doctor coming into the room.

He shook hands with us and introduced himself as Dr. Mohammad. He was a handsome man who looked to be in his forties, with thick dark hair and brows. He wore a yellow bow tie and a stuffed kangaroo peeked out of his pocket, likely for soothing his pediatric patients. He had kind, dark eyes that reminded me of Len's in the same melty chocolate, hot espresso way. He examined Prim, asking a bunch of questions in a silky accent.

I said, "I don't understand what's happening. This all began a few days ago. Now she can hardly walk, sit, or stand without pain. The medicine given to her doesn't seem to be effective. We need to know what's going on. She has a doctor's appointment on Wednesday, but I'm not sure we can wait that long."

"I completely understand your frustration," he said with compassion. "I assure you we will figure out what's going on before we send her home. It could be a slipped disc, arthritis, or spinal degeneration of some kind. I'm going to order blood work and an MRI, then we'll go from there. I'm only the ER doctor, so I'd like to admit her to the hospital so she can be treated and observed by a specialist. That way we can get her tests run first thing in the morning. We can also manage her pain better here in the meantime."

I hugged myself and bit my lip. "Okay."

Cam put a reassuring hand to my back and the doctor spoke to a nurse in a rush of medical lingo and gave us a quick nod and wave before moving on to his next patient.

Once he left Prim's bedside, another flurry of activity descended to issue drugs, schedule tests, take more vitals, and begin the paperwork for admitting her to the hospital.

I sat in the hard-plastic chair at her bedside and put my face in my hands while techs and nurses scurried around us. I didn't know how we were going to pay for all this. Fear warred with my self-loathing for pondering financial concerns when my grandma desperately needed medical attention.

Cam sat beside me, rubbing circles across my back. "It'll be okay."

I couldn't bear kindness right now. Couldn't bear to be comforted, and I couldn't think straight. I needed a quiet room free of all sensory stimulation so I could unravel the knots of thoughts and feelings clogging my brain and throat. I shrugged away from him. "Please, don't." I rubbed my forehead with the heels of my palms.

He dropped his hand and sat back, sighing. "I forgot. You're Mrs. Tough Girl."

"No…" The unspent emotions formed stones in my shoulder blades. "It's not about being tough." I lowered my voice, hoping Prim couldn't hear. I didn't want to explain near her I was breaking down but was trying to remain strong for Prim because I didn't want my emotion to scare her more.

"You're so difficult sometimes." He sat back, dropping his head back against the wall, shutting his eyes.

Fine. Sulk. But that was preferable to him coddling me and making me cry.

Around midnight, an orderly rolled Prim to her room. She was awake but doped out of her mind. I helped her get comfortable while Cam hung around the other side of her bed, pouring a cup of ice water and helping to arrange her bedside table.

The nurse, a beautiful middle-aged woman with skin as dark and shiny as a blackberry, entered the room. She spoke in a sultry, melodious voice, introducing herself to us and Prim. She said to me, "You should probably go home and get some rest. She'll sleep tonight, and in the morning, we'll run the requested tests and a specialist, probably Dr. Lopez, will look at the results. He may want to keep her another night."

"I should stay."

Prim said, "Go home. Now. You have to go to work in the morning. You just started. You've got to keep your job. Go."

I looked between Cam and the nurse. "I don't know…"

"Don't you worry, baby. We're going to take wonderful care of your grandma."

Prim waved her spindly arm, heavy with the I.V. "Go. Go on."

I felt like a stray dog being chased away from a warm house. "You're sure?"

"If I have to tell you one more time, I'm going to take a switch to you."

We all laughed. Prim had never raised a hand to me, though she'd often threatened to do it.

The nurse said, "I see she still has plenty of spunk."

"You've got that right." I hesitated. "Against my better judgment, I'm going home. I'll be back as soon as humanly possible."

Cam said, "I'll be here first thing tomorrow."

"You don't have to do that."

"You're right. But I will."

I kissed Prim's forehead and left a final message with the nurse to call me immediately if anything happened.

As we walked down the bright, fluorescent hall, Cam said, "I imagine you need a ride home?"

Cam pulled into my driveway at near one in the morning. He turned off the truck. The only sound was the chorus of crickets and tree frogs outside. My body slumped in the seat. So many thoughts required my attention and I couldn't process a single one. I ignored them all and stared blankly at the moths dancing around the security light on the shed.

"You okay?" Cam asked.

"Yep." I dipped back into my abyss. "I'm…" Tears bubbled up. "Exhausted." Stomach acid crept along the back of my throat, and I sighed. I wanted something loaded with dark chocolate and caramel.

He reached across the seat and took my hand.

I squeezed his hand. Hard. Willing my tears to retreat. But the tears had a mind of their own. A few rogues scrambled down my cheeks. I turned my face away and swiped at them.

"Rook." Cam's voice was soft, filled with sincerity. "You've been so strong for so long…No wonder you're exhausted."

"Don't…" I whispered.

"Stop. Stop trying to hold the whole world together all the time. It's not your job."

I grabbed the door handle. "I need to go."

"Why do you have to be so hard all the time? Did you ever wonder if that might've contributed to our divorce?"

I snapped my head around to glare at him, seething. "How dare you?"

"Like it or not, it's the truth. I used to think maybe you were only trying to be strong and tough. But if you won't cry or show any real emotion, it's going to eat you from the inside out like acid. No wonder you're angry all the time. I wish you could let it all go."

I shoved open the door. "I don't need this right now." My heels wobbled on the driveway as I landed. I slammed the car door so hard I staggered backward. I removed my heels and stormed toward the house, the gravel digging into the tender soles of my feet.

He met me in front of the truck. "Look, I'm not trying to upset you. I'm simply trying to be a friend."

I tried to step around him, but he cut me off.

"Get out of my way. I can't deal with this right now." I faked him out to the left and skipped right, running around him.

"Dang it, Rook!" His voice echoed through the darkness. "I love you."

I froze on the top step and opened the door to the screened porch. I didn't know how to respond. My mind flooded with conflicting thoughts and feelings. I was scared for Prim. Worried about financing her treatment and how I could work and care for her. I'd had a great evening with Len and liked him enough to give him a chance. At least I was finally trying to move on. Cam was engaged to be married. I still cared for him, of course, but there was too much history, too many feelings to work through. I closed my eyes.

Cam's phone rang. He hissed a curse.

My head ached with the pressure of stifled tears; my body was heavy with emotions I fought to contain. My feet hurt. More than anything, fatigue had burrowed deep in my bones. Soul-tired was Prim's name for it. I couldn't process anything right now. I ached only for my cool cotton sheets and fluffy comforter and ached to slip into oblivion.

I didn't look at Cam. "Thanks for everything, Cam. I appreciate you helping me with Prim. I hate to imagine what might've happened if you weren't here tonight. Go home to your fiancée." I stepped inside and closed the door.

Chapter Nineteen

The next morning the house was hollow and lifeless, as if saddened by Prim's absence. I dressed quickly and went to the hospital to check on Prim before work. I texted Len to let him know the situation and that I'd be a little late.

He texted back **Take your time.**

He seemed like a pretty good guy. In spite of what Cam thought about him, Len deserved a chance.

Prim reported a decent night but complained of poor sleep because of all the nighttime nurse visits. I fluffed her pillows and wiped her face and arms with a damp cloth. The nurse came in to take a blood sample and roll her down to radiology for the MRI. I waited in the room until Prim returned and was served breakfast. The morning doctor visited and said Prim would be kept for the rest of the day. With a promise I'd return at lunch, I kissed her goodbye as she picked at her scrambled eggs.

When I pulled into the parking lot at work, I was relieved to find I was only twenty minutes late. I entered the lobby of the main building. It was a comfortable space, where a receptionist sat behind a high countertop flanked by two ferns. The Four Wild Horses logo on a giant faux bourbon barrel lid sat under bright lights.

Dewey leaned on the reception desk talking with Lucia. His hard stare bored into me as I passed. His long Rumpelstiltskin nose twitched.

I said, "Good morning."

But he continued to scowl, as if his gaze alone could choke the life out of me. "Hey, you. Girl."

I stopped and faced him, my heart thudding.

He approached. His gnarly teeth were tobacco-stained and his lips red as butchered meat. "I hear you been asking questions about me." His Adam's apple bulged grotesquely in his neck and waggled like a fishing bob. He didn't like me.

The feeling was mutual.

"Yeah, so?"

"Why?"

"There was some stuff I wanted to know."

"Like what?"

My heart rabbited now. He could be the killer. If so, it would be stupid to let him think I suspected him. I needed to be very careful how I proceeded. "I was talking to Randall, wanted to know what sort of person you were."

"What's it to you?"

"Because you were really angry with my friend, Bryan, the other day." I braced myself for his response. I glanced at Lucia, hoping she was paying attention in case I needed a witness. She was on the phone.

"Are you the one who told the cops on me?"

"What are you talking about?"

"Some cop contacted me and wants me to come to the sheriff's department for questioning."

"And? They're in the middle of an investigation. I'm sure they're calling a lot of people to come in."

He snorted through his long, pointy nose. "Well, I didn't do anything to that jerk. Though I wish I had. He shorted me on pay. I've got a family to support."

"I guess you should've done your job right." What sort of lapse of sanity was I having? Where was this coming from?

He edged forward. "And maybe you need to mind your own business."

"My friends are my business. Always."

He pointed a knotted, grimy finger. "Hey, I did my job. I'm one of the hardest working people at this place. You ask anyone."

"I would, but you get mad when people ask questions about you." I stomped away.

"Hold on. We ain't done here. I want to know…" He shouted after me, "Hey, girl. Come back here. I ain't done…"

Ignoring him, I scooted into the break room to grab a coffee. Holly and Len were in there, whispering.

"Morning." I beelined to the coffee bar, my hand shaking as I reached for the coffeepot.

"Good morning," they said in unison, moving apart.

I poured my coffee, mixed in creamer, wishing I had a nip of bourbon to calm my nerves. But ironically, unsolicited drinking on the job at the distillery was frowned upon. I turned to Len. "I'm sorry our date last night was interrupted. But I wanted to let you know I had a wonderful time." I remembered that knee-buckling kiss and my face warmed a little.

He glanced at Holly. "Yeah. Me, too."

Holly stretched her glossed lips into a too-wide smile and her penciled brows lifted. She looked like a clown from a Stephen King novel. She touched my arm, her hands icy. "You two make an adorable couple." She cut her eyes at Len. "I'll leave you lovebirds alone. Len, when you get a chance, there's some paperwork you need to sign."

"Sure thing." Len reddened a bit and watched her walk away. He faced me. "I had a fantastic time. I'd love to see you again. How about tonight?" He pulled his phone out of his pants pocket.

Weird. He didn't ask after Prim. *Rude.* Maybe he was distracted. We were at work, after all. Holly needed him. He was reading something on his phone.

We strolled toward the marketing pit.

"I'd like to, but I'll probably be taking care of my grandma tonight."

"I guess I'll have to wait until the barbeque on Saturday in order to finish our kiss."

A slow grin spread across my heated face. "I guess you will. But I heard good things come to those who wait."

At lunch, I left the office to run by Wendy's to order a cheeseburger combo for myself and a small Frosty for Prim. It seemed the days of relaxing and reading during lunch were gone for the foreseeable future. Surely the hospital staff wouldn't deny Prim a little treat. Cam called as I pulled into the hospital's parking garage. I let it go to voice mail. He probably wanted to discuss last night. I couldn't deal with that yet.

Prim sat up in her bed, watching *Judge Judy* and eating lunch.

"Hey, Prim," I said as cheery as I could manage. I presented the Frosty. "Looky what I have for you."

"Thank goodness." She shoved back the plate of a half-eaten chicken salad sandwich, potato wedges, and fruit cocktail. Her gown hung off one shoulder and her hair was mussed. She reached for the Frosty with both hands like a child.

"Is the food that bad?"

"It's okay, but that Frosty sure will be better." She smiled, looking at me over the rim of her glasses.

On the bedside table was a vase of daisies and roses with a big pink bow tied around the neck of the vase.

"Those are pretty flowers," I said. "But there's no card. Who gave you those?"

"Cam." She spooned a bite of Frosty into her mouth. "He brought them to me this morning."

Recalling the scene last night, my heart sank into my shoes. He'd been nice, sincere, all the things I'd ever wanted him to be when we were married. Maybe he'd been those things and I couldn't appreciate it at the time because I'd been too focused on myself. I rubbed my face as if I could rub away all the worries and drama, too. I conceded. "That was mighty nice of him." I chewed my burger and watched *Judge Judy* tell off a slum lord. When the commercial came on, I asked Prim, "Have they told you your test results yet?"

"No. Not yet."

"How are you feeling?" I sat in the chair by her bed and pulled my food out of the bag.

"I feel fine as frog hair."

I laughed. "Are you in any pain?"

"Nope." She spooned the chocolate Frosty into her mouth.

I ate my food while she chatted away, telling me the gossip she'd learned about the nurses. As my visit ended, a nurse entered the room.

"When is Prim being released?" I asked. "I have to go to work now and need to make arrangements to pick her up."

"We can't release her yet."

"Why? She says she feels fine."

She chuckled. "She sure does feel fine. She's on powerful pain meds. But the tests we ran this morning are still under review. With luck, she might be released tonight. Honestly, I wouldn't be surprised if the doctor keeps her another night."

I fretted over Prim all the way back to work and for the rest of the day. In the afternoon, the doctor called to say the results had still not come back. He wanted to keep Prim another night and he'd release her sometime the next day. My brain cried out for chocolate and coffee, so I made my way to the break room. Drinking my coffee, I stared at the row of sundry candy bars in the vending machine. Admittedly, my craving was triggered by stress. But I was already fighting too many things. I couldn't fight my cravings too.

Clarence sidled up to me as I fished the Milky Way Midnight out of the machine. He smelled like garlic. He smiled. "Hey there, princess."

"Hey."

"I suspect you have something that doesn't belong to you."

I peeled back the wrapper. "I don't know what you're talking about."

He leaned against the vending machine. "I'll tell you a story. I had some things in my office. A laptop and a folder. Yesterday, I was going to make use of those things and realized they were missing. I asked around and discovered you had been snooping around my office on Wednesday night. This person said you were leaving my office with a very thick computer bag."

Holly. She had to be the snitch because she was the only one who'd seen me near Clarence's office. "Interesting story." I bit into the candy bar for a surge of sugary courage. "I have a story, too."

He glowered at me. "Oh yeah?"

I tipped my head. "See, my best friend Bryan died on Monday. Had a laptop and a folder in his office. But when I checked, those things weren't in his office. Nor did the sheriff's office have them. But guess what else? He also had a thumb drive in his desktop computer." I sipped my coffee. "I wonder what happened to the thumb drive with all that important financial information?"

"There was a thumb drive?"

I scoffed. "Yeah, right. Like you don't know. Like you didn't have the laptop and the folder, too, right?"

He pushed his glasses up, his brown eyes blinking rapidly. "Okay. Okay. I can't deny the laptop and folder. But I never had the thumb drive. I didn't know about it." He muttered to himself. "I wish I had."

I blinked at him. "You mean, you really don't have it?"

"That's what I'm saying." He licked his lips and smoothed his mustache. "I don't have it, either."

Barely suppressed rage clouded his face. He spat, struggling to keep his voice low. "Are you kidding me?"

"I'm not kidding."

"What happened to it?"

"I don't know. I thought you took it."

He gritted his teeth, his mustache twitching. "If you give back the computer and folder, I'll give you some money. How much do you want?"

I took another bite of my candy bar. For a brief second, I considered it. Then I shoved the thought away. Finding Bryan's killer was more important. "Mr. Ford, that offer is insulting to both me and the memory of my friend." I didn't want him to know I'd already given it to law enforcement. He'd know soon enough.

He hit the vending machine and swore under his breath. He pointed a finger at me. "I've got to have that stuff back. One way or the other." He stormed away.

Sipping my coffee to hide the shudder shooting through me, I wondered how I was going to keep myself out of danger while trying to find justice for

Bryan.

Chapter Twenty

It was near six by the time I left work. I texted Jimmy on my way out to tell him I had another piece of evidence. To save myself time, I asked if it was possible for him to swing by my house. I needed to run by the house first to pack Prim's crochet project, clothes to come home in, and a brush and barrettes to fix her hair. She'd appreciate that. Supper was coming from a drive-thru as I had neither the time nor the energy to cook.

Upon reaching my car, a sheet of white paper flapped under the windshield wiper. The paper read: You're next. But it had been typed in Chiller font. I'd managed to aggravate both Clarence and Dewey in a short span of time. If I had to bet on who left this note, I'd put my money on one of them. Holly hated me, too. So, I tacked her name on to the list.

Though the sun hung low in the sky, the air remained humid and thick. The birds had fallen silent. In spite of the hot summer evening, a cold, spookiness descended. My good old-fashioned women's intuition tickled my gut. My skin stretched tight and uncomfortable as control top pantyhose. I scanned the parking lot.

A truck, dark-blue with turquoise swooshes on the sides, idled at the far end of the parking lot. The blacked-out windows made it impossible to discern the driver's identity. The engine gunned. The truck swooped out of its space.

Fumbling with my keys, trying to get the key in the door lock, reminded me of all those cheesy, frustrating horror movies where the characters dropped their keys while running. I never wanted to be that girl. But fear weighed heavy in the body and prevented nimbleness in my fingers.

The truck pulled toward me, slow and menacing.

Finally, managing the lock, I jumped in my car, locked the door, and drove the key into the ignition. The truck pulled behind me, barricading my exit. The grass embankment blocked my forward movement, and the wheel stops in the parking spaces beside me prevented my escape left or right without considerable damage to my car. Different escape possibilities flashed through my mind. I could try running, but I was too out of shape and the air was so humid, I'd probably pass out within 100 yards. How was I going to get out of this? What if someone jumped out of the truck to attack me? What could I do? I reached in the back seat for my giant ice scraper. Guess I was going to sit until I had to fight.

The passenger window rolled down. I shifted in my seat to see inside the truck, but the driver was cast in shadow. A white Styrofoam cup flew out, landing on my back window. Brown, gritty juice flowed down the glass. Ew. Dip spit. My stomach churned. The truck's tires squealed as the vehicle flew off in a wave of muffled rock music. I squinted to read the license plate and tried to take a picture with my phone, but I couldn't get the phone out of my purse fast enough. Besides, the truck was too fast anyway. That was okay. It didn't take a genius to figure out Dewey was the culprit. Jerk.

I stared at the slow descent of the brown spit on my back window in my rearview mirror. Dang it! Now I had to add a trip to the car wash before picking up dinner and going to see Prim. I waited until the truck had disappeared then I flew out of the parking lot toward my house. My phone rang. Cam. I'd call him later. I had my hands full right now.

My phone chimed indicating Cam left a voice mail then immediately chimed again to signal a text. Jimmy. **Serving summons be there in 20 mins.**

Once home, I put the note in a plastic storage bag, along with the paper I'd taken from Holly's legal pad, and laid the bag on the kitchen table. I jogged upstairs to pack Prim's things. There was a knock at the back door in the kitchen. I ran downstairs and peeked out the window. Jimmy. Thank heavens. I let him in. "Hey. I'm really glad you're here."

He filled the doorway.

I stepped back to let him inside and shut the door behind him.

"What's up?" He scanned the room, his hand resting on the butt of his gun. "You okay?"

I handed him the bagged notes. "This." He took it and read them as I spoke. "This one I found on Holly Parker's desk. She's the admin assistant at the distillery. But I'm not sure she's involved. It could've been an accident the paper was on her desk or it could've been planted."

He made a note in his notepad.

"This one was on my windshield when I came out of the office tonight." I found the picture on my phone of the spit attack on my car and showed it to him. "And this. The driver, who I'm certain is Dewey Stiggers, threw a cup of dip spit on my car."

He studied the picture.

"You have no idea who could've put the note on your car?"

"I have a couple of suspects. It's either Clarence Ford, the bookkeeper, or Dewey Stiggers, the delivery driver. They both have been acting suspicious. I kind of had run-ins with them today."

"What sort of run-ins?"

I told him what happened between Clarence and me and the words I'd exchanged with Dewey.

He listened intently, making notes. "You must be pushing somebody's buttons. Otherwise, why would someone bother to threaten you?"

I shrugged.

"Describe the truck for me." He jotted notes as I described the truck. "Is there anything else you can tell me? License number, anything?"

Hugging myself, I shook my head. "No. He drove away too fast to catch any numbers or letters."

"Okay, well…" He sighed and tucked away his notepad and pen. "I'll look into it for you, Rook. I'll let you know if I find out anything."

"Did you find anything useful on Bryan's laptop?"

"All I can tell you is we did find financial documents and we're having a forensic accountant look at them. We're hoping to know something soon. But it could take a week or more."

I rubbed my forehead. "I wish I could find the other thumb drive for y'all. There might be something else on it to tie everything together."

"Rook, this is getting serious. You've had run-ins with two men in one day. One or both of them could be involved in Bryan's death. You need to back off right now before you get yourself hurt. Or worse."

"Thank you bunches." I grabbed the stuff I'd collected for Prim. "And thanks for coming by. I hate to rush you off, but I have to go to the hospital now."

My house phone rang. Jimmy waved and stepped out of the house as I answered the phone.

"Hello," I waved bye to Jimmy with one hand and balanced the phone between my shoulder and ear while I dug in my purse for my car keys.

Batrene said, "Hey there, hon, I've been trying to reach y'all. Is everything okay? I saw an ambulance out there last night."

"Prim's in the hospital with her back again."

"Oh dear. I was afraid of that."

"I'm sorry I didn't call you earlier. I got home late and then rushed off to work this morning. It's been a hectic day."

"That's okay. I only wanted to check on y'all."

"I'm going to the hospital tonight. Is there anything you want me to tell her?"

First, she wanted all the details of Prim's condition and wanted to tell me about the other people she'd known with similar conditions and the medical procedures they had to go through.

Then she said, "I saw the deputy at your house. Have they discovered anything about Bryan?"

"Not really. They're having a forensic accountant look at the documents on Bryan's computer. I found it at the office and turned it in to the sheriff's department. I'm hoping we hear something any day now. I do want you to know I'm staying on them and we're going to get answers. Hopefully, real soon."

Her voice cracked. "Your mamma would be so proud of you."

I hadn't thought about my mom's case in a long time, but now that I was helping with Bryan's case, mom's case niggled at my mind. I was in a better place now so maybe I could help her, too. "How well did you know my mom?"

"Very well. I was her babysitter for a while and, of course, we went to church together. Heaven only knows what she saw in your daddy. No offense to you, because you know I think the world of you."

"I'm not offended."

"I know that once she got involved with him, it was like a light went out in her. I mean, she had been dating that Decker boy—"

"What Decker boy?" I'd never heard anyone mention this Decker guy.

She hemmed. "Well, I guess I've kept you long enough. I'll let you go. You give Prim my love and tell her I'm sorry I can't come visit in the hospital."

"Don't worry. She knows. Hopefully, she'll be home tomorrow."

I hung up with Batrene, perplexed, and rushed to the hospital to squeeze in before visiting hours ended.

Cam called again on my way to the hospital, but I didn't answer. I had too much on my plate already. I'd try to call him from the hospital.

Prim was sitting up in bed, watching television. Cam was there, too.

I sank, nearly dropping the bags. "Uh. Hey. What are you doing here?"

He stood and took the bags from me, setting them by the bed. "I was concerned about Prim so thought I'd visit. I was calling to see where you were."

"Oh. Okay. Well, I'm here now. I wasn't ignoring you. It's been a hectic day." I stood on the other side of her bed, taking her hand. "Prim, I brought your puzzle book and crochet. I brought stuff to fix your hair, too. You want me to fix it now?" I brushed a wisp of hair from her face.

"No. I'm fine."

"Has the doctor been here today to give you the test results?"

Cam said, "He came in about an hour ago and said they should have results in the morning. I asked when he'd be back. He said he starts his rounds at about seven in the morning."

Prim said, "I need to get out of here so I can go to Bryan's visitation. I want to be there for Batrene. She can't be alone right now."

I said, "I spoke to Batrene tonight. She understands. She knows you'd be there if you could. We'll go tomorrow. If you're strong enough. You don't want to wear yourself out or you won't heal."

"We'll see." That was Prim code for she'd do exactly as she wanted. She sunk into her pile of pillows and closed her eyes. "I'm so sleepy."

"That's okay." I tucked her in. "You go to sleep. I'll stay here a bit longer. Then I'll go home and come back first thing in the morning."

Cam's phone rang and he stepped out into the hall to talk while I stared blankly at the television. I didn't know what I was watching. A stream of thoughts whirled one into the other in an incoherent jumble of Dewy, Clarence, the truck incident, Batrene, and the information she'd dropped about some Decker guy and my mom, and Cam and his profession of love. Like flashing minnows in a creek, I couldn't grasp any one thought long enough to trace it. Briefly, I entertained asking Prim about the Decker guy my mom had dated, but that would be wrong. Prim needed peace and rest right now. I'd have time later to talk to her about all that, but she was already half-asleep. My eyes grew heavy.

A nurse entered to remind me visiting hours were ending in ten minutes. She offered me a pillow and blanket if I wanted to stay the night. I declined, knowing I wouldn't sleep if I stayed. But, truth be told, I was a little scared to stay in an empty house after the events that had unfolded earlier in the evening.

Cam returned. "Visiting hours are over. Are you staying?"

"No. I feel like I should, but…"

"C'mon. I'll walk you to your car."

Any other day I might've declined the offer, but I welcomed the company this time around.

We walked through the sterile, fluorescent hall, engaging in small talk about Prim, Batrene, Bryan's funeral, work—all the usual things—anything to keep the subject off earlier tonight. We crossed the pedway into the parking garage, our voices echoing in the concrete space.

"Here I am." I veered toward my lime green car.

"The old June bug car," he chuckled.

"Yep. Still have it all these years later. It's been good to me." I unlocked the car and opened the door. "Thanks for escorting me. I'll see you later."

"Rook," Cam held the door. "Wait. Please."

My shoulders tightened. I made myself look into his face.

"About last night…"

"Cam, please. Let's not do this right now. I'm exhausted."

"Please listen—"

"You shouldn't have said what you said, Cam." I leaned against my car and fiddled with my car keys. "You're engaged. I'm trying to move on. Granted, not very successfully so far, but still…"

"I know it was wrong. But, it's true. I never really stopped loving you. I couldn't remain when you no longer loved me."

"I did love you. I lost sight of things for a while, but…"

"What are you saying? You still love me, too?"

Oh no. This had the potential to be all kinds of ugly. Did I still love him? Had I ever stopped? I had a bad habit of closing off feelings I didn't want to deal with, choking them down with food. Or they morphed into anger fuel. Or I cut them off like a hangnail. After the divorce, I kept going. I didn't consider my feelings or how we'd failed each other. I thought about other things and kept moving.

I searched his eyes, the color of blue jay feathers. It wouldn't matter if I still loved him or not. He was in another relationship, on the verge of another marriage. "I don't know…"

He scratched the back of his head, frustrated. "I do know I can't imagine my life without you."

I shook my head and stared at my sandals.

"Jacie wants us to move to Cincinnati after the marriage. Sell the bar, everything. And move."

I averted my face, unable to imagine my life without him either.

"Did you hear me?"

"Yeah." I didn't have the energy to sift through all my conflicting emotions right now. I was dealing with Prim's illness, Bryan's death, my new job, and trying to find Bryan's killer. And, Cam was engaged, promised to another, but was saying he loved me. If he was happy with her, I couldn't stand in the way of that. I couldn't, once again, destroy his happiness and my own chance for happiness. I needed to move on. I shrugged. "I don't know what to tell you, Cam. I guess you have some stuff to figure out. I can't help you with that."

"Maybe if you still loved me…"

Anger surged in my gut, shooting into my chest. "I'm carrying way too much on my shoulders to worry about my feelings right now." The anger was now pouring from my mouth. "My grandma is sick. I don't know what's wrong. That freaks me out. She's my only real family left on this earth. I have no one else. No one."

He held my hand and spoke softly. "Hey. You have me. You'll always have me."

"No, I don't. Not really. We're friends, of course. But…you know what I mean. Besides, what if you move with Jacie to Cincinnati?" I pulled my hand away. "Anyway, if that's what you want to do, you should do it. You have to consider your future with her. Jacie has you. But that's the least of my concerns right now." I was fired up. "Prim's medical issues are mounting. I've had this job only days, thanks to my friend who was likely murdered there. Now, I think the killer may be after me, and you want to talk about our feelings?"

He perked. "What? What do you mean?"

I told him about the letter and the truck.

"Are you kidding me? You have to quit. You can't go back there."

"I can't quit. I need the work now more than ever. To pay you back. To help Prim and to pay my godforsaken student loans."

"Don't worry about what you owe me."

"Cam." I sighed. "I already rely on you too much. We're divorced. At some point, I have to act like it and stand on my own two feet. These feelings you're having are probably my fault because I've been asking a lot of you lately. We've been seeing a lot of each other. I never meant to lead you on."

"You haven't led me on. You need help. I'm happy to do it. I love Prim." He touched my cheek, his gaze longing and loving. "Rook…"

For a few seconds, I allowed myself to relax into his touch, the warmth, the familiarity. An ache of longing yawned in my gut.

My eyes popped open and my body battened the hatches on that longing, shutting it out. I drew away from him and lowered myself into my car. "We can be friends. No reason not to be. But you need to go home...to your fiancée."

I drove home alone, hating myself for losing Cam and everything we could've been, wishing more than ever he was coming home to me again and that I had the courage to try to love him again.

Chapter Twenty-One

Exhausted, but too wound up to sleep, and brain too scattered to read, I hunkered down on the couch and dammed my feelings with a bottle of Kentucky Red Ale, a large bowl of Cheetos and popcorn, and a moon pie while I watched reruns of *Law and Order: SVU*.

As I'd done every night, I filed through the copies I'd made from Bryan's red folder. I'd already read several links about bookkeeper fraud and found that sometimes shady bookkeepers established phony businesses and paid those businesses from their employer's account. I began sifting through the invoices and researching the companies to see if they were legitimate. I started first with websites and made a list of their phone numbers and their hours of operation. Thankfully, a few of them had Saturday hours. I planned to call those in the morning to verify their legitimacy. The rest would have to wait until Monday.

After my research, I snuggled under one of Prim's handmade afghans with my bowl of popcorn and Cheetos to watch television. I'd made it through my first week of work. What a crazy week it had been. At some point, I'd fallen asleep because the next thing I remembered, I was waking to a man screaming enthusiastically about a car shammy.

I groaned and rolled off the couch. It was already seven in the morning. I still needed to get to the hospital and to get Prim and me to Bryan's visitation. I'd hoped to place a few calls to check on the legitimacy of the companies on the invoices and would try to get around to that later in the day. After a quick shower, I threw on a Beatles T-shirt and shorts and set off for the hospital, stopping by McDonald's for a sausage biscuit and coffee.

Prim was watching television and picking at her breakfast, her gown slipping off her shoulders. She looked like a child in her big sister's nightgown. A nurse came in and checked Prim's vitals and I.V. bag. Before leaving, she said the doctor should be in soon to review her for release.

The doctor entered the room as the nurse left. He wore blue scrubs, a green scrub cap, and tennis shoes. He carried an iPad under his arm. He pushed up his wire-rimmed glasses and shook my hand. "Hi, I'm Dr. Lopez. How are we doing today, Mrs. Vertrees?"

"Oh, very well." Prim fidgeted with her applesauce lid.

He glanced at his iPad. His pinched lips and knotted jaw told me the next words wouldn't be good ones. "Mrs. Vertrees, I have some difficult news. I've looked at the test results. We've detected several tumors in your left breast. Those bumps under your arm are swollen lymph nodes. Your white blood cells are considerably elevated."

I melted in my seat, gawking at the doctor. Each of his words was like a pickaxe chiseling away at my entire world. Prim stared straight ahead at the wall, her spoon slipping from her hand onto her bed covers.

The doctor rambled on and on about this and that test. I was catching only snippets of what he was saying. "...possible the cancer is in your bones or blood, which is why your back is hurting...depending on the stage...start an aggressive course..."

I wanted to bury my face in hands, to cry, to run screaming from the room. I wished I was one of those delicate women who fainted so I wouldn't have to hear anymore. I couldn't do any of that. I needed to be strong for Prim. I sat there as stupid and cold as a stone.

The doctor finished his speech. "Are there any questions?"

I found my voice. "How long does she..." But my mouth wouldn't form the words my mind and heart couldn't conceive. I stumbled. "How long will she..." My throat closed off.

Dr. Lopez had probably been asked the question many times. "It's difficult to say. A few months? If you're very lucky, maybe a year or so. It'll depend on how well she responds to treatment."

"What sort of treatment..."

He looked at his chart and sighed. "It's tough to say. We'll refer you to an oncologist who can suggest a possible course of treatment."

Prim stirred her applesauce. "Can I go home today?"

We arrived home from the hospital in enough time to shower and change into our black dresses for Bryan's visitation.

Tanbark Funeral Home was packed. Almost everyone from the distillery attended: Holly (surprisingly), Lucia, Pierce, the marketing team, and the warehouse folks. Clarence and Dewey hadn't shown up. That didn't surprise me and, in fact, only further convinced me one of them was likely the culprit.

The room was chilly and smelled of musty roses. The same way my mother's viewing had smelled. The same way my Pappy's wake smelled. Musty roses were the scent of death. Quiet chatter and laughter filled the room. Flowers, plants, and gifts lined the walls and surrounded the casket.

Standing at the head of the casket, Batrene wore a black dress with a sparkling rhinestone broach. A lace handkerchief in one hand, she received guests with serenity, shaking hands and exchanging words with people as they paused at the casket to pay respect to Bryan.

Batrene hugged Prim then sandwiched her delicate hand in hers. "Oh, Prim. I'm glad you came. You shouldn't be here with your back, though. How are you doing, hon?"

"Oh, I'm very well. The doctors believe it's cancer." She'd said it as casually as discussing their gardens.

Concern melted Batrene's features. "Oh, sugar. How bad is it?"

Prim pressed her pink lips together and patted Batrene's hands. "That's nothing to worry about right now. If there's anything at all you need, we'll help in every way we can."

"We'll talk soon." Batrene squeezed my hand, too. "Thank y'all. I don't know what I'd do without the two of you."

I guided Prim away to allow Batrene to greet the other guests. We stood by the casket, looking at Bryan's frozen features.

"He looks good, doesn't he?" Prim asked.

"Yes," I lied. He looked like a wax figure of Bryan. He looked unnaturally peachy and powdery from the makeup, and his hair was combed over and heavily sprayed like an evangelistic television preacher. His suit was peculiarly straight and unruffled. His favorite University of the Bluegrass Thoroughbreds shirt was pinned to the inside of the casket lid. I put my hand on his cold, lifeless arm. "I'm sorry this happened to you, BB. I swear I'll find out the truth if it kills me."

I led Prim over to a blue velvet settee placed underneath a landscape painting, where I helped her sit and promised to bring her a soda. I bought a couple Cokes and ran into Cam in the lobby. He was dressed in a green plaid button-down, gray blazer, and jeans.

"Hey." He smiled. "Apologies for the casual wear. I have to go to work."

"Don't worry about it." I offered a reassuring smile as we turned back to the parlor. "There are all sorts of people here in their work clothes."

"I won't stay long. I only wanted to pay my respects."

"Batrene will be happy you came."

Len came in, tucking his sunglasses in his suit pocket. He flashed a dazzling toothpaste ad smile. He sidled up to me and wrapped his arm around my waist, pulling me close. He kissed my cheek. "Hey there. You okay?" He and Cam nodded at each other by way of greeting.

Holly stood across the room, speaking with Pierce and Lucia. She shot daggers in our direction. Then she turned her back on us.

A hint of sadness washed over Cam's face. "Well, I'm going to..." He motioned toward the viewing room and stepped away.

My phone buzzed. Jimmy. I texted that I'd call him later.

Len followed me to where Prim was sitting. They greeted each other and he opened the Cokes, giving one to Prim.

He checked his watch. "How long are you going to stay?"

"Visitation will last a few more hours. Afterward, people will gather at Batrene's for a while."

Disappointment flitted over his face. "I was hoping you and I might hang out tonight."

Really? I winced. "I can't do that." In fact, it was the last thing I wanted to do.

"Hey, I understand. I'll call you tonight or tomorrow." He left.

I sat next to Prim. "Len didn't go pay his respects at Bryan's casket. Isn't that odd?"

Prim said, "People grieve in different ways. He may have a hard time looking at a dead body. My uncle was like that. He fainted every time he saw a dead body."

I bit the inside of my lip, watching Holly leave the room. "Maybe."

We stayed at the funeral home until three. Everyone was too tired to stay longer, so we went to Batrene's to eat and visit with each other a little longer. By six, Prim was wiped out, so I took her home and helped her change clothes, take her medicine, and get settled in her recliner in front of the television.

"I'll be back in a couple hours, okay? I'm going to go help Batrene clean up."

By the time I reached Batrene's, all her guests had left the house and she and her younger sister, Bonnie, were scraping dishes.

I walked in the house, Maxine panting at my heels. "I've come to help," I said.

Bonnie smiled, big dimples in her cheeks. "I swannee, it's like looking at Annette Daniels. You look exactly like your momma."

"Doesn't she?" Batrene said.

I said to Batrene, "You look tired. Why don't you go rest? You've had a long day and tomorrow..." I squeezed her arm, my throat clenching. "Tomorrow's going to be a hard day."

She nodded. She drooped everywhere, the weight of her sorrow pulling at her face and shoulders. She didn't squabble but shuffled out of the kitchen.

The television clicked on in the living room. Bonnie ran water in the sink as I finished putting food away in the fridge.

Thankfully, most of the plates and utensils were disposable, but there were a few casserole containers, cake plates, and utensils that needed to be washed. Bonnie was short and chubby, with chestnut hair feathered back from her round face. She dipped her hands into the soapy water and scrubbed at a casserole dish.

I recalled my earlier conversation with Batrene. "Batrene told me she used to babysit my mom. I guess y'all knew her really well."

"Oh, yes. Batrene babysat me, too. We weren't much younger than her, so she was more like a supervisor to keep Annette and me out of trouble."

"How old were y'all at the time?"

"Batrene was eighteen and Annie and I were about fifteen." She rinsed the dish.

I dried the glass bakeware and put it on the kitchen table. "Were you and my momma close?"

"We were pretty close for a lot of years. We started growing apart when she started dating your daddy. That sort of thing happens to people when they get real serious, so I didn't hold it against her or nothing."

"Of course. Do you remember a guy named Decker? Batrene mentioned him earlier and I've never heard of him. I was curious who he was and how my mom knew him."

She grew silent, suddenly focused on scrubbing a serving spoon.

"Bonnie?"

"Your momma and daddy broke up for a bit. He was the guy she dated before your parents got back together."

I was surprised. "Really? I never knew that. How long did they date?"

"Oh gosh. I'd say at least six months."

"What was his name?"

"Will Decker. He was…" Batrene came into the kitchen and Bonnie snapped her mouth shut.

Batrene said, "What're y'all talking about?"

I started to speak, but Bonnie cut me off. "Oh, nothing. She was telling me all about Prim. Weren't you?"

Stunned, I nodded.

Batrene glowered at her sister and cleared her throat. She poured a glass of lemonade and sat at the kitchen table. The conversation shifted. I wanted desperately to know why the relationship between Will Decker and my mother was shrouded in secrecy. Why Batrene thought it was necessary to hide the information. Why Prim had never mentioned this man. But I didn't want to broach the subject now. My instincts told me it was a delicate subject that might upset folks, and Batrene was already dealing with enough. I let it drop. For now.

Chapter Twenty-Two

It was a good day for a funeral. The church was full for the sermon. Batrene insisted we sit on the front pew with her and her sister because we were as good as family. Cam came to pay his respects, sans Jacie, looking ruggedly handsome, albeit uncomfortable, in a suit. He sat in the pew behind us. Six of Bryan's friends and cousins carried his casket out of the church and loaded it into the waiting hearse.

I drove Prim and Batrene to the cemetery, where the closest family and friends gathered around the open earth like a murder of crows. Cam stood close to me, occasionally stroking my back. I wanted to cry. I wished I could because my head ached from the dammed emotions.

The preacher said a final prayer over Bryan and a blessing over the mourners, and we were released to join the land of the living again.

Cam said, "I'll meet you over at Batrene's. I have to stop by my parents' house. My mom got a gift for Batrene and made a dish, but they can't manage to come by."

"That's okay. She didn't have to do anything."

"I know, but you know my mom."

After the burial, Prim and I relocated to Batrene's house, where she and Bonnie would receive guests. We rushed to set out all the sympathy food that had been dropped off by well-wishers.

"Oh, shoot," Batrene said. "My ice maker ain't working. I need more ice. I know this house is going to be full of people, and we can't do without ice for drinks."

"I'll go get some." I grabbed my keys and purse. "If there's anything else you need, call my cell."

"Thank you, sweetie," Batrene said.

Guests were already arriving as I backed out. We navigated around each other and I sped off down a two-lane country road with lush foliage and a hedge of trees with long branches intermittently overhanging the road, providing sparse shade. On the way inside Tom's Convenient Store, I checked my phone. Batrene had texted that I should also bring more plastic cups and stop by the grocery for yeast rolls. I grabbed the ice then shot over to the grocery. I dashed inside, hunted down the yeast rolls and plastic cups and passed through the checkout, giving one syllable answers to Rosie Beale to cut short her attempts to start an in-depth conversation.

I rushed out to the car. The temperature on the parking lot asphalt was already scorching, and the sun seared my eyes and skin. I jumped in the car and blasted the A/C and Bob Dylan for the drive home.

When I turned off Reynolds Road onto Aberdeen Road, I glanced in my rearview mirror to see a car approaching behind me. Normal enough. I kept singing and glanced away to turn the music up and the A/C down. When I looked up, the grill of the other car was super close to my bumper. It was a large vehicle, a gold SUV-type. The vehicle was getting closer, fast. It shifted to the right, locking its fender with my bumper. I jolted with the hit.

It all happened in a blink. The other car increased its speed and pushed me to the left, into the other lane. A large truck barreled toward me, honking. I tried to speed up to get around the vehicle, which now pulled alongside, blocking me in. I jerked the wheel and swerved off the road as the honking truck passed me. My car rolled down a grassy shoulder, lodging into a shallow ditch, the front of the car landing in a bush of honeysuckle and poison oak.

The vehicle sped past. I couldn't get a license plate number or a make or model of the car. But I did catch a glimpse of a sticker on the back windshield. It looked like a bee or a wasp. Maybe a hornet.

I sat at the wheel, shuddering, panting, trying to rally. I performed a quick mental scan of my body, searching for unusual pain or numbness.

Honking sounded behind me. A truck eased to a stop beside me. Cam.

His mouth dropped open. He pulled in front of me and parked his truck on the shoulder. He jumped out and sprinted toward me. He looked like the star of a *Law and Order* show in his suit and sunglasses.

He opened my door. "You okay?"

"Yeah, I'm fine. Shook up more than anything."

"What happened?"

"Some jerk ran me off the road. On purpose." My fear and panic were giving way to the gradual rise of my anger.

"What?" He looked around as if he might still spot the perpetrator. "Why?" He held out his hand and helped me out of the car through the passenger side. The driver side was blocked by the bramble.

"I don't know."

He lifted his sunglasses and looked me over to make sure I was in one piece. "Did you get the plates or anything?"

"No. They came out of nowhere, rammed me, and pushed me off the road."

"What did the car look like?"

"A gold SUV-type car, kind of boxy, like a Cadillac Escalade." I pulled my ponytail to tighten it. "You know I don't know cars." I huffed, looking around, and planted my hands on my hips. "It had dark tinted windows all around."

"Anything else stand out?"

"There was a hornet decal in the lower left corner of the back windshield." I rubbed my collarbone, where the seat belt had gripped me.

He moved around my car to inspect it. "Looks like the car should be okay to drive, but it's damaged. Rear bumper dent and paint scratches along the driver's side. Good thing you stopped here. If you'd gone twenty feet farther, you would've rammed that tree." He pulled out his cell.

"Who are you calling?"

"The sheriff's office."

I rubbed my face. Sweat beaded around my hairline. The katydids screeched all around me. I checked the ice. It was still in good shape.

Cam rejoined me, searching the deserted road, for the official vehicle.

"Maybe it was a day drinker out causing trouble."

"No." I shook my head. "I'm sure it was personal."

"What are you talking about?"

"I don't want to get into it right now." I licked my dry lips and wiped my forehead.

A dark-brown SUV appeared around the corner, lights flashing. Cam stepped out and waved.

The car pulled onto the shoulder behind me.

Ugh. Sheriff Bulldog Goodman. He stepped out, clapped on his hat, and tucked his sunglasses into his shirt pocket. He saw me, snorted a laugh, and shook his head. "Why am I not surprised?" A roll of skin puckered over the top of his shirt collar. "Rook Daniels. Are you ever not in a mess?"

"It's Rook Campbell. I didn't ask for this. Or for anything. I'm trying to live my life."

He took out his notebook and sighed, exasperated. "What happened this time?"

Cam stepped up. "This time, Sheriff, someone forced her off the road, trying to kill her."

Goodman rolled his cold, dead gaze over me, but he spoke to Cam. "Now, why would anyone want to kill her? Maybe she's a bad driver and is fibbing."

"Why would I do such a thing? That's crazy." I told him what happened.

"A bee. You want me to look for a gold SUV with a bee decal on the back?" He tucked the notebook into his chest pocket. "Miss Campbell, I'm a busy man. We're investigating your friend's death, and we have other cases to pursue. I'm going to tell you this issue probably won't be our priority—"

Cam interrupted. "Sheriff, what if this is linked to Bryan Bishop's death? Maybe the person who killed Bryan thinks she knows something—"

"What do you know that you're not telling us, Miss Campbell?" Goodman leveled his cold gaze on me.

I'd been working with Jimmy, and I trusted him to pursue the case, however much he was annoyed with my interference. My backside was covered and I didn't need to say anything to Goodman. I crossed my arms over my chest. "I've told you everything I know. Now, if you don't mind, I need to get back home. Mrs. Bishop needs ice for her funeral guests."

Goodman squinted. He was like a bird dog picking up a distant scent of prey. "Uh-huh. If that's how you want to play it..." He tapped the corner of his eye. "But I know there's something you're not telling me."

I dug my nails into my biceps and clamped my mouth shut for once.

"Let's get this straight, Cam. There's no evidence Mr. Bishop was, in fact, murdered. We're investigating it because Miss Campbell seems to believe there's a reason for it. We're looking into it."

"Yeah," Cam sniffed, rolling his shoulder back, pulling his suit jacket tight across his shoulders. "I'm sure you're working real hard on it."

Goodman's neck reddened. His voice boomed. "Son, don't you ever question the diligence and dedication of my department. We're doing everything we can with the limited resources we have to work with. But we can't chase every flight of fancy—"

Cam dropped his arms and stepped forward. I grabbed his arm to hold him back as he balled his fists at his sides, saying, "Now hold on a minute—"

"No, you hold on." Goodman pointed his short, thick finger at him. The red flooded into his cheeks. "Up to this point, we've found no evidence Mr. Bishop met with foul play. In fact, everything I've seen points to natural causes. And now, this cockamamie story? All I see is an attention-seeking woman with a vivid imagination."

Now I was angry. I was a lot of things, but I was no attention-seeking drama queen. "Has the coroner's report come back yet?"

"The preliminary results point to heart failure. But we're running a toxicology report. That could take weeks."

"You don't know for certain he wasn't murdered, do you? That tells me there could be a killer running free among us, and he could kill again at any moment."

Chapter Twenty-Three

Sweeping into a parking space at the distillery on Monday morning, I was only five minutes late.

Len greeted me as I exited my car. "Hey there, beautiful. How you are you this morning?"

"Fine. You?" I gathered my things and exited the car.

"Good Morning." He kissed my cheek.

"Morning." I straightened my black wrap dress and touched my iridescent blue necklace.

He wore a shell-pink button-down and khakis. He smelled fresh and inviting. While I felt like a rumpled sweater covered in cat hair and stale cigarette smoke found in the corner of an attic.

"You okay? You seem…stressed."

I chuckled. "I leveled up from stressed about a week ago."

"Is there anything I can do?"

"Thank you. I'm fine." The common refrain of the deeply distressed.

Len launched into something about work, but I wasn't listening because I noticed Dewey and Randall standing outside the rickhouse, talking. Seeing them reminded me to figure out which one had left the letter on my windshield. Dewey had thrown the spit on my car. He'd made no secret of his dipping habit. But that didn't mean he'd left the note on my car.

I doubted it was Dewey anyway because he was on the road almost all day. I wasn't sure he even had computer access. It was possible he typed it at home, but that would be a lot of work. Nah. He was the sort who'd write it with a marker or pen.

Then there was Clarence. He might've been angry enough with me to put the note on my car. Especially after I'd taken the laptop and folder from his office. He certainly had a reason to come after me. But I had no way to prove it.

The only other person on my suspect list was Holly. She didn't like me, but why would she want to threaten me or hurt me? What would she possibly have to gain from it? Unless there was another suspect who should be on my list…someone who killed Bryan and now wanted me dead.

I spent my lunch hour at the Golden Dragon making phone calls to the list of companies I'd collected from Bryan's folder. The first five companies I contacted were all legitimate. On the tenth call, I received a message the phone number was unavailable. I put a star by Tree of Life, Ltd. It was supposedly a spice company. I finished the call list before leaving the restaurant, finding one more questionable company.

On my way back to the distillery, I left a voice mail for Jimmy about the two companies I found and how I suspected invoices were generated and checks were paid but the money went into another account, probably Clarence's.

The rest of the workday was pretty uneventful, which was nice. I managed to get all the social media blasts sent before I left at five. I still had a few calls to make to food and porta potty companies for the event. But I needed to hurry. I wanted to leave right at five so I'd be in the parking lot, waiting on Dewey, where I could confirm if the black truck with turquoise swooshes belonged to him.

His car was parked near the shade tree at the top of the parking lot. I sat in my car, watching in my rearview mirror. About fifteen minutes later, Dewey came striding up the hill toward the truck, lighting a cigarette.

Just as I'd thought. Jerk. Switching on my phone's video camera, I pulled my car behind his truck and rolled down my window.

He stood by his truck and glowered suspiciously at me. "What do you want?" He drew from his cigarette, repeatedly opening and closing the lid on his Zippo lighter. It was silver with a gold snake coiled around it.

I lifted my phone, videoing him, the truck, and the license plate. "Is this your truck?"

"Yeah. What's it to you?" He stepped toward my car.

There was a lot I wanted to say to him. Mostly accusations about him being not only a killer but a coward. However, ruffling his feathers was a bad idea since I could very well be talking to Bryan's killer.

"That's all I needed to know."

"Take that camera off me or else." He charged toward me.

I didn't drive away because I wanted a clear capture of his face. "Is that a threat, Mr. Dewey Stiggers?"

He lunged at my car and I stomped the peddle, racing away from the distillery, my heart rabbiting in my chest. Afraid Dewey might've followed me, I drove straight to the sheriff's office and ran inside the building. It was crisply cool and beige.

I spoke to the receptionist behind the glass. She was gathering her things to leave.

"Hey, Rosa. Can I see Jimmy?"

"Sure." She dialed a number. "He'll be right with you." She left the desk and a few moments later, Jimmy opened the side door.

"Hey, what's up? You look a little freaked out."

I glanced over my shoulder. "I am. A little."

He frowned, the scar at the corner of his mouth deepening. "Come on back." He held the door for me and then led me down a beige, fluorescent-lit hallway. He stopped and motioned to a door on the right. The room was small with an open floor plan dotted with several desks, all full of officers typing on their computers or talking on the phone. The space was well-lit, almost too bright. He led me to a desk along the wall by the door, where we sat across from each other.

"Tell me what's happening." He rolled his chair forward to lean on the desk.

I pulled out my phone and played the recording I'd taken of Dewey and told him about my most recent findings. He leaned back, rocking, listening intently, rolling a pen around and around in his hands.

When I finished, he chuckled. "You've had a busy day." He sighed, propping his elbows on the desk. "Here's the thing, the spit thing is gross, but it might be a misdemeanor, if that. A small fine. Enough to annoy him. Sounds like this Dewey guy is the sort who'd make you his special project. We certainly don't want that. If we can wait to nail him on something bigger, something we can lock him away for, that would be ideal. In the meantime, and I can't emphasize this enough, stay away from him. Don't give him any reason to focus on you."

He licked his lips and smoothed his hand over his dimpled chin as if stroking a beard. "Now, as for Clarence, I think we can nail him. I'll have the forensic accountant look into those names you gave me. Forward the names and the recordings to my phone, please. But, it's going to take time. We can't rush this. Rushing equals mistakes. Mistakes equal dropped charges and mistrials. I want to make sure I wrap this up tight with a pretty bow. But it's probably best if you leave him alone, too."

"What about Holly?

"From everything you've told me about her, she's obnoxious, but that's not a crime."

"What about the petty cash stuff?"

"That was resolved to the company's satisfaction. They didn't press charges, so there's nothing I can do."

"Can you at least call her in for questioning?"

"Okay." He jotted a note on a sticky. "But every time I question someone of little or no interest, it takes time away from pursuing the actual killer."

I cradled my purse in my lap. "Do you have any more information about Bryan?"

"Not yet, but I promise we're working on it. We're interviewing people every day. I will make certain Clarence and Dewey are next on my list."

"I wish I could find the thumb drive."

He turned the pen around and around in his hands. "I want you to know something. I spoke with the medical examiner, Leigh Powers, and she says Bryan likely died of poisoning. She's ruled out natural causes, like a heart attack or stroke."

I slapped my chair arm. "I knew it!" Shaking my head, anger burned in my chest again. "And Sheriff Goodman didn't want to believe it. I told him.

Does she have an idea what it is?"

"Based on some of the physical signs, she thinks it might be cyanide. But she wants to do a toxicology screening to be sure. So..." He sighed. "We're waiting on the final results, which could take weeks. It'd be great if you could keep that information under your hat."

"Sure. Of course. Have you told his mother? She deserves to know."

"I will as soon as we're done. Now..."

We stood.

He patted my back, walking me out to the lobby. "I want you to go home. Relax. And, please, if at all possible, stay out of trouble."

I smiled. "I'll try. But I can't make any promises."

Chapter Twenty-Four

I staggered down the stairs. The only light came from the bulb over the sink. Prim sat at the kitchen table in her robe. The stove clock read five-thirty a.m.

"Prim? What are you doing?" I flipped on the light.

On the table stood a large rusty coffee can and three piles of money.

"Sorry I woke you, hon. I couldn't sleep."

"What are you doing with all this money?"

She patted a stack. It struck me how old and frail her hands seemed. It was amazing how such things went unnoticed when sharing a life with another person. "I've been saving this since your Pappy died. Every time I received one of his social security checks, I'd cash it and put the money in here."

"Okay…" I sat at the table. "Why do you have it out?"

"I'm giving it to you." She gathered the piles and shoved them in the can. "I was waiting until the right time." She pushed the can toward me.

I stared stupidly at the cash, too tired to fully register my thoughts or emotions. "I can't accept this. You're going to need this now more than ever. Your treatments are going to be quite expensive."

Her lower lip pushed against its counterpart. She pushed herself to stand. "The money is yours. I want you to have it. Use it how you see fit." She patted my arm and retired to her recliner, flipping on the television.

Staring at the money, I warred with my feelings. I wanted it, needed it. I'd deposit it in an interest-bearing account and use it to pay for Prim's treatments. Except…I counted out five hundred to repay Cam and added a couple hundred extra for sitting with Prim every day. Granted, it wasn't much, but I had to make every dollar count.

Since I couldn't go back to sleep, I decided to go in early to work. Dressed in a comfy red rayon dress, a white cardigan, and nude sandals, accessorized with a long silver necklace and matching earrings and bracelet, I was ready to go well before Cam's arrival. I left him a note. I considered leaving the money I owed him, too, but changed my mind, wanting to express my appreciation in person.

I left Prim's pills and a glass of water by her chair and kissed her. "Cam will be here soon. If you need anything in the meantime, call Batrene or me. Okay?"

She smiled at me drowsily and patted my hand. "Don't worry about me, hon. Have a good day."

The scent of lilacs from Batrene's yard hung in the morning air as the sun peeked over the horizon, splashing gold and rosy light over the stone walls, pastures, and grazing horses contentedly swishing their tails.

There were only a few cars in the parking lot when I arrived at the distillery. I grabbed my purse and coffee and headed toward the main building.

Someone shouted. Two men were outside the rickhouse in each other's faces, pointing, shoving, and shouting. I put a hand to my brow, blocking the sun. Randall and Dewey. It was impossible to discern who the instigator was, and I couldn't make out what they were saying.

Running to the edge of the parking lot, I shouted, "I'm calling the police…" I pulled out my phone and dialed 9-1-.

Dewey spun and pointed at me. "Mind your own business…" He added a choice name for me.

Randall said something to Dewey.

I couldn't hear what Randall said, but he swept his arm before him, indicating Dewey should leave.

Walking away, Dewey shouted one last time at Randall. "This ain't over." He stormed up the hill toward his truck, jumped in, and sped away, flipping his middle finger at me as he flew by, his wheels spitting out rocks and dust. His truck disappeared down the drive. He was quickly ascending my suspect list to the primary spot. He was hot-tempered, ill-mannered, and violent.

The sort of person who might murder.

"You okay?" I shouted at Randall

Randall lifted his hand in response. He spit on the ground and disappeared inside the rickhouse.

Len's car rolled down the drive.

I dialed Jimmy instead of 911. I left a message on his voice mail to call first chance he had.

Len shouted and waved. I crossed the parking lot toward him.

"Hey," he kissed my cheek. "Why so early?" He glanced at his watch.

"Wanted to get a jump on the day. You're here pretty early, too."

"I needed to prepare for a meeting with the Historical Society tomorrow. Could you help me with some presentation slides?"

"Sure."

He slipped his arm around my waist and guided me toward the administration building. "I was thinking, how about we go out tonight. Maybe a movie and drinks. I'm down for anything."

"Sure, sounds great. If I can get Batrene to watch Prim for me." Honestly, I didn't feel like having fun. But I couldn't cope with my current reality. I didn't want to deal with all the feelings. I was afraid they'd destroy me. Bryan was gone. Prim was...fading. Cam...who knew what was going on there. The bills were mounting, and my life might be in danger. I needed a distraction. We stopped by the break room for coffee.

He leaned close. "Maybe we can finish our kiss from the other night." He rested his hand on my waist. "It's been on my mind a lot these last few days."

Recalling the kiss made me smile. I looked at him under my lashes. It had been a nice kiss. But, truth be told, I hadn't thought much about it. It was hard for a sinking woman to think about a budding romance.

"Don't you two paint the sweetest picture?" Holly's smile was squared off and tense. "I hate to interrupt the little love fest here, but I need coffee. Excuse me..." She pushed between us and headed for the coffeepot.

I glanced between them. "I need to get to work. Let me know the details of the presentation as soon as possible and I'll get started."

"You've got it." He leered.

As I passed out of the break room, Holly hissed, "How dare you?"

I stopped short and pressed against the wall to eavesdrop.

Len said, "This was the agreement…"

"You're enjoying it a little too much."

"What do you want me to do?"

"Stop…"

Pierce was headed in my direction. We waved at each other. I didn't want to be caught eavesdropping, so I continued down the hall toward the marketing pit. Maybe I was crazy, but to my ears, Holly sounded jealous.

Tangled Up in Brew was lively for a Tuesday night. Loud talking, scurrying servers and bartenders, and cooks sweating over a variety of fried and fatty foods in the kitchen. The first football game of the season between Auburn and the University of the Bluegrass Thoroughbreds was on the television behind the bar and the Rolling Stones's "Paint It Black" blared on the jukebox in the corner by the pool tables.

I wanted to pay Cam back as soon as possible, so, on our way to supper, I asked Len to stop by the bar.

Cam lifted his chin in greeting as Len and I entered. The scent of burgers and onion rings tortured my grumbling stomach. Tangled Up had one of the best burgers in town.

With a towel slung over his shoulder and a toothpick jutting from his full lips, Cam filled glasses from the tap. When he finished his current order, he stepped down to talk to us. "Hey, y'all. What brings you two out here tonight?"

I said, "We're on our way to supper, but I wanted to stop here first. Is there somewhere you and I can talk? I only need a minute."

Jacie was at the bar, waiting on an order, pretending not to watch us.

He waved me behind the bar, and I followed him through the kitchen full of workers buzzing around the grill, prep line, and sink, clanking dishes and shouting at each other.

Cam closed out the noise, shutting us in his office. The space was tiny and grimy. He had a small desk, piled with papers and empty Kentucky Spice bottles. A bulletin board above the desk was covered with papers pinned askew. Duct tape covered rips in the rolling chair's vinyl, and the seat was concave from extensive use. The garbage can overflowed and a filing cabinet with a dent in the side stood in the corner by a safe.

"This place is kind of gross." I laughed, leaning against his desk, smoothing the skirt of my red sundress.

"Yeah, but it's all mine." The chair creaked loudly under his weight. He leaned back, resting his ankle on his knee. He shifted the toothpick to the other side of his mouth. "What did you need to talk about?"

I pulled the money out of my purse. "I wanted to pay you back."

His brows shot up. "Wow." He took the money. "Perfect timing. The compressor went out in the A/C at home the other day. It's been hotter than the ninth level of Hades." The office chair squeaked as he rocked. "And with the wedding..." He shook his head. He waved the money. "This should make Jacie happy. She'll get those flowers ordered now." He sniffed a humorless chuckle and tossed the money on the desk. "Thanks."

I rolled my eyes. "A/C is way more important. I mean, it's August. We still have to get through September."

"That's what I've been saying." He clasped the chair arms, his knuckles whitening. "She's so..." He rubbed his face then sighed again. "Any way..."

"If you need more money..."

"Nah." He waved his hand. "I'll be all right." He paused, chewing on his toothpick. "You remember the time you and me stayed in the cabin at the Gorge? The next morning it was all cold and frosty outside. We hiked down that big hill to the water."

"Cold? More like icy."

"But remember how amazing the coffee and hot shower were afterward?"

I smiled wistfully, gazing into the past. "My sweatshirt and blanket were cozy and warm." For a moment, I was transported back to the fuzzy warmth of that sweatshirt and blanket in front of the fire. Cam's chair squeaked and my mind rushed back to the present. "That was ages ago. Why're you bringing that up?

"I don't know. I was thinking about it last night while I was lying in bed sweating under the ceiling fan."

"Why?"

He looked at his foot and toyed with the fraying hem of his jeans. "I don't know. I was pondering the broken A/C and how thankful I am for it in the summer. How much more I appreciate it now that I don't have it. How I can't wait to get it back."

The smile slid from my face. "Yeah. That was a good time." Desire stirred deep in me—a desire I'd only ever felt for him. I studied my red ballet flats.

He stood and moved to stand beside me. I stared at his shoulder, not daring to look him in the face. I was afraid that if our gaze met, we might land ourselves in a heap of trouble.

"I should probably get back to Len."

"Do you like him?"

"I think so. We're still getting to know each other. But he's smart, handsome…"

"Rich?"

"I don't know about that, but that wouldn't be my primary factor in dating him, and you know it."

"But money doesn't hurt." He smirked.

I rolled my eyes. "It's time to move on. You know?" I didn't want to have this conversation. "By the way, I'm taking Prim to the oncologist in the morning. The good news is you get the day off."

"I don't mind. Let me know what the doctor says."

Jacie appeared in the doorway wearing a tight pink T-shirt and white shorts, perfectly displaying her fake tan. She looked between us; accusation and anger flinted in her eyes.

Cam said, "Hey, babe. What's up?"

Her pink-glossed lips twitched into a tight smile. "Hey, Rook." She smacked her gum. "Honey, we sure could use you out here. We're awfully busy." She tossed her ponytail. "What're y'all doing?"

He tucked his hands in his pockets. "Rook came to pay back the money she borrowed."

She snapped her gum, surprised. "Thank heavens. I was sure we wouldn't see that money again." She snorted a laugh.

"Jacie…" Cam warned.

She blinked innocently. "What? I only mean that it's a lot of money. It's hard to pay back so much at once."

Yeah, right. "I need to get back to Len, anyway."

As Len and I were being seated at a secluded table in the Pink Pigeon, an upscale gastropub in downtown Lexington, my phone rang.

"Sorry." I pulled my phone from my purse. It was Jimmy. Silencing the ring, I texted him I'd call him after supper and asked how late was too late.

His response: **Never too late. Except when I'm at the gym.**

I smiled.

"Looks like a good message." Len opened his menu. Do I have a competitor?"

Laughing, I dropped the phone in my purse. "No. It's Jimmy Duvall."

He cocked his head, puzzled. "The deputy?"

"Yeah." I scanned the entrees.

"Does he have information about Bryan?"

"I don't know. He's supposed to return my call."

His eyes glimmered with interest. "Oh? Anything to be concerned about?"

"Maybe." My head swam with all the food choices. "Dewey threw dip spit on my car Friday. I was reporting it."

"Why did he do that?"

My intuition nudged me to be careful about saying too much. "Not sure. I might've upset him somehow."

He looked at me, closing his menu. "What did you do?"

I changed the subject. "How harshly would you judge me if I ordered the Korean BBQ chicken sandwich and fries instead of something fancy."

He chuckled. "I'll only judge you a little bit."

After some discussion about our food choices and placing our order, he said, "I hope Dewey didn't hurt you or your car."

"He didn't."

"He's a hothead, for sure. My brother-in-law Randall has had a few run-ins with him."

"I know. I witnessed one this morning."

"What happened?"

"I don't know the particulars, but it looked intense. There was some shoving. Dewey pointed his finger at Randall and yelled that it wasn't over."

Our food was delivered. I pounced on my fries.

Len cut into his steak. "That guy is a piece of work. I don't know why Randall keeps him around. He's always causing problems and slacking on the job. I can't recall a person he hasn't had a fight with."

I tilted my head. "If he's such a shoddy worker, why doesn't Randall fire him?"

He hemmed, chewing his food. "Well, I-uh-I don't know."

I couldn't put a finger on it, but his demeanor shifted, a shadow slid behind his eyes. He knew something.

Chapter Twenty-Five

D r. Napier's office was located in a major complex in Lexington, consisting of four large buildings with connecting pedways and a parking lot large enough to offer a shuttle service.

Dr. Napier was a quiet, reserved man with gray hair, gray eyes, and a big bow tie. He explained Prim's treatment options: chemo, hormone therapy, target therapy, and possibly radiation and surgery. Or some combination.

He showed us a chart of the different subtypes. "Mrs. Vertrees, you have an invasive metastatic triple negative form. That means it's spread through your body and in your blood and lymph nodes. Which is why your lymph nodes are swollen under your arms and your back hurts. The triple negative means hormone therapy isn't likely to work. We'll try a few weeks of chemo, followed by radiation. Because of your age, surgery should be a last resort."

Overwhelmed, my mind clamored to grasp the words and their meaning. Waves of emotion slammed down on me, drowning me. I squeezed Prim's hand. This was a problem I couldn't solve for her, something I couldn't fix. My throat closed off and my head throbbed in the swell of feelings and thoughts.

Prim matter of factly said, "How long do I have?"

Dr. Napier grew somber.

She added, "And don't sugarcoat it."

"Not long. Maybe several months, maybe a year, if you're very lucky."

I closed my eyes.

Prim said, "Can I go home and think about it?"

I snapped my head around to look at her.

159

Dr. Napier said, "Certainly. I wouldn't take too much time, though. The sooner we can get to this, the better." He pulled several pamphlets out of the acrylic containers on the wall and handed them to Prim. "These will cover what we discussed and will help guide your decision." He opened the door for us.

"At least it isn't raining." I helped Prim across the vast parking lot and into my car. I rounded my vehicle and climbed in the driver's side.

Prim sat, deflated, holding the slick, colorful pamphlets covered with the smiling, hopeful faces of cancer. I tried to make small talk to distract both of us, but she wasn't participating, so I left her alone to stare out the window as we drove home.

When we got home, Prim threw the pamphlets in the kitchen garbage and poured herself a glass of tea.

I was stunned. "What are you doing? Why are you throwing those away?"

"I'm not going through all that. I've seen what these treatments do to people. I don't want you to go through that either."

"But it could buy you more time."

"What? Maybe a few more months at most? A few more months of sheer misery and being sick and hurting all the time?" She shook her head. "Nope. Not going to do it. If I was your age, or even forty or fifty, that extra year might be meaningful, but I'm an old woman, Rook. I've lived a full life. I've fought my way through most of it. I'm tired. Soul-tired."

"But…" I wanted to scream, *You can't leave me, too.*

"You're going to be fine, child." She squeezed my upper arms. "This is life. You're going to do like I've done, like your momma did. You're going to keep going until you can't. That's all anyone can do. Now…" She shrugged. "I'm going to go water my flowers."

Wishing I could stay with Prim, I arranged for Batrene to keep an eye on her while I reluctantly went to work. On my way to the distillery, I exploded into tears and was forced to pull into the Waffle House parking lot.

I needed to speak with someone, someone who understood what Prim and I meant to each other. First, I tried my best friend Millie, but it went to voice mail. She was probably at work anyway. I missed Bryan more than ever. If he were still alive, I'd be snuggled in one of his brotherly bear hugs and he'd have soothing wisdom to impart.

There was one other person I could call.

Hesitating, I stared at my phone's favorites list, which included four numbers: Prim, Millie, Cam, and Bryan. That left Cam. My thumb hovered over his name, while uncertainty twisted knots between my shoulder blades. *Don't cry.*

I almost chickened out and was about to hang up when Cam answered. A dog was barking in the background.

Cam said, "Hey, hold on a second." There was a muffled conversation and a door slammed. "I'm back. I'm at Mom and Dad's. Lots of distractions," he chuckled. "What'cha need?"

As soon as I heard his voice, I cracked. "Cam, it's Prim."

Alarm shot through his voice. "What's the matter, Rook? Is she hurt? Are you okay?"

"Yes, I'm okay." I swiped at my tears. "Prim's not hurt, exactly. She's…" I gulped air and blurted out. "She's refusing treatment."

He paused. "Where are you?"

"I'm at the Waffle House. I was on my way to work—"

"Wait for me…"

He'd already hung up.

Within fifteen minutes, Cam's truck raced to the back of the Waffle House lot, where I was parked. Blowing my nose and wiping my eyes, I stepped out of my car. Traffic on the road buzzed by. The time on my phone said nine-thirty. I'd received clearance for the doctor appointment, so everyone at work knew I'd be late. What was another hour when my whole world was crumbling around me?

Cam jumped out of the truck and charged toward me, sweeping me into his arms, clutching me to him.

I broke into fresh tears, knowing my time with Prim was limited, even with treatment. And more limited without it. The thought was too much to bear.

His cologne, sweet and spicy, wrapped around me. "I'm sorry." He squeezed me closer.

"I didn't expect you to actually come here, though."

He pulled back. "Of course. I know what Prim means to you. And to me. I love Prim. She's like my own grandma." He put his hands on his hips. "Tell me what's going on."

I leaned against the car, hugging myself, and told him everything about the type of cancer and the treatments the doctor recommended. "When we got home, Prim said she wasn't going to go through all that."

He sighed and leaned on the car beside me, his shoulder against mine. "Man, that's rough, babe. But you know those treatments can be horrible. We don't like it, but we have to respect her wishes."

"I know. I do respect them. But I..." My voice broke. "I don't know what I'm going to do without her. She's all I have left, Cam." I dropped my face into my hands.

Cam rubbed soothing circles on my back. "I know. It's hard. I get it. But you won't be completely alone. You'll still have me. And Millie. And Batrene. I know it's not the same, but you're not completely alone. We'll get through this."

A deep silence fell between us where I cried quietly into my hands and he rubbed my back.

When my nose began running, I rifled through my purse for a tissue. Finding a couple fast food napkins was the best I could manage, but it'd get the job done. I blew my nose and wiped my face. "She said she was soul-tired and tired of fighting. The doctor said she only has a few months, maybe a year. She's been strong for so long, and she's made her decision. You know what that means?"

"Yeah. She sure is a stubborn old lady." He nudged my shoulder. "You get it honest."

"I remember a time when you thought my stubborn streak was endearing."

Humor lit his face. "Still do. You going to be okay?"

"No. But I'll keep going anyway."

He kissed my forehead. "That's my girl." He smoothed my hair and locked his gaze on mine. "You listen to me. If you need anything. No matter how big or small. You call me. Okay?"

I'd hoped he hadn't noticed my hesitation, but he did. He squeezed my arm, his thumb stroking my skin. His hand was smooth and hot. "I mean it, Rook. Anything at all. I want to help Prim and you in any way I can. She's done a lot for me. For us."

The air around us grew tense, electrified with desire. A look of expectancy, like the moment right before a first kiss, filled his features. He was making it hard to be divorced and move on with my life.

"I've got to get to work. Thank you for being there to pick me up all the time."

Chapter Twenty-Six

Prim's decision to forgo treatment had emotionally drained me, and I had nothing to give to Bryan's murder investigation. I kept to myself and focused on my work, which was no easy task either since my mind kept returning to Prim.

In the afternoon, while I was working on a vendor list for the Bourbon, Bands, and BBQ Festival, Len leaned on my cubicle wall. "Hey. You're awfully quiet today."

"Yeah, I'm...tired."

"I was wondering if you wanted to go to the barbeque at Randall's this weekend? I know he mentioned it to you, but I wanted to know what to tell him."

I didn't really want to go, but I also didn't want to sit with my feelings either. The more distraction the better. "That'll be fun. Should I bring a dish?"

He shrugged. "Sure. If you want." He stood and paused. "You sure you're okay?"

"I'm fine." The common song of a woman dying inside.

After work and an early dinner, Prim walked over to Batrene's for a visit. She insisted and I wasn't going to fight her. She should be free while she could. I was sitting at the kitchen table, with sponge separators between my toes, waiting for the shiny red polish to dry.

Just as I'd settled in with my distillery study guide to learn about the history of Four Wild Horses, a knock sounded on the back door.

I walked on my heels, like Frankenstein's monster, to the door. I peeked out the curtain on the door. Jimmy. He was red-faced and sweaty and dressed in a grass-stained, dusty softball uniform. The shirt was black with the word Hornets scrawled in yellow across the front over the image of a snarling cartoon hornet.

Opening the door, I smiled at him. "I hope the other team looks worse."

"They do. We whooped 'em good."

I laughed. "You look like you could use some iced tea."

"That'd be fantastic." He stepped inside, removing his ball cap. He smelled of earth, sun, and sweat. It was a heady mixture.

I poured two glasses of tea, handing him one. "To what do I owe this unexpected visit?"

He sat and crossed an ankle on his knee. "I was on my way home after the game and thought I'd swing by to see why you were trying to contact me yesterday."

I gasped and smacked my forehead. "Oh, no! I forgot to call you back. I was on a date and couldn't call. By the time I got home, I'd forgotten."

He swallowed the tea. "On a date, huh? Who's the luckiest guy in Rochdale?"

"His name is Len. I work with him. You met him the other day."

He was silent for a moment. "Oh, that guy. Tall, dark hair."

"Yes. Him."

"Is it serious?"

I shrugged one shoulder. "I don't know." I sat beside Jimmy, sipping my tea. I recalled Len's bright smile, his seductive voice, his silky kiss, the feel of his lean muscles beneath my fingertips. My face warmed. "There's potential." I shifted the topic back to him. "Are you dating anyone?"

"Not since Beth."

"But you two broke up a year ago. Haven't you at least had an interest in anyone?"

He trailed his finger through the condensation gathering on the glass. "Eh. There's someone I'm kind of interested in, but the timing has always been… off."

"You never know, maybe it'll work out."

His hazel gaze met mine, steady. "Maybe. It's okay, though. I've been pretty focused on my work these days. I'd like to be sheriff someday."

"I know a lot of people who'd prefer you to Goodman."

"What did you want to tell me?"

"I wanted to tell you about something I witnessed at work yesterday. When I arrived, I saw Dewey arguing with a guy. There was a shoving match then he jumped in his truck and tore out of the parking lot like a bat out of hell."

"Is that it?" Jimmy licked his lips and rubbed his chin. "There's not much there."

"It shows he has a violent temper and he's aggressive enough that he might actually hurt someone. There must be something going on. Otherwise, why would he be attacking the guy?"

He winced. "It's circumstantial, at best."

"Well, haven't you been looking into him?"

He rubbed his brow. "Bryan died last Monday. We know it wasn't a heart attack. But as I've already told you and Mrs. Bishop, it takes time for the tox screen to come back."

"Can't you put a rush on it?"

He chuckled. "It doesn't work that way. But I promise you, we're working as hard and as fast as we can."

"What have you done? Who have you spoken to?"

The intensity of his glare, the pink flush, and the bulging vein in his neck indicated I'd touched a nerve. "I don't have to tell you any of that. We've processed the scene, booked the evidence, performed the autopsy, and ordered the tox screen, and we have an accountant looking at the documents you gave us. Those were a big help. Plus, we've performed preliminary interviews and are now doing call-back interviews on our biggest suspects. We're also looking into the backgrounds of the people who are highest on the suspect list. Is that enough?"

I was thoroughly chastised. "Okay. When you put it like that..."

"I understand your impatience. I really do. I'm impatient, too. You need to understand that these men may be top suspects on your list, but that doesn't mean they're our only suspects. We're looking at everyone connected to this. But we have a small office and we're giving it everything we have. Bryan's case isn't the only one we're dealing with. I swear to you, if Bryan Bishop was murdered, we're going to do everything we can to find the killer. I swear it."

"I understand, but—"

"Rook, please. I know you mean well and you're trying to help. I also know how stubborn you can be. You have to let this go and let us do our jobs. You need to back off before one of these guys seriously hurts you."

"Okay." That's all I would say, giving him the impression I'd back off. But I had no intention of letting anything go.

After Prim returned home, she and I retired to the living room to watch television. Prim snuggled under an afghan in a near-dozing state while I worried about her.

An interesting *20/20* was coming on when the doorbell rang.

In a drug-addled fog, Prim said, "Who in the world is here at this hour?"

I shrugged. It was only nine, but to Prim, who went to bed at nine, it was late. After all, she was already in her little yellow nightgown and yellow floral robe, her feet stuffed inside a ratty pair of gray memory foam booties. I made a mental note to get her a new pair of booties for her birthday in September.

"I'll get it." I pushed myself to stand. I opened the door, my jaw dropping. "Hey, Jacie." I scanned the yard. "What are you doing here?"

The sky was dusky purple. Crickets and tree frogs screamed from the shadows, and bugs pinged against the porch light. Jacie stood on my porch in a white tank top, which practically glowed against her tanned arms. Her jean shorts showed off her well-toned thighs, and her hair was pulled into a sleek ponytail.

She smiled tightly. "I wanted to bring back this cake plate." She handed me the plate.

"Thanks," I said slowly. How did she know where I lived? I played it cool, reigning in my suspicions. "You didn't need to come all this way, though. I could've picked up it up another time."

"Well, I wanted to give you some advice."

Here we go. I remained calm on the surface, but inside, adrenaline began dumping into my veins in preparation. Putting the cake plate on the ornamental table by the door, I told Prim, "It's a friend. I'll be out on the porch." I stepped outside while pulling the door closed. "What's the advice?"

Her head jerked side to side. "I advise you to keep away from my man."

Now that was interesting. Because, at one time, he'd been my man. But I didn't want to give her the impression I was fighting over him. However, I also wasn't going to let her or anyone order me around. In addition, I was super-annoyed she showed up at my house, at night, uninvited, to dish out directives. Trying to stay calm and defuse the situation, I sighed. "Jacie, I don't want Cam. He's yours."

"That's funny. Because a friend of mine saw you two out at the Waffle House getting cozy. In broad daylight."

"He was being a friend. That's all. I've had a rough time lately."

"I bet."

"If you have a problem with it, why aren't you discussing it with him?"

"Because I'm discussing it with you." She pointed her finger at me. "You've been trying to get him back ever since he left you."

"No, I haven't." If I were vindictive, I might've told her Cam had recently admitted he still loved me. "You need to go have a conversation with Cam."

She stepped closer. "You will stay away from him. Or else…"

"Or what?"

"Or I will kick your butt."

Puffing up, I stepped off the porch. "If you think you're the one to do it…" Here's the thing, in spite of my education and rearing, a fire deep in me made it impossible for me to back down from a fight. This had nothing to do with Cam but had everything to do with my pride.

I smiled. "I'm right here."

Jacie took a step back. "I'm serious. I'm getting married soon, and I'm not going to let you ruin it."

I opened my arms wide and stepped closer. "Bring it."

CHAPTER TWENTY-SIX

She slapped me.

Rage shot through me like a bottle rocket. I launched myself at her and tackled her to the ground.

She screamed out and grabbed for my hair. I punched at her wildly, not sure where my hits were landing. It was as if I'd gone blind. She squealed and scratched and slapped.

Prim shouted from the porch, but I hardly registered the words, as if I was no longer in my mind or body. Jacie had locked her hands into my hair. I felt nothing. Pulling my fist way back, I was primed to punch her with everything I had.

Suddenly, water gushed into my face, in my mouth, and up my nose. I couldn't see or breathe. I rolled onto the ground and Jacie squirmed away from me.

I shouted. "Stop spraying me!"

Prim lowered the hose. "I want you two to stop this trashy stuff this instant and start acting like you've got some sense. Y'all ought to be ashamed of yourselves."

I wiped my face on my arm and shirttail. Jacie pushed herself to her feet. She pointed at me and said, raspy-voiced, "You're crazy."

"I'm crazy?"

"Now you hold on, missy," Prim shouted at Jacie. "You listen here. I'm not saying Rook was right." She cut her gaze at me. "She wasn't. She knows better and was raised better. But you can't poke a hornet's nest and cry about getting stung." She waved the hose nozzle as she spoke. "You come out here picking a fight and expect her to be happy about it? And now you're upset she ain't going to lie down and take it? Well, that ain't right, either. Now, you take yourself home, and don't you come back here no more. I mean it. Next time, I won't stop her."

Jacie scowled at us. "You tell her—"

Prim raised the nozzle in the air like a scepter. "No! No more talking. You go. Now. Off my property, you little Jezebel."

Jacie pointed her finger at me. "This ain't over."

Prim sprayed her. Jacie danced away from the water, squealing.

Prim scowled. "It is over. Now git before I grab my rifle."

I started to cross the lawn toward Jacie. She sprinted and got in her car. I turned back.

Prim shut off the water. "I can't believe two grown women fighting each other over a man."

"She was fighting over a man. I was fighting for myself."

Prim pinched her lips into a line. "Mm-hm. And you believe that?"

Chapter Twenty-Seven

The next couple days passed without incident. I'd observed Clarence and Dewey from a distance, but nothing stood out as odd. I was growing weary and antsy waiting on the police to do their job. I wanted to know who killed Bryan, how they killed him, and why. But I couldn't do anything to help Bryan except keep an eye on things at work and to help Batrene with managing her finances. Nor could I do anything more to help Prim except take on more of the household management. This was becoming my new normal.

After a busy Saturday morning of caring for Batrene and Prim, I dressed for the barbeque date with Len, donning jean shorts, a gauzy peasant top, sandals, and silver accessories, finishing the look with a messy bun and light makeup. While the macaroni baked and I waited for Len, I folded the laundry and put it away. I was ready for an afternoon of lazing in a lawn chair at a family barbeque and not feeling guilty about it.

Randall and Vonda Tilkey lived in a simple brown brick ranch with a covered porch in Miltonville, a sleepy bedroom community between Frankfort and the Four Wild Horses Distillery. We pulled into the gravel drive.

Len leaned over and kissed me. "You're going to love my sister, Vonda. She's excited to meet you."

We entered the house via the carport.

Len opened the door and called out, "Hey."

Two women left their work at the kitchen counter to greet us in a whirlwind of happy chatter, introductions, and hugs.

171

Vonda and Kim, Len's sister-in-law, were both still stuck in the days of pretty-boy glam bands and acid wash jeans. They still wore their hair long, permed, feathered on top, and clipped back in a barrette. Vonda had dyed red hair and Kim was a gold-streaked brunette. Both were big-breasted and chubby. Vonda wore a white Mickey Mouse shirt and capris and Kim wore a navy-and-white-striped shirt with white Bermuda shorts. Vonda had been plating deviled eggs while Kim put the final touches on the pasta salad.

Vonda said, "Len, grab the buns and that platter of meat and y'all come out back. Randall's about to fire up the grill."

We exited through the back door onto the patio. Thankfully, the sun was on the other side of the house, casting the patio in shade. But even in the shade, it was as though I'd put on damp clothes fresh from the dryer.

The house sat on about a half-acre of land, allowing plenty of room in the backyard for shade trees, a playhouse for the kids, a detached garage, a small deck, and horseshoes. Screaming children chased each other through the yard with squirt guns. "The Devil Went Down to Georgia" blared from the radio on the umbrella-shaded table.

At the other end of the patio stood an enormous silver grill, flanked by two men with competing paunches holding cold beers and chatting. Both wore T-shirts, cargo shorts, and ball caps.

Randall's bottom lip protruded with a wad of dip. Yuck. He spit in a cup and accepted the plate of meat from Len. He uncovered the meat. "Oh, yeah. Let's get these burgers and dogs on the grill." Soon, the comforting scent of grilled meat filled the air.

My stomach grumbled.

Len introduced me to the other man, Kim's husband, and Randall's brother. "This is Keith Tilkey. He's a driver at the distillery."

Keith lifted his beer and said in a thick drawl, "How do." Keith was short and lean, with tufts of fawn, curly hair puffing from under his ball cap. He wore a pair of cargo shorts, a blue U of B T-shirt, and white socks, with black Caterpillar brand work boots. After fishing around in his shorts pocket, he pulled out a box of unfiltered Camels. He flipped the lid. Tucked inside were a few remaining cigarettes and several sticks of Big Red cinnamon gum. He offered the box to me. "Gum? Cigarette?"

"Neither. Thanks."

He paused and drew out a stick of gum. "The ol' lady's always on me about quitting smoking. This is about the fifth time I've tried. I figure if I put my gum in with the cigarettes, I might make a better choice."

"Sounds like a good idea. Maybe I can try that with my bathroom scale and my box of moon pies." I patted my belly to indicate my overweight status.

He laughed through his nose, stuffing the gum in his mouth. "Might do."

Keith looked at Len. "Hey man, how'd you wrangle one this pretty to spend time with you?"

The men sniggered. I smiled.

Len said, "It wasn't easy. I had to sit real quiet and patient-like. When she got close enough, I reached over and snagged her." He grabbed me around the shoulders.

The men guffawed. Len's phone chimed. He checked it, silenced it, and sent a text before dropping it in his pocket. His pocket buzzed. He ignored it.

Randall leaned over and opened the lid on an enormous igloo cooler at his feet. "Y'all want a beer?" There was enough booze on ice for a small army.

I selected a blackberry wine spritzer.

Randall's kid, Caleb, ran up to us. He was chubby, sweaty, and red-faced. "Hey, Dad. My gun's messed up. It's not shooting water."

Keith said, "Let me take a look at it."

Once it was fixed, Caleb trotted off while Keith and Len started a game of horseshoes. Len texted between throws. Who on earth was blowing up his phone on the weekend?

This was a perfect opportunity to dig for information about Dewey. "I saw the shoving match between you and Dewey. Is he always so unpleasant? I've tried to talk to him, but he's kind of mean."

Randall shrugged and spit brown juice into his cup. "I wouldn't put too much stock in it. That's just Dewey's way. He yells and curses and threatens, but I've never known him to actually do anything."

"You sure? Usually people with bad tempers are prone to physical violence."

"Nah. Not Dewey." He spit the wet, brown, dip flakes into the cup. It looked like wet soil. "All bark, no bite."

My stomach churned. I sipped my spritzer to hide my disgust with the happy taste of bubbling blackberries. "He seemed pretty intense yesterday. He pushed you."

He took a swig of beer, swished it in his mouth, and swallowed. "First off, he's about half my size. He knows I'd whip him." He adjusted the flame on the grill. "But I won't have to worry about him anymore." He drank from his beer and lifted a burger with the spatula to check the underside.

"Why's that?"

"He was mad because I fired him."

I was pretty sure Randall wouldn't tell me why he'd fired Dewey, so I didn't bother asking. But maybe I could take an indirect route. "That's a shame. I understand he had a family."

"He should've thought of that before he fell asleep on the job and faked his mileage chart. Again." He wiped the sweat from his forehead on his arm. "I told him when it happened the first time it had better be his last time. I cut him some slack and well…" He shrugged and drew from his beer.

Bryan had been right to dock his pay. Not that I doubted it, but it was good to have confirmation.

"Dewey…" He sniffed a laugh and used a fork to roll hot dogs on the grill. "He's a pain in the neck. He's been that way since high school. But he grew up rough. That's why I helped him get on at the distillery."

I began to pity him. But then I remembered Bryan. I couldn't let pity for Dewey's situation distract me from my investigation. "Would he ever hurt someone if he felt they wronged him?"

Randall was quiet for a moment. "I doubt he had anything to do with Bryan's death, if that's what you're getting at. A bad temper doesn't necessarily make a murderer." He leveled a side look at me, drinking his beer.

Understood. Sipping my spritzer, I contemplated Dewey's character and his proclivities. It occurred to me that if Dewey was prone to violence when crossed, Randall might be in danger. "Are you worried Dewey might retaliate?"

Randall snorted. "Nah. Like I said, he's a blowhard. Talks a big game." Then he announced lunch was ready and moved away with the platter, effectively shutting me down.

Chapter Twenty-Eight

After dinner, we adults all sat around the table, sipping drinks and eating Caleb's birthday cake. The children's plates were filled with partially eaten dinner and cake. They'd been too eager to resume their squirt gun battle. The sun settled into the horizon. Lightning bugs darted and flickered, and the scent of honeysuckle and roses wove through the warm evening air. The bug zapper behind us fried insects.

Kim and Vonda discussed Jessie Belle's upcoming makeup party and the men ruminated over the forthcoming basketball season (a veritable religion in Kentucky) and who their favorite picks were. I was content to nurse another spritzer as I sat back and listened to the rhythms of language, the kids screaming and playing, and the radio competing with the tree frogs and crickets.

When basketball and football had drained the men of conversation, they made their way to the detached garage. Randall wanted to show something to the other two. Vonda and Kim didn't linger long.

Vonda stood. "I guess I'd better get this stuff cleaned up and get the food put away."

That was our cue to offer help, which she would politely decline—and that declination would be politely ignored.

We all filled our hands and carried everything inside. The house was chilly and scented with a weird potpourri of onions, cinnamon candles, and cleaning chemicals. The kitchen was decorated smartly in country chic, with two white walls, a large red accent wall, and another accent wallpapered in red and white toile. Roosters and chickens decorated the walls and shelves

176

and lots of thick, distressed wood furniture. The appliances were all stainless steel. I liked it.

We wrapped leftovers in foil and plastic wrap and stuffed them in the refrigerator. Vonda and Kim started washing the dishes while I stepped outside to collect trash from the patio. The kids had created a gigantic mess where they'd sat.

I was working at sweeping crumbs from under the table when the security light on the roof of the detached garage flipped on. The men were awash in a fluorescent glow as bugs darted and flitted around the light. The main door was open, revealing a cluttered interior.

Keith lit a cigarette. Randall tucked a pinch of snuff in his lip. Len texted. Their closeness, the set of their shoulders, gave off a "thick as thieves" aura. The discussion seemed serious. They disappeared into the garage.

Curiosity getting the better of me, I approached the garage, carrying the garbage bag with me as an alibi if I was caught snooping.

The men spoke in hushed tones, so I couldn't make out what they were saying.

The garage smelled of fresh-cut grass, sweat, and motor oil. It was cluttered with old machine parts, oil splotches on the ground, and a dirty riding mower and weed-eater along one wall. Tools lay everywhere in boxes on benches, stuffed in corners, on worktables, and hanging on the walls alongside shelves of various seeds, sprays, and boxes of junk. On the other wall, a clunky refrigerator hummed. A fluorescent light flickered over the worktable.

All three men were in one corner hunched over a large box covered with a drop cloth.

I announced my entrance in a singsong voice. "Knock, knock."

All three men sprang up, startled, and dropped the cloth, edging around the box, as if to hide it from my view.

"Hey," Len came toward me. "We're looking at the car parts Randall got the other day."

Randall said, "Yeah. I'm thinking about getting into restoring this old car a buddy of mine has."

Keith said, "Yep. An old sixty-five mustang. It's blue right now, but you oughtta paint that sucker cherry red."

Randall nodded. "Yeah. That'd be real nice. I do like a red car."

I'd never doubt Randall and Keith's enthusiasm for cars. They were the sort of men who didn't mind getting dirty. Len, however, was their opposite in every way. His grooming was pristine. Hardly the sort of guy who'd appreciate motor grease under his nails and on his clothes. Further, their reaction to my entrance wasn't normal for a bunch of men looking at car parts. Rather, it was more like the reaction a mother might get in catching her son with a porn magazine.

Len guided me toward the door, his hand stroking my back. "What are you doing out here?"

I shrugged, wrapping the garbage string around my fingers. "Only curious to see what's going on."

He put his arm around my shoulders. "Aw. You miss me already?" He kissed my head.

"Absolutely," I joked. "But I should probably go soon. Check on Prim."

"Okay." He popped a kiss on my lips, holding me close. "We'll leave in a bit." His pocket buzzed again.

"Who keeps texting you?" It wasn't any of my business, so I downplayed my nosiness. "It seems rude for them to keep bothering you at a family function. It's been all day. Is there an emergency?"

He ignored the phone. "It's, uh, a couple friends." His eyes darted. He kissed me again, deeper this time. "We'll go soon. Promise." He pulled away from me, nudging me toward the door, and playfully slapped my rear.

That was a clear signal for me to go back to the house and wait on him. I didn't like it, but I complied. Well, I pretended to.

Turning away from the garage, I started toward the house. But when I glanced over my shoulder, none of the men were in sight. I ducked behind a tree, dropped the garbage bag, and crept through the shadows to trace the side of the garage to the back window.

By now, the purple sky had extinguished the sun and a thin mist bedewed the grass. Lightning bugs danced to the tune of the tree frog song. The kids were still running through the yard screaming and playing, draining every minute from the summer day until their parents called them home.

Flattening myself against the back of the garage, I peeked in the window. The men had gathered around the mysterious box again. Randall uncovered a corner and was pointing and talking. I stood on my tiptoes to see what was inside. Dang it, I couldn't see.

"Blauw, blauw, blauw," a little boy screamed, spritzing me with water from his pistol—the combination of his voice and the cold water made me jump nearly out of my skin. Caleb.

I shooed him away.

The chubby blond swathed in green camouflage clothing grunted. "What are you doing?" He lowered his squirt gun. He stunk of wet dog, sweat, and the cloying sweetness of birthday cake.

Crap. I put my finger to my lips to indicate he should be quiet. I smiled and whispered conspiratorially, "I'm trying to sneak up on the guys. I'm going to scare them."

"Oh." He hunched his shoulders, silencing his giggles with his dimpled, dirty hand.

"You go around that way." I pointed to the side of the building. "Wait at the corner. When they come out...you blast 'em."

He sniggered, tiptoeing around the corner to his position.

A car pulled into the driveway and honked twice. The men sauntered out of the garage.

Randall called out to the visitor. "Hey, man! How you doing?"

I couldn't see Caleb, but I heard him shout, "Blauw, blauw, blauw." He roared with laughter. "I got you good, Dad."

Randall said, "Dadgummit, Caleb. Get out of here. Go play." Exasperated, he said to his visitor, "Kids."

Caleb scooted off, howling with laughter and calling out to the other kids.

"Yeah, I've got a couple myself. I understand." The visitor said in a deep, booming voice.

I returned to peek in the window at the back of the garage.

The visitor was a tall man, with white ball cap on his head, a bumpy nose, and a big belly. He wore a white golf shirt with green horizontal stripes and khaki shorts that showed off white, wiry legs. He carried a large manila envelope.

He shook hands with Randall. "I came by for my shipment."

Shipment?

"Burt, this is my brother-in-law Len and my brother Keith. You'll probably be seeing them around. We're partners."

The men all shook hands.

Burt clapped his hands together. "Let me see what you got." He seemed in a big hurry for whatever it was.

Randall said, "C'mon in. It's back here."

I ducked low, peeking in a corner of the window. The men gathered around the box again, but their bodies blocked my view. Maybe Burt ordered a car part? Maybe Randall fixed cars on the side? He definitely wouldn't be the first or only home mechanic in Kentucky.

Burt said, "Ain't that a beaut? This is going to impress the pants off a lot of people. I'll take two."

Two what?

I craned my neck. Burt held something, but I couldn't get a clear view of what he was holding. Keith walked away then returned with a bag.

Burt handed the envelope to Randall. "Here's your money. The whole three grand."

Three grand! What the devil did that bag contain? The bag wasn't very big, about a foot square. Surely no car part cost three grand. It had to be something else. Were they dealing in stolen jewelry? Guns? Drugs? Was I witnessing a *Breaking Bad* moment?

Burt said, "Thanks, fellas. Great doing business with you. I'll be in touch. I know someone else who's interested in…distribution." He started to walk away then stopped. "If I wanted to get my hands on a large amount, what would I need to do?"

"How large?" Randall asked. "It took us a couple of months to get this together."

"Two, three dozen."

Randall's voice jumped a few pitches. "What?" He paused. "I don't know, man. Like I said, it takes a long time…"

Burt said, "Think about it. There's a lot more money where that came from. Well, fellas, I've got to run. The wife and I have a meeting out at Helmsdale Baptist tonight." He got in his car. When Burt drove away, the men in the garage hooted.

"Did y'all hear what he said?" Keith guffawed. "We won't be able to count the amount of money he's looking to spend."

"Don't get too excited," Len said. "We may not be able to get our hands on enough product."

Len might be into shady dealings. My heart raced. Had Bryan known about this? I needed to get away from this garage before they caught me or I might not leave here if they thought I'd threaten whatever hustle they were engaged in. But then Randall spoke and my curiosity won over my fear.

Randall said, "Burt's crazy. There's no way we can score the amount he wants. Not without getting busted. We shouldn't try it."

"Don't be too fast to discount it," Keith said. "We need to think about it. Talk it through. There may be a way."

Randall snorted. "Let's separate this cash real quick before the ladies start to miss us." He withdrew the money and waved it. "Three large, my friends."

The back porch light flipped on and Vonda stuck her red head out and shouted, "Rook? Rook? Where you at?"

That was my cue to get out of there before I was caught.

Fortunately, the light didn't illuminate the entire backyard, but the fact she was drawing attention to my absence annoyed the bejeezus out of me. I cut away from the building, across the back of the lot, into the deepest shadows, jumped behind a tree and ducked behind a woodpile then cut along the fence-line into the neighbor's yard. I bolted around behind their garage, along the edge of their property, across the neighbor's front yard, and into Randall and Vonda's front yard, popping out from behind an oak tree there into the light cast from the front porch.

Kim yelled out, "Here she is." Vonda and Kim stepped onto the front porch. Vonda said, "Girl, what're you doing?" The porch light haloed her poofy red hair and cast her face in shadows.

"Oh," I chuckled, panting from the activity. Man, I was out of shape. "Playing hide and seek with the kids. But it looks like they abandoned me. I guess I hid too well."

"Girl, get in here before the mosquitoes eat you alive."

I jogged toward the house as the men came around front.

"There you are," Len said. "I thought we'd lost you."

"Nope." I smiled, not daring to venture another word.

"You ready to go home?"

"Yeah. I'm beat." That wasn't a lie.

Saying goodbye in the South had always been a ritual loaded with hugs, farewells, gossip, more hugs, handshakes, more talking, making plans for future gatherings, a discussion on so-n-so's health, and another round of farewells. The length of acquaintance, or the closer blood-kin, the longer it took to extract oneself from a gathering. Fortunately, I'd only known Len's family a few hours, enabling us to depart in no less than twenty minutes with plenty of "y'all come back and see us anytime."

Vonda hugged me. "See if you can get my baby brother to behave."

"I'll give it my best shot." I laughed.

We spent the car ride in silence. I bit my tongue to keep from asking about what had transpired in the garage. The desire to know was killing me. But knowing might, in fact, kill me. I needed to tell Jimmy what I'd seen, but it was already late and he'd seemed a little put out with me the last time we spoke. It could wait until tomorrow.

Chapter Twenty-Nine

Before leaving the house for work on Monday, I made toast and coffee for Prim and ensured she took her medicine. She picked at her toast.

Batrene called while I wolfed an egg sandwich and downed a bottle of diet Kentucky Spice soda.

"You still need me to watch Prim?"

"No, but thank you for the offer. She seems okay now. But it might be helpful to call her a couple times, if you remember."

"Oh, sure, hon. I'd be happy to. I may come over for a visit anyway a little later. I need the company, too. With Bryan gone and all. I can't believe we're starting our third week without him. Have you heard anything?"

"I haven't. I've given evidence, documents, and such, to Jimmy. I have no doubt he'll do a good job, but, like he told me, it takes time to examine evidence and interview people. They're a small force and they have other cases. They're doing the best they can. We need to be patient a little longer."

"But how much longer?" Her voice tensed. "I want to know what happened to my son and why he was killed. When they catch the scumbag, I want to go to the trial and confront the monster. I want to watch them go to prison for the rest of their miserable lives. I wish I was younger and healthier. I'd hunt the animal down myself."

"I understand. I want all those things, too. I promise, if I hear anything, I'll let you know immediately."

I flew to work, fueled by caffeine and Led Zeppelin. It was a balmy morning in the mid-sixties with low humidity after the overnight rains.

The mellow cast of light and the yellowing trees announced autumn would soon be on its way. Very soon, with any luck.

Once I arrived at the distillery, I sat in the parking lot checking my phone for the hundredth time. Jimmy still hadn't returned my text or my call.

Glancing around the parking lot, I didn't see Len's car. I'd determined to keep a close eye on him for a few days, while maintaining my emotional distance. He was involved in something shady, or at least questionable. Randall and Keith were connected to it, too, but since they worked in the rickhouses, it was virtually impossible for me to observe their movements.

I went inside to start my day.

After greeting my teammates, I asked, "Have y'all seen Len?"

Jeff, the social media guru, said, "Len is out…" He made air quotes around *out*. "An appointment, supposedly."

"He's always out." Marla's eye roll was apparent in her voice.

After a bit of mumbling and head-shaking, we all dove into our work.

When lunchtime rolled around, Marla slung her bohemian purse over her shoulder. "Rook, you want to join us for lunch? We're going to Babylon Café. The best Greek food ever."

"Oh, no thanks. I brought my lunch." I needed to save money wherever I could. "I'll join y'all another time."

When I finished my current task, I gathered my book and lunch bag. Though the day was warming up quickly, it was far from the hottest it would get, so it was tolerable enough to eat outside. I walked to the back of the property toward the pond.

As I rounded the corner of the farthest rickhouse, I heard a woman's angry voice. "Tell me what you're doing…"

I stopped short, ducked behind the building, and peeked around the corner.

"Hold on." Len rubbed his face and looked at the sky. Classic male exasperation. "It's all an act."

Len? I thought he was out today!

Holly flipped her hair and snorted. Her tan, muscular legs took a power stance in her gray miniskirt. "You're one heck of an actor. I've seen the way you look at her. The way you touch her. Now you're taking her around your family. Are you insane?"

He looked at the sky again and steepled his hands over his nose. Classic male "you've been busted" stance. After a moment, he looked at her and opened his hands as he stepped toward her. "Wouldn't it look weird to date someone and not kiss them?"

"You're enjoying it too much. You really do like her, don't you?"

Hey. They're talking about me! What a jerk!

He said, "Only to keep down suspicion. You know you and I can't be seen together."

My mouth dropped open. Were they having an affair and using me as a pawn in some twisted game they were playing? Over my dead body. A brief fantasy of popping out of my hiding spot, marching up to Len, and punching him in the face flitted through my mind, but I held my place.

"Are you sleeping with her now, too?" Holly added mockingly, "You know, so it all looks legit?"

"No. I swear. I've only kissed her. Nothing more."

That was true. He hadn't attempted anything else. I'd assumed we were taking it slow, and I'd been happy with our progress, or lack of it. Wow. Tears stung my eyes. Not because I was sad to lose him but because I'd been such a fool. And because Cam had been right about him. That was the biggest gut punch to my pride. I'd been so focused on Bryan and Prim that I'd been completely blind to Len.

"Besides, her friend is the deputy. I'm trying to find out what all she knows, if anything."

"She knows something." Holly looked around. "The way she's been poking around..." She shook her head. "I don't trust her."

My mouth dropped open. *She* didn't trust *me*? She was stepping out on her husband with a coworker and *she* didn't trust *me*? Len wasn't the only one I wanted to punch right now. Fury and hurt tore through me like a hurricane. I quaked under its power. The utter betrayal. My heart raged against my chest, crashing against it over and over like a rabid animal. I balled my fists, the pressure building in my head.

"I need a little more time." He moved forward and put his hands on her waist, pulling her close.

He continued speaking softly to her, but his words were indiscernible. She relaxed into him. He kissed her cheek and her neck. Soon they were practically making out.

His phone rang. The call, whatever it was, thrilled him. He said something to her that made her happy, too.

She shouted, "Ohmigoodness," and threw herself against him.

They kissed again.

I pressed myself against the rickhouse as he walked away.

He said over his shoulder, "I'll see you tonight."

"You'd better," Holly said.

I peeked around the corner at her. She was kicking at a clump of grass. She checked her watch then she left, too.

As her heels clicked quickly past on the cobblestones, I again pressed myself against the rickhouse, wondering how to exact my revenge. I didn't want Len. Not after what I'd witnessed at the barbeque. And *definitely* not after discovering his and Holly's adultery. I wanted to devise a glorious way to crush him. Filthy, stinking, rotten, scum-sucking… Then it hit me. I needed to keep him close enough to gather information, if I could. I deflated. Now he was near the top of my list, sitting close to Clarence and Dewey. Maybe not for murder, but he was definitely involved in something criminal. More importantly, I needed to find out why he needed to spy on me and figure out what I knew. What did he hope to gain from it? What in the Sam hell was going on at this distillery?

Chapter Thirty

Jealousy was an awful disease, and I was about to unleash a plague. Prim wouldn't be proud of my vengeful moment. I wasn't proud of it either, but I was happy to give my anger full rein. *Game on.*

After lunch, I found Holly in the break room, where she was reloading her water bottle. "Hey, Holly. Have you seen Len?"

Her smile tightened in the corners of her mouth. "No. I haven't seen him all day."

Liar, liar, pants on fire. I put on a wistful face and pulled a coffee mug from the shelf. "Huh, odd. He texted me saying he's going to take me someplace special." The lie tasted sweet on my tongue.

A maniacal light sparked in her eyes. "Oh? How fun."

"Yeah," I breathed, pouring caramel-flavored creamer into my cup. "He's…" I shuddered. "Sexy. We've only been out a few times. But it's really…" I sucked in my breath and poured the coffee. "Hot."

Her smile ratcheted another notch, growing closer to the mad clown end of the smile spectrum. "That's…just…great."

I chuckled. Time to ice this cake real thick. "I know. TMI, right? But I can't help it. The chemistry is crazy intense." I leaned against the counter, holding the steaming cup near my lips, blowing on the coffee. I lowered my voice. "He's an amazing lover."

Of course I had no idea if he was or not. But Holly didn't know that. Not for certain.

She was seething, shuddering with the struggle to control herself. She pinched her lips together, her nostrils flaring. She snapped closed the lid on her water bottle. Clearly, she was angry enough to claw my eyes out.

That's not appropriate talk for the office. Her eyes flicked down to my coffee cup. "You have a great rest of the day." She looked at me again, this time a genuine smile spread slowly over her thickly glossed lips—a smile verging on insanity.

Check.

Len had come in to work after lunch. After a quick greeting, he dove into his work without another word. After work, I stopped Len as he tried to hightail it from the office. I caught up to him and linked my arm with his.

"Hey there. I've hardly seen you today."

"Yeah. I've been super busy." He was texting.

"What are you doing tonight? You want to come over to my house? I'll cook dinner. We can probably find a movie on Netflix or something." I had no intention of doing anything with him.

He flushed a little, opening the door for us. "I'm, uh, pretty busy tonight."

We stepped out into the warm evening, deep gold pools of light puddling around the shadows. We started toward the parking lot. Next to Len's Impala, Holly was sitting in her car, the engine running.

He stopped at the tail of his car. "I'll see you tomorrow, Rook. Okay?"

I threw my arms around his neck. "Will you call me tonight?"

Flustered, he stammered. "I-uh-well…I'm not sure. I'll try. I have a lot of work to do."

"Do you ever stop working?" Laughing, I ran my fingers into his hair. "When are you going to relax? I can definitely help you with that." I pressed my body close to his and planted a forceful kiss on his lips.

He shuddered, straining against the kiss. But he wasn't pushing me away either. He wasn't my target, though. Holly was. Her jealousy was out of control. The more jealous I made her, the more miserable they both would be. She was watching us kiss and he was going to smell like me. Now, when they were together tonight, they were going to argue. She wouldn't be able to stop ruminating about the kiss. There was no way she was going to let him touch her. In addition, I planned to send sultry texts every hour on the hour. It certainly wasn't going to be the night of romance they'd planned on.

Knowing my barb had more than landed, I broke off the kiss and said, breathless, "You have a great night."

Checkmate.

Chapter Thirty-One

The next day, I went to work early in hopes of speaking to Pierce without Holly or Clarence around. I also remembered during my drive that I needed to double-check inventory counts for the forthcoming festival. The first count was fifty sampling bottles of Devil's Kiss, but the last count I received was forty-five. I needed to verify with Randall what we had and what we were supposed to have.

Unfortunately, I had overestimated the number of early risers. Even the dock crew hadn't started yet. There was only one other vehicle in the lot. I recognized it as Randall's white Ford pickup. He must have come in early to take care of paperwork. Since he was the dock supervisor, he probably always had plenty of paperwork to do.

I sighed, looked around, and checked my phone. No messages. The digital clock in my car said seven thirty-five. At least Randall was at the rickhouse. Maybe he wouldn't mind me checking the inventory if I stayed out of his way.

I strode to the rickhouse. The sun oozed over the horizon, tinting the sky and trees with a mélange of red, orange, pink, and gold. It was a pretty morning, though humid, the air almost too thick to breathe. A faint mist cloaked the grounds behind the distillery and dew jeweled the grass.

The rickhouse door was unlocked. I stepped inside and paused a moment to adjust to the dim lighting. The earthy oak and sharp bourbon odor hung in the air. The interior of the building was all thick oak beams and oak barrels, their round bodies lying quiet and snug in their racks. A radio played in the background.

I shouted over the music. "Randall?" My sandals clomped on the wood floors. Flanked by floor-to-ceiling barrels, I passed down the center aisle toward the dock at the back of the rickhouse, where the supervisor's desk would be. Not hearing a response, I called again, "Randall?"

As I approached the desk, The Animals' "House of the Rising Sun" greeted me. The desk was empty. Though I'd reached the back of the building, there was one dark, narrow corridor just beyond the desk. A door slammed at the end of the dark hall.

"Randall?"

I peeked around the corner. There was a door, cracked open, allowing in the burgeoning daylight. It had been stopped from closing completely by a brick. Outside, a vehicle door closed and an engine started. I picked my way in the darkness toward the door. About halfway down the hall, there was a greater mass of darkness to my right and a large mass I couldn't quite make out. I dug in my purse for my phone. Finding it, I opened the flashlight function, easing deeper into the alcove. Inch by inch, the light made apparent the wood floors, scattered papers, a wad of red gum on the papers, and a shoe print, partially smudged. I could make out C and half of a letter that looked like an A but might have been an H.

Bourbon vapors tickled my nose. I moved the light up and to the right, finding a wet bourbon barrel.

Legs hung out of the barrel.

Gasping and staggering back, I dropped the phone, the light beam shooting into my eye. Picking up the phone, I dashed toward the form. "Randall! Randall!" I threw my purse to the floor and grabbed his arms and his shirt, trying to pull his torso out of the barrel, but he was too heavy. The barrel was full of bourbon. He wasn't struggling. He was either passed out or drowned. I tried again, grabbing his collar and bracing myself against the wall with my foot to get leverage.

I jerked backward as hard and as fast as I could, and he fell back against me. I lost my balance, falling to the floor with him on top of me. My head thumped against a shelf on my way down. Pain blasted through my skull then dwindled into a rhythmic throb. Randall lay on top of me. Bourbon trickled all over me and dripped, puddling on the floor. My back hurt from the fall, and I couldn't catch a good breath because Randall weighed on my lungs. Grunting, I rolled out from under him.

I hovered over him, panting, slapping his face. "Randall, Randall!" He was unresponsive. "Please be drunk. Really, really drunk." I flourished little slaps all over his cheeks. I checked his pulse and listened for breathing. He wasn't dead drunk. Just dead.

Chapter Thirty-Two

I leaned against the outer wall of the rickhouse, staring at the blue and red flashing lights of the two patrol cars, an ambulance, and the coroner's vehicle. By now, other employees had arrived and Deputies Ladonna and Jimmy were questioning them. Another deputy was putting yellow tape around the building. The parking lot had already been barricaded to limit access to the building.

Sheriff Goodman was talking to me.

I looked into his bloodshot eyes, hardly able to register the words rolling from his thin, chapped lips.

"Miss Daniels, I need you to tell me again what happened here. Walk me through it one more time."

"My name is Campbell! Rook. Campbell!" My voice echoed across the valley.

People stopped and stared.

"And I won't speak to you a minute longer until you get that right."

His mouth pursed, white around the edges. "Alrighty then. Miss Campbell…" He spat the name as if it tasted rotten. "Will you walk me through the scene one more time?"

I explained everything. How I'd come in early to speak with Randall about inventory for the upcoming event. How I'd heard the door slam and a vehicle start. How I'd tried to extract Randall from the barrel. And how, when I was finally able to get him out of the barrel, it was too late.

The angle of his head and the narrowing of his eyes signaled the sheriff's disbelief and suspicion about my presence at the murder scene and my

193

version of the story. "Why were you here so early?"

"I told you. To get information about the inventory for the event." My clothes and skin were uncomfortably wet and sticky with the bourbon. I made plans to go home at lunch to change clothes.

He tapped his pen against a notebook. "And you couldn't have done that later, when the workday had already begun?"

"Like I told you already, I came early before the dockworkers became too busy. I didn't want to get in their way. I thought it would be best to take care of it early."

He stilled the pen. "And he wasn't breathing at all? No pulse? Nothing?"

"There were absolutely no signs of life. I think he must've been dead for a while."

He jotted notes. "And you say you heard a door slam?"

"Yes."

"And a vehicle started up behind the building by the door?"

"Yes."

"What sort of vehicle was it?"

"I don't know. But it sounded big."

He snorted. "You can tell the size of vehicle based on the way it sounds when it starts?"

"Well, can't you? I mean, within reason." I motioned toward the parking lot. "A utility vehicle motor sounds a lot different than my little sedan. It sounded like a bigger vehicle. Like a big truck, possibly one of our smaller delivery trucks. That's all I know."

I looked at the ground, at the sparse blades of grass peeking through the gravel at the edge of the pavement. I swallowed the hard lump of emotion pulsing in my throat.

Crime scene technicians swarmed the area, both inside the rickhouse and all around the perimeter. The throbbing spread into a dull ache all over my head.

Pierce stood in the parking lot, rubbing his brow as he spoke with Deputy Ladonna. Holly, crying, stood with Len by the trunk of her car, sucking up consolation.

Sheriff Goodman closed his notebook and tucked his pen in his breast pocket. "I don't have any further questions right now. But don't go on vacation or anything. I might have more questions later." Goodman called over to one of the senior rickhouse workers to interview him next.

A yearning for coffee and chocolate settled into my gut. I walked uphill to the office building, stepping through a barricade guarded by a deputy. I wanted to speak to Jimmy, but he was interviewing someone. Instead, I entered the office building, stopped by the restroom to wipe the sticky bourbon off my bare skin, grabbed a coffee and Milky Way Midnight, and returned outside to the bench outside the visitor's center.

Lucia, the receptionist, stood beside me. "I can't believe this." She toyed with the gold lion's head on her necklace. "I heard you found the body."

"I did." I shuddered, recalling the feeling of Randall's lifeless body in my grip, lying against me, wet and heavy. I bit into my candy bar. I could only think of those novels about women dating vampires, touching their cold, undead bodies, and I felt sick. I'd have to side with the werewolves. At least they were warm and had a pulse.

Lucia, thankfully, interrupted my bizarre train of thought. The red lipstick crusting the lines of her lips, she whispered, "Is it true you found him drowned in a barrel of bourbon?"

"Yeah." I shuddered again. The chocolate wasn't taking effect. Maybe my taste for bourbon was also dead now. I was pretty sure memories of this horrible day would come floating back any time I got near a shot glass. And his family. Poor Vonda losing her husband. And Caleb, oh heavens, Caleb. Losing his daddy. Acid crept along the back of my throat. I understood all too well the devastation of losing a parent as a child. He'd go his whole life… Tears stung my eyes. I leaned my elbows on my knees and hid my face in my hand.

"Geez, what a horrible way to die. I couldn't imagine." She took a deep, jagged, breath as if she too might drown. "I feel sorry for Pierce. He's beside himself. Of course, he's upset about the death. Who wouldn't be? But our little distillery is quickly getting a reputation for dead bodies."

I rubbed small circles into my temple. Bryan had been one of those dead bodies. Of course, she didn't mean anything by it, but I wanted her to go away now. Thankfully, someone called out to her.

She patted my back. "You be strong, sweetie. Let me know if you need anything. Okay?"

I nodded by way of answer and she left. Numb, I sat there in front of the visitors' center, for an indeterminate time, sipping my coffee and staring at the large oak tree at the end of the parking lot.

Jimmy approached. "We meet again. Under some pretty gruesome circumstances."

"Yep." I drank my coffee.

"What happened?"

"Do I need to tell the story all over again? I've already told everything to Sheriff Goodman."

He looked around, squinting in the sunlight. "It'd be helpful if you did. It could jog your memory about a significant detail."

With a heavy sigh, I recounted everything for Jimmy.

"When did you notice the ten barrels were missing?"

He had my full attention. "There were barrels missing?" I was flummoxed. "I-I-I didn't know there were any missing. I'd been so concerned for Randall, I hadn't realized, but it all makes sense now. The truck I'd heard must've been the getaway vehicle." I performed some quick math. Those ten barrels were worth many thousands of dollars. I couldn't imagine that much money. Losing such a large amount of revenue could sink Four Wild Horses, in spite of its past success. That was at least fifteen years of the aging process gone. Time was the one factor that could never be retrieved, never be bought. I glanced at Pierce, who leaned against the back of a police vehicle with his face in his hands. Time was the ultimate and rarest of commodities. Stress and pity twisted knots into my stomach.

Jimmy's gaze followed mine. "Mr. Simpson's had a rough time lately."

"Yeah," I stared into my coffee. "Hopefully when they find Randall's killer, they'll find who stole the bourbon. I hope it can be retrieved."

"I got your text the other night. I'm sorry I didn't call back. It's been a hectic weekend. Some personal stuff and there must've been a full moon.

CHAPTER THIRTY-TWO

People were pretty wild."

"It's fine."

"What was on your mind?"

"I went to a barbeque with Len on Saturday. That guy over there…" I nodded in Len's direction. "The tall one with the blonde."

Jimmy glanced over his shoulder. "Okay."

"We went to his sister's house. His sister is married to the deceased, Randall. As it turns out, Keith, that man by the rickhouse…" I nodded at Keith, who was pacing back and forth, his hands tucked under his arms, "is Randall's brother. He was at the barbeque, too."

"Tight-knit bunch," Jimmy sniffed.

I stood, stepping closer to Jimmy, lowering my voice. "Those three are acting squirrely." I told him everything I'd witnessed at the barbeque.

Jimmy was very interested. He ran his hand over his chin, as if he had a beard. "Oh, man. I wish you could've seen what was inside that box."

"Me, too, but I didn't want to get caught. Especially since I don't know how dangerous they are or how deep this all goes."

"Good decision. If we had reasonable suspicion, we could maybe get a search warrant, but as it stands right now…I mean, they could've been selling car parts." He dropped his hand to his hip. "I'll definitely take a closer look at them. Man, the list keeps getting longer."

The sheriff finished his business and headed across the parking lot toward us. "Duvall. C'mere." He stuffed a wad of tobacco into his jaw.

"I'll do anything to get this case solved faster and get justice for Bryan and his mother."

He walked backward in the sheriff's direction while talking to me. "Please. You've done enough. Let us handle this."

Chapter Thirty-Three

Pierce closed the distillery for the rest of Tuesday and all of Wednesday. I wished I could visit Vonda, Randall's wife, to offer my condolences and maybe discover a little information. But, desperate as I was to figure out what had happened to Bryan and maybe Randall, I still had to give the poor woman at least a day to grieve.

It wasn't quite noon yet, and the heat was mounting. Even on a sitting mower and wearing Prim's big floppy hat, sweat trickled down my back, between my breasts, and behind my knees, where sweat bees repeatedly stung me.

Batrene walked over to the property line, waving a newspaper like a fan. Her grass was getting high, too.

I'd mow her yard next. I parked under the shade tree and shut off the lawnmower, "Hey, Batrene. How are you?"

"How's Prim?" She panted, her cheeks red.

"Okay. Tired."

"I've tried to talk to her about taking treatments, but she won't budge. I didn't want to push her too hard because that'd only make her dig in deeper. You know how she is."

"I know. Thanks for trying, though."

She gave me an envelope. "I want you to have this."

"What's this?" I opened the flap to reveal three hundred dollar bills. I gaped. Snapping my mouth shut, I shook my head and handed the envelope back to her. "I can't accept this. You need your money."

"No. I want you to take it. You've been doing a lot for me and you're going to take it." Her bottom lip quivered. "I know Bryan would want you to have it, too."

I wiped my sweaty face and emerging tears on the sleeve of my shirt. My legs were covered in grass clippings. "I miss him."

"I know you do, baby. I do, too. He's still with us in spirit." She put the envelope in my hand. "So, you have to take this."

Reluctantly, I accepted the money. "When I'm finished here, I'll come mow your yard."

"Oh, that's mighty good of you. I'll make sure there's plenty of cold lemonade for you. When you're done, I want you to go through Bryan's room. See if there's anything there you want. He's got books, and I know you like to read. Maybe you'll want to take those."

Emotion choked off my ability to speak, so I nodded.

She patted my cheek with a violet-scented hand and made her way back to her house.

When I'd finished mowing the yards, I searched the shed for the weed-eater, but I couldn't find it, and Batrene's didn't work. I remembered Cam had borrowed ours a couple weeks ago.

I phoned Cam to ask him to return the weed-eater.

He hedged. "My hands are kind of full right now. Can you come out to Mom and Dad's to get it?"

"Sure. I'll be there in about fifteen minutes." There was no need to spiff up since I still had more yard work to do when I returned. I jumped in my car, and set off across town, passing out of Rothdale into the countryside.

Cam's family home sat at the bottom of a winding, hilly road in Gestonburg on the west side. Taking the gravel drive on the right, I passed the cow pastures ending at the white farmhouse edged with shrubs. The yard was shaded with several old oak trees. I pulled beside Cam's truck and was greeted by a black and white border collie.

"Hey, Maisie girl." I scratched her ears. "Looks like you've had babies."

She wagged her tail and smiled at me with shining brown eyes.

Cam was unloading boxes from the back of his truck.

I greeted him. "Hey, what's going on here?"

"Jacie and I split." He jumped from the bed of truck. He wiped his sweaty forehead on his bicep. "I'm moving in with Mom and Dad for a while. They can use the help anyway."

My eyes widened. "Oh. I'm sorry…" I was too stunned to say anything more.

"It's okay. Let me get the weed-eater for you."

I followed him to the shed. "Do you want to talk about it?"

"Not really." He opened the door and we stepped inside the stuffy building. He flipped on a light.

I was partly relieved he didn't want to discuss the fallout with Jacie, but I was also riddled with guilt for any part I might've unwittingly played in the separation. I pressed forward with the issue. "Did you break up with her or did she break up with you?"

He pulled the weed-eater off the wall and popped the cap on the string case. "I used all your string. I'll replace it for you." He pushed around loose parts on the workbench, found the string spool, and fiddled around with replacing the old one. "We broke up because she came home all wet one night and fired up. Griping and complaining about you." The new string in place, he snapped on the cover and wiped the dried grass from the weed-eater head with a dirty cloth. "I didn't know what she was talking about. I was watching *Cheers* and minding my own business. She throws out a demand, insisting I stop being friends with you. I asked why." He handed me the weed-eater. "Anyway, we got into a big argument and long story short, I'm living with Mom and Dad again." He smiled crookedly. "This is what winning looks like."

"I live with my grandma, so I guess I'm winning big, too."

We laughed.

He stepped out of the shed and closed the door. "I don't know what set her off. She never would tell me."

Initially, I'd had no intention of telling him about my tussle with Jacie. Because, contrary to what Jacie believed, I'd never had designs to separate them. But I was a human with flaws. And one of my flaws happened to be a vengeful and vindictive nature when I'd been provoked. I definitely

200

considered Jacie's recent behavior provoking. "I don't want to rub salt in the wound, but..." I told him the whole story about Jacie coming out to my house to confront me and Prim hosing us down.

"You've got to be kidding me."

"'Fraid not."

He paused and scratched the back of his head. "I don't have anything else to say. Except..."

"It's fine. It's over. No one was hurt. Except maybe Jacie's pride. I'm glad to forget about it and move on." I walked back toward my car.

"I would've paid anything to see Prim spraying you two and ordering Jacie off her property." He guffawed. "She's something else."

A few puppies played around the porch, nosing in the plants and around the shrubs. I picked one up and nuzzled its head. She wiggled around, licking my nose with bologna-scented kisses.

Cam said, "I think you need one."

I chuckled. "I'd love to have one, but I can't handle one more bit of responsibility right now."

Cam's mom stepped out on the back porch. She was tall and lean, with thick, salt-and-pepper hair. "Rook Campbell, as I live and breathe, get in here, girl, and come sit a spell."

"I wish I could, Momma Iris, but I'm filthy and I need to get back to finish my yard work. I came to get the weed-eater."

"I heard about Prim. I hate it for her. She's a good woman."

Coming from Iris, that was high praise. She didn't give compliments lightly. "Thank you."

"If y'all need anything, you let us know. I've always thought highly of her."

"I appreciate that. Cam's already done a ton for us, though. I couldn't impose any more."

She smiled. "Yeah, I guess Cam's a pretty good boy."

He said, "Proving the rumors are true that I wasn't born to this family. I was discovered under a cabbage leaf in the garden."

We all laughed.

One of the pups pulled a loose branch from under the shrubs.

Iris said, "Hey, Cam, get those pups away from that shrub. It's poisonous. It'll kill them."

Cam and I pulled the puppies away. I looked closely at the shrub. It consisted of thousands of little needles identical to the needles on Bryan's office floor the day he died; the same sort of needles that had stuck to my skirt.

I said, "Iris, what kind of shrub is this?"

"English Yew. It's deadly."

I wanted to compare the needles to be sure. "Can I have a sprig of this?"

When I'd finished the yard work, I showered and made a simple supper of hamburgers and roasted potatoes then sat at the computer to research English Yew. I then compared the sprig collected from Iris's shrub to the needles that had been on Bryan's office floor the day of this death; they appeared to be the same plant. Then I jumped on Google. After a bit of research, I verified that English Yew was innocuous externally, but if ingested was every bit as dangerous as Iris had claimed. Ancient soldiers used the plant to commit suicide in order to avoid capture from enemy armies. Also, only a few sprigs of the plant could kill animals much larger than Bryan.

I picked up my phone to call Jimmy. Len had left a voice mail and texted. He wanted to see me.

I scoffed. "Nope." I dialed Jimmy instead.

He answered, "Hey there, Nancy Drew."

I laughed. "Well, believe it or not, I've found another clue. A pretty important one."

"Yeah?"

"You should have the toxicology lab scan Bryan's samples for English Yew. It's a highly poisonous shrub."

"What makes you think that's what killed him?"

"I found yew needles on his office floor. They were stuck to my skirt. I kept them and still have them, if you want to come get them."

"Interesting. Yeah, I'll come over in a bit. Who had access to a yew plant?"

"Practically anyone. It's pretty common."

CHAPTER THIRTY-THREE

"How would he have ingested it?"

I recalled the tumbler spilled on the office floor. "Maybe someone made a tea of it and slipped it into his tumbler?"

"That's possible, I suppose." He squinted. "They were probably in a hurry. Maybe the needles were stuck to their shoes or clothes and they didn't know it. And because they were in a hurry, they didn't realize the needles dropped."

"I guess my question then is who at the distillery not only has access to the plant but had the motivation to use it?"

"That's the million-dollar question."

Chapter Thirty-Four

The overnight storms had done little to ease the late August heat. In fact, the air was so thick with humidity it was like breathing under a wet, wool blanket.

Because Rothdale was tiny, our stores and the products they carried were limited. So, residents often drove about ten miles west to the Walmart in Frankfort. I arrived around ten that morning to a packed parking lot. But I didn't want to go to Vonda's empty-handed. Whatever I gave them would seem like a shallow gesture. There was nothing I could say or do to minimize their pain. After all, whatever Randall might've been involved in, it wasn't their fault.

The asphalt was hot against the soles of my shoes and the humid air left a film of moisture all over me. Sweat sprang along my hairline as I stepped across the parking lot and onto the shaded sidewalk. A blast of delicious cold air from the store hit me as the automatic door slid open.

I considered taking food to them, but their kitchen would be a cornucopia of sympathy pies and casseroles. Instead, I searched the Home and Garden aisle and, after much deliberation, finally settled on a pretty copper-colored wind chime with a butterfly at the center of the rods. I proceeded to the card and party supply aisles and selected a card. I wanted desperately to put the gift in a gift bag since a rabid raccoon could do a better gift-wrapping job than me. Fortunately, I found a silver gift box, where all I had to do was fold it, stuff it with tissue, and put a bow on it. Prim wouldn't be happy with me for opting out of the classier gift paper option, but what she didn't know wouldn't hurt her. Besides, wasn't it the thought that counted?

I wound around to the far left of the store, where the snacks were kept, grabbing a bag of chips to replace the bag I'd finished at lunch yesterday. I moved farther down the aisle to the Little Debbie snacks, trying to decide between fudge rounds or nutty bars, when a cart slowly approached. I stepped closer to the shelves to get out of the shopper's way, but the cart stopped.

Behind me, a lady's voice said, "Aren't you..."

It was Kim Tilkey, Keith's wife. She shook a glittery red-tipped finger at me. "Len's girlfriend, uh..."

I wanted to correct her misconception of my relationship with Len, but it was too much to address in the snack aisle with a near-stranger. I let her remain misinformed. "Rook. Campbell."

"That's it." She smiled and splayed her hand on her ample chest. "I'm Keith's wife, Kim."

"Yes." I smiled. "I remember you. How are you?"

"I'm pretty good. How's Len?" Her perfectly penciled brow arched. Her makeup was applied immaculately, as if she were about to do a glammed-up photo shoot for *Vogue*. It was out of place with her jean shorts and Myrtle Beach T-shirt.

"He's good." I lied. "Keeping busy." I was sure that wasn't a lie.

She lowered her voice as if sharing a juicy secret, but her eyes bespoke pity. "How's he handling Randall's death?"

"As well as one can under the circumstances." I honestly had no idea how he was handling anything. Nor did I care. Since the barbeque, I hadn't talked to him outside of work. At the office, I avoided anything unrelated to work. When he asked me about my cool behavior, I made excuses about being busy, preoccupied, or tired. "How's Randall's family doing?"

She shook her head. "Vonda's holding up as well as she can. I visited last night. Took over a chicken casserole and an apple crisp. Poor Caleb misses his daddy, of course. They were supposed to go fishing this weekend. He'd been so excited."

An ache yawned in my heart for Caleb. I knew what it was to lose a parent as a young child. "I feel for them. It won't be easy going forward. I wish there was something I could do, but I've only met them once. I got this card and windchime. You know, a gesture."

"Oh, how sweet. She'll like that. Are you going to the visitation or the funeral?"

Considering my current feelings for Len, that wouldn't be appropriate. "Probably not, since I don't know the family well. Len and I only started dating recently. It's not serious."

"I see how that could be awkward for you." She nudged me with her elbow. "But he must like you if he brought you around to the family so soon. It's a good sign."

I smiled and nodded, going by the old rule: if you don't have anything nice to say, you should say nothing.

"Oh, you know what…" She ducked her head and rummaged through her purse about the size of a small suitcase. "You look like a stylish girl, a girl who appreciates makeup and such."

False.

"You should come out to my place this weekend. I'm hosting a Jessie Belle party on Sunday afternoon around four. These parties only last a few hours, but I think you'll have fun."

Oh, lord, no. I'd rather fall into a beehive.

She extracted a card and pushed it at me. "Here's my card with my address and all my contact information. You don't have to buy anything, but it's a good way to meet people. I'm going to have about twelve other girls there. I'll serve tacos and fajitas and frozen margaritas. I'll have all kinds of makeup, lotion, and perfume samples. I'm also giving away one free facial and one free makeover."

"Oh, I don't know…"

I didn't want to go because I wouldn't know anyone there and that was the closest thing to hell on earth for me. However, Kim was Keith's wife and Keith was involved in suspicious activity. At best, he might be stealing bourbon. At worst, he might be connected to murder. Being at her house might provide me with an opportunity to find out more about what was going on. I could probably endure one afternoon of hell to maybe discover what the men had sold from Randall's garage the night of the barbeque, what Len and Holly were always whispering about, or why Randall was killed.

"C'mon, it'll be fun. There'll be someone you know. She works with you and Len, but I go to church with her and her husband and kids. Holly Parker?"

My skin crawled. "Yeah, I know her. What church do you go to?"

"Helmsdale Church."

Holy bourbon balls! A lightning bolt of excitement flashed through me. I blanked my face, though on the inside I perked like a hound tracking a rabbit. I'd heard that name before when I was spying…erm…gathering information on the men at the barbeque. Burt, the guy who paid them a wad of cash for a mysterious package, went to that church.

On a whim, I said, "Do you know a man named Burt who goes to Helmsdale? He's kind of tall with a booming voice. He stopped by the night of the barbeque to see the men."

"Oh! I bet that's Burt Anderson. I know them real well. His wife, Linda, and I are in Ruth's Daughters together. She's such a sweetie. You'd love her."

"Ruth's Daughters?"

"A women's only Bible study group. You should come. We always have a hoot. In fact, Linda Anderson will be at the Jessie Belle party this weekend. You should come and I'll introduce you."

"Sure, okay. Can I bring a dessert? I make a mean apple spice cake. My secret ingredient is bourbon."

"Sounds delicious. The party's at six, but people come earlier." She wrinkled her nose and lowered her voice. "Don't bring Len, though. The men get in the way."

My mouth eased into a smile. "Oh, I hadn't planned on bringing him."

I hated myself for what I had to do. Vonda, a grieving widow, deserved to grieve in peace. I tried to justify my rudeness by believing that Batrene and I needed to know what had happened to Bryan. To justify it further, maybe if I discovered who killed Bryan, I might also find out who killed Randall, thereby helping bring closure to Vonda, too.

I got lost, of course. I should've known better than to set off to a place I'd visited only once. However, Miltonville was tinier than Rothdale, so I found my way soon enough. I pulled down the drive, parking in front of the brown brick ranch with a covered porch. A pair of yellow mums flanked the two steps to the door. I rang the doorbell.

Caleb, red-faced and calf-eyed, answered the door, dressed in a camouflage Ninja Turtles shirt and jeans. "Hey," he whispered, downcast.

"Hey. Do you remember me?"

"Yeah."

"I'm sorry about your daddy."

He looked at his feet, his bottom lip pushed out. Sniffling, he hid his face in the bend of his elbow.

Vonda said from inside the house. "Caleb, who's at the door?" A minute later, she appeared, wearing a blue and white tie-dyed Dollywood shirt and a pair of white shorts. Sallow-skinned and pale, she looked like a different person without her makeup and teased hair. Her face was also red and puffy.

"Hey, girl. C'mon in. I apologize for my house. Everything is such a mess right now."

"I know this is a bad time. I came by to offer my condolences."

Her mouth trembled. She pulled a tissue out of her shorts pocket and pressed it to her eyes. "Please, come on in."

"I won't keep you long." I stepped into the air-conditioned house. "I know we only met once, but I wanted to bring by a little something and offer you my deepest sympathies for your loss." I held out the gift box, hearing Prim's voice in my head accusing me of acting like I'd had no raising.

She accepted my offering. "Aw, thank you, sweetie." Her voice cracked. "Thank you. You didn't have to do that. Would you like some iced tea?"

"Sure, please." I followed her into the kitchen. The table was already full of food.

She set a glass of iced tea in front of me. "How's Len? Is he okay?"

"He's just fine." I climbed onto the barstool at the counter. "He said he was going to stop by to see if you need anything. But he had an errand to run first, so he couldn't come with me." The lies were flowing so easily these days. If Prim knew, she'd tell me I needed more churching.

"No worries." She poured herself a glass of tea. "I guess you heard how it happened?"

"I was actually the one who tried to pull him from the barrel."

Her mouth drew downward. She reached out and squeezed my hand. "Oh. Bless your heart. I don't know what I'd do if I had to…"

"I can't express how upset I am that I couldn't save him."

She leaned on the counter and touched my wrist. "Well, of course you couldn't. I don't blame you. Not one bit. Randall was a big guy. I'm sure you did the best you could."

I looked into my tea. "It was too late."

"I can't believe it, though. I mean, he'd been working there for years. He'd never had one safety violation." She stood behind the counter, facing me. She drank her tea, silent for a moment. "There must be more to it."

"What do you mean?"

"I don't know. Women's intuition, I guess. He was arguing with someone on the phone the night before he died."

It couldn't have been Clarence Ford because they had little interaction. They worked in two separate buildings. The person on the phone could've been Dewey. After all, they'd recently been involved in a shoving match after Randall fired him.

I started with Dewey since he was highest on my list. "Do you think he might've been talking with Dewey Stiggers? Or…was there someone else he might've had disagreements with?"

She shook her head. "I don't know. But I know he's had problems with that Stiggers fellow in the past. It wouldn't surprise me one bit if he was to blame."

Last week, I would've agreed with her but, based on what I'd witnessed at the barbeque, I was beginning to have my doubts.

"You don't remember anything he was talking about?"

She tilted her head. "Why?"

"I'm sorry. I don't mean to pry. But since yesterday, when I pulled him out of the barrel, I've been torn up, trying to figure out who would want to do such a thing to such a great guy."

"I understand. I've been trying to rack my brain, too." She sighed, looking past me. "I remember him saying 'We had an understanding. We were going to wait because we can't get that many bottles all at once.'" She shrugged. "Stuff like that."

Sounded like he might've been talking to Keith or Len. They seemed to have differences in the garage the night of the barbeque. They were uncertain about getting their hands on a bunch of something. Maybe that something was bottles of bourbon and maybe their disagreement had escalated into murder.

Vonda added, "By the time he hung up, he was angry and he shouted 'That's not what we agreed on and if you can't accept the terms we discussed, you'll have a big problem on your hands. I'll blow this whole thing up and see how you like them apples.'"

"What an odd statement. Do you know what he wanted to blow up?"

She shook her head, her gaze distant. "I have no idea. I asked but he wouldn't tell me what it was about or who he was talking to. When I pressed the issue, he got mad at me, so I left it alone."

Chapter Thirty-Five

The next day at work, I had one job. Keep my head down and eyes open. And stay out of trouble, if at all possible.

Len leaned over the top of my cubicle. "Hey, gorgeous. How are you?"

He was paler than normal, with evidence of sleepless nights under his eyes.

"Good. You doing okay since Randall's death?"

He nodded, not looking at me. "I'm good. I guess." He wore his sadness like a costume.

"I'm sorry about his death. Especially to die in such a horrible way. My heart goes out to Vonda and Caleb. It's going to be rough for them."

"Yeah." He paused. "I tried calling you yesterday. And I sent a text. Did you not get them?"

"I did. I was super busy."

He pursed his lips and nodded slowly. He wasn't buying it. "Yeah. So I heard. Vonda told me you visited her."

My heart beat faster. The thin ice was cracking under my feet. "It was the least I could do. To offer my condolences."

"Uh-huh." He studied me like a cat watching a bird, not with curiosity but predation.

Jeff shouted for Len.

Len said, "We'll talk later."

There seemed to be a threatening tone to his voice. But maybe I'd imagined it. I shuddered, making plans to avoid him at all costs.

211

That afternoon Jimmy phoned me. I stepped outside for privacy, pacing under the large oak at the end of the parking lot. Sweat slicked under my breasts and arms.

He said, "If you say I'm calling in any capacity other than friendship, I'll deny it."

"Okay. What's the matter?"

"I wanted you to know I've heard back from the forensic accountant. They compared the two thumb drives, the one from the office and the one you gave us. Most of the files were identical, but there were a few new files on his work thumb drive that completed the story. Someone at the distillery is definitely up to shady dealings. I won't tell you who until we've questioned him or her. But I wanted to thank you for giving us the documents and laptop because we've discovered someone has been skimming money from the distillery with a crooked vendor deal."

"What do you mean? Explain it like I'm a three-year-old."

"There are two competing vendors who want to sell you something to help your business. Vendor A and Vendor B. They both have good products, but one is more expensive than the other. Well, the cheaper one, Vendor B, comes to John Doe at your establishment and says if you give us the deal, we'll charge the same price as Vendor A but you actually pay the Vendor B price. This creates a surplus of funds. The surplus is then kicked back to John Doe, who helped secure the deal for Vendor B. Vendor B gets a steady influx of business and John Doe gets money under the table. Everyone wins. Except the company, that is."

Clarence. It had to be him who killed Bryan. Clarence's family owned The Flying Eagle cooperage. Before Bryan died, he was trying to encourage Pierce to reevaluate supply purchases from The Flying Eagle. They charged the same as the Farleigh-Jackson cooperage, but they had poorer quality, charged a delivery fee, and made more mistakes in the orders. Clarence had been angry about Bryan's interference and appeared to take Bryan's discovery as a personal affront. No doubt, he was probably getting a kickback from his family's cooperage in exchange for sending business their way. Clarence might have killed Bryan as a means of protecting his family's business.

Jimmy was still talking. "Are you still there?"

"Yes. Go ahead."

"There's more. There are false invoices from false companies billing the distillery. The distillery paid this false invoice, but the money was funneled into a bank account that appeared like a company account."

"Clarence Ford? He's in charge of accounts payable/receivable. All invoicing goes through him. Did he kill Bryan?"

"I can't divulge that information."

I laughed. "Whatever. I know I'm right."

"This distillery is a cesspool of corruption. I don't know what's going on there. But we've also discovered, as I'm sure Bryan did, that there were discrepancies with inventory as well as reports filed that bottles were missing when shipments were delivered."

"So?"

"So, if there were only one or two missing bottles or cases, I'd blame it on a clerical error. However, in the past year, several cases and dozens of bottles have been reported missing either in inventory counts or in client deliveries. Which tells me there's some sort of fraud involved. Either the company is intentionally shorting their clients or a worker on the inside is stealing the bourbon for personal use or, more likely, resale."

It was a slap in the face. Immediately, my mind jumped to the night of the barbeque. Len, Randall, and Keith all worked at the distillery. They'd been acting suspiciously the night of the barbeque, whispering, huddled around a box in the garage. They'd sold something for a hefty price to Burt. But if that was what they were doing, how were they getting the bottles to sell?

"You still there?"

"Yeah." I glanced out across the parking lot toward the rickhouses. Keith was standing at the back of his delivery truck at the main rickhouse, talking on the phone while his truck was being loaded with small-batch crates and regular-batch boxes with the black Four Wild Horses stamp on the side. "Hey. I need to go. Thanks for calling."

"Is everything okay?"

"Yeah, sure. I'll call you later. Okay?" I hung up

I sprinted back to my desk as fast as my thong sandals would allow. Grabbing my purse and keys, I said to Len, "Sorry. I have an emergency and need to go."

He swiveled in his seat. "What's going on?"

"Thanks," I yelled, running down the hall. My phone chimed.

Jimmy texted **Watch your back at the distillery. Dangerous place.**

Jumping in my car, I flew down the driveway and fell in behind Keith's delivery truck. Allowing a few cars between Keith and me, I followed him out of Rothdale limits and a few miles along an old country road into Franklin County. I pulled my phone out, holding it in my lap, ready to take a picture or video if necessary.

About fifteen minutes later, we came to an abandoned gas station on the right side of the road. It was a white building with an arched APCO sign at the front and rusted red pumps, dating back to at least the sixties. The windows were all broken out and weeds had grown high around the building and the pumps. A rusted-out car without windows or wheels buried in weeds stood beside the building. Keith pulled the truck behind the building.

I couldn't stop, for fear of being seen. But my phone at the ready, I snapped a picture of the truck pulling into the abandoned lot and kept driving. My phone chimed and flashed a low battery notification. Ten percent. Ugh. I hadn't realized it was that low. Great. For a special bonus, the bars on my phone indicated No Service.

"Of course!" I pulled into a gated pasture access. Cows stared at me through the wooden fence, lazily chewing their cud. I searched for a charger cord but didn't have one with me. "Shoot, shoot, shoot." I hit my steering wheel. Checking the time, I decided to wait for fifteen minutes then go back.

When fifteen minutes had passed, I backtracked to the gas station. The truck was gone. But there must've been a reason why he'd pulled in behind the building. I eased my car into the parking lot and around the back of the building. There were two crates of small-batch and a box of regular-batch. Both boxes looked new and had the Four Wild Horses stamp on them. I looked around. But why would he leave it all the way out here?

Getting out of the car, nerves on edge, I glanced over my shoulder and approached the boxes. I didn't want to touch the boxes or take them with me because I was afraid of tainting the evidence. But I couldn't stay here either. He might've been dropping it here for someone else to pick it up. There was a high chance that person was dangerous. Instead, I took a picture and tried to send it to Jimmy, but it stalled. My battery power was now at six percent. Still no cell reception.

Growling, I stormed back to my car and tore out of the abandoned lot and headed back toward town. At the end of the road was a small convenience store where I finally received cell reception. But the power was down to five percent now. I took a chance and called Jimmy.

Thank heavens he answered. I didn't give him a chance to speak. "Hey. My phone's dying. Listen close. I'm at the Red Bird Convenience Store on Route 27. I need you here ASAP."

"Copy." He was in police mode. "Stay there. Don't move."

While I waited, I went into the store to find a charger cord. Since there wasn't one, I bought a snack pack of roasted cashews and a diet Kentucky Spice and waited in my car for Jimmy. I parked facing the road. Only two cars went by. A red Toyota pickup and a gold SUV with blacked-out windows and a hornet in the window. I'd seen that vehicle before. I fumbled with my phone to take a picture with whatever remained of my battery, but the SUV sped by too fast. I had no doubt it was the same car that forced me off the road after Bryan's funeral. I desperately wanted to follow it, but Jimmy told me to stay at the Red Bird until he got there. For once, I was going to listen and stay put, since the driver had tried to kill me before.

"Hurry, Jimmy. Hurry." I stared down the road.

After a few minutes, the gold SUV passed me again, leaving the area, again moving too quickly for me to get a picture or a view of the license plate. I dropped my head to the steering wheel. Several minutes passed and I heard sirens in the distance. Soon, Jimmy flew into the parking lot, sirens blaring.

Finally. He jumped out and ran to my car, hand on his gun, eyes scanning the area. "What's wrong?"

"Get in your car. Follow me. I want to show you something."

I led him to the abandoned gas station and we parked behind the building. The box and crate were gone. We got out of our cars and stared at the wall.

I explained how I'd happened to come across the boxes. "I can't show you the picture right now because my phone is dead. But there was a crate and a box here. They were both stamped with the distillery logo."

"Are you certain they contained bourbon?"

"I can't say for certain, but the chances were pretty high since they came straight from the distillery. I was afraid to touch them in case they were evidence."

"There could've been something else in the boxes. Or they could've been empty."

"I suppose that's a possibility. Also, remember the SUV that tried to run me off the road after Bryan's funeral? The same vehicle drove by the Red Bird and after about five minutes, it came back."

"You're sure it was the same vehicle?"

"I'd bet my life on it. It had the hornet sticker on the back. Like the one on your softball uniform."

He stroked his chin. "Interesting."

A silver glint in the grass caught my eye. "What's that?" I stepped forward and knelt. I used a nearby stick to push the grass aside. "Give me your flashlight."

"What is it?" He squatted beside me. "Lookie there." He pulled a pair of gloves out of his back pocket. He snapped on the gloves and lifted the item out of the grass to inspect it. It was a silver lighter with a gold rattlesnake wrapped around it. "It's a lighter."

"Nope. You're wrong," he said. "That's evidence."

I smiled. "I'll do you one better. That belonged to Dewey Stiggers."

He stood. "Now, what are the chances that Dewey, who once worked at the distillery, has been to a place where allegedly stolen bourbon has been dropped and picked up?"

"Have you been able to locate him yet?"

"No. I'm still trying."

"I hope you find him soon before another person dies."

Chapter Thirty-Six

Prim and I sat in front of the television with soup and sandwiches for supper. I was simply too tired to prepare anything else, and Prim's appetite had waned considerably. She nibbled at her grilled cheese and had eaten only a few spoonfuls of tomato soup before pushing her plate and bowl aside. Seemed all she wanted to do anymore was sleep.

We switched on the evening news.

A beautiful, middle-aged black woman with sparkling dark eyes came on. "This evening, police discovered a body in an abandoned vehicle in the parking lot of the Green Valley Motel in Miltonville. The man has been identified as thirty-six-year-old Dewey Stiggers of Rothdale. Right now the police are not commenting on the cause of death but we will report on the situation as the story develops."

Listening intently, I froze, a lump of grilled cheese in my mouth.

"The sheriff's department isn't releasing details about the cause of death but has determined foul play. Law enforcement officials ask that if anyone has any information related to Mr. Stiggers' death to please contact the tip hotline. If necessary, you can remain anonymous."

I finished my supper with Dewey on my mind. If Dewey was dead, what did that mean? If he was missing days ago, he probably didn't kill Randall. So, who did?

I stepped out on the porch to call Jimmy.

"Rook, it seems this is the beginning of a beautiful relationship."

"Jimmy." My voice was a warning. "This is serious. Dewey has been missing and now is found dead? This, on top of finding his lighter at the

218

drop site earlier? Do you think he could've killed Randall before he went missing?"

"It's not likely. The preliminary examination is suggesting he died well before Randall."

"But he was clearly at the drop site at some point. Maybe he was working with someone, they had a disagreement about something, and his partner or partners killed him and relocated the body. That someone might've been Keith, since he's the driver I saw at the abandoned lot."

"Possibly. Maybe Keith is being blackmailed by an outside person or persons. It's also possible Dewey was killed at the motel and the killer stole the lighter and lost it here. I can state, with some certainty, that Dewey knew about the missing bourbon and the players involved. Since he was a delivery driver, he might've been a participant."

"But to what degree?"

"That's the big question. I've seen things like this before among drug rings. This is likely a deal gone wrong. Maybe Dewey was involved and wanted more money. Or maybe he was skimming off the money he owed to his partners or was holding out on the goods, probably to sell and make the money for himself. Or it could be an outsider wanted what he had and killed him for it."

"Have you questioned Keith yet?"

"I went out there when I left you and he wasn't home. I'm going to call him in the morning and ask him to come out to the station. I want to keep it relaxed so I don't alert him we're on to him. If he refuses to talk, I'll apply a little more pressure until we have proof and can arrest him. I need you to lay low and, for the love of all that's holy, stay away from him."

"I don't feel comfortable—"

"Got to go. We'll talk soon." Sirens started as he ended the call.

Uneasiness settled over me as lightning bugs emerged against the setting sun and honeysuckle eased around me. Bryan, Randall, now Dewey. All worked at the distillery and all were dead. Keith and Clarence were primary suspects, but how did they connect? One was committing fraud the other involved in stealing inventory. Though, Len was also at least involved in

219

the bourbon theft. He was there in the garage at the barbeque. It had to be stolen bourbon they sold to Burt. But how deep did Len's involvement run? Bryan had discovered those crimes and was about to expose it all. So, he was killed. It was possible Randall or Dewey killed him. Or what if Len was involved in the murders, too? My stomach lurched as if taking the first drop on a roller coaster.

Of course, the killer could be an outsider, as Jimmy suggested. I hoped that was the case. That it was someone I'd never seen or met. But it was also possible the killer was alive and well and still working at the distillery. He could be sitting in the cubicle next to me.

The next morning, on my way to work, the skies were deep gray with the threat of storms. I hoped it would rain. We needed it. Jimmy called. I silenced The Traveling Wilburys' "End of the Line."

"Hey, do you have any free time this morning?"

"Why? What do you need?"

"I need you to come downtown to the sheriff's office to answer a few questions."

"About what?"

"It's best if we talk about that when you get here."

Odd. "I'm on my way to work. Can this wait?"

"We won't take much of your time."

"Why won't you tell me what it's about?"

"Rook—"

I put it together. "Are you saying I was involved with Dewey Stiggers' death?"

"Not necessarily."

"Or maybe you think I know something? I don't know anything. I was as shocked as anyone when I heard."

"Can you be here in about ten minutes?"

Annoyance prickled under my skin. "I can't believe you're doing this to me, Jimmy. You know me and you know I've been trying to help."

He sighed. "I'm doing my job."

CHAPTER THIRTY-SIX

"Fine," I snapped. "I'll be there in a bit."

The sheriff's office was a white stucco building with a bowed glass front. It was built about ten years ago as part of the downtown redevelopment project. Inside, the building was cool, crisp, and as sterile as a hospital. I waited in the lobby until Jimmy came to collect me.

He held the door open and motioned for me to come inside. "Thanks for coming in. I'm sorry to trouble you like this."

"I hope it won't take long. I hate to miss any more work."

"I understand." He opened a door on the left. I'd seen closets bigger than the interrogation room. It was a white room with a gray table by one wall and three blue chairs. I took the chair by the back wall. Jimmy sat in front of me. Though air-conditioned, the room was close, suffocating, especially with Jimmy and his muscular frame in there with me.

Jimmy said, "Can I get you anything to drink?"

"Coffee with cream, no sugar, would be great. Thanks."

He disappeared for about ten minutes and then re-entered the room with a Styrofoam cup full of coffee. He sat the cup in front of me. "I apologize for the wait. I had to make a new pot."

"Can we please get started? I need to get to work." I tasted the coffee. Grimacing, I pushed it aside.

He chuckled. "I probably should've warned you about the coffee. It's no Starbucks." He sat, one arm stretched out on the table. "I hope you can answer a few questions for me about Dewey Stiggers."

"I doubt it, but I'll try."

"You had a run-in with him recently, didn't you?"

"I did, but so did Bryan and Randall, and they're both dead. From what I understand, there were few people at the distillery who didn't have issues with him."

"Right," he said flatly.

The door opened, and Sheriff Goodman stepped in. He was as broad and tall as Jimmy but flabbier, though he probably had a strong physique in his youth. I took a deep breath, the feeling of suffocating intensifying. He sat with a sigh and took out his notebook.

"How did Dewey die?" I asked.

"We were hoping you could tell us." The sheriff sat back, legs spread, his notebook balanced on one leg, pen primed to write.

"I don't know. If you think I have anything to do with this, you're crazy." My voice tensed a few notches.

Sheriff Goodman said, "Let's start at the beginning. Shall we? How long have you worked at the distillery?"

"A little over two weeks. My friend Bryan helped me get the job after I quit my last one."

"Why did you quit the last one? Where did you work before?"

"I was an adjunct English instructor at U of B."

The sheriff eyed me with disbelief. "You quit teaching to work at a distillery? That doesn't track."

"I don't know what that has to do with anything."

"Points to your character."

"I quit because I got angry. I consistently performed full-time work for part-time pay, no benefits, and no voice on the committees, and I had to pay to park. My compensation fell far below the poverty line. I was fed up. I desperately needed money, steady work, and a viable income."

Goodman's face lit up. "You have a short temper?"

I glanced at Jimmy, who was focused on the sheriff. "Yeah. Especially where injustices are concerned."

"Would you say you have a violent temper?"

"Not especially," I said. "Certainly not enough to murder someone, if that's where you're headed with this."

Goodman leaned forward, his elbows on his knees. "You said you were desperate for money. Why so desperate?"

I bounced my leg. "For the same reasons any human needs money. Bills, food, shelter. I now have my grandma's medical bills to pay, along with a mountain of student loan debt. Oh, and I like to eat, have a car, and have a roof over my head."

"I get that. How desperate were you?"

"What do you mean?"

He sat up and glared at me with suspicion. "Desperate enough to steal a bunch of rare bourbon and kill anyone who gets in your way?"

"No! Are you insane?" I squeaked. "Jimmy, tell him. You know me. I'd never do the things he's suggesting."

Jimmy sat quietly, listening and taking notes. Why wasn't he supporting me?

Jimmy said, "I know. It's okay. Go on and answer the questions."

Goodman said, "I know you because I know your family. Poisonous fruit from a poisonous tree. Your father's in prison for being a crook. I'm thinking maybe one of his former associates reached out to you and offered you a bunch of money if—"

Icy rage crawled along my spine and shot out of my mouth. "I'm not going to listen to this trash. It's absurd." I looked again at Jimmy, hoping he'd intervene. "Jimmy, you're my ex-husband's best friend. You were in our wedding. You hung out with us all the time. How can you sit there and let him accuse me of these things?"

Jimmy said, "Rook, no one's accusing you. We're conducting an investigation, trying to figure out who stole the bourbon and killed those men."

"Here's what I know." Goodman raised his voice, shouting me down. "This distillery didn't have any problems until you got hired. Then you come along and, within a couple weeks, there have been two murders and a bunch of rare, expensive bourbon stolen."

"You mean three murders. Bryan Bishop was murdered, too."

"That's inconclusive."

I gaped at the two officers. "I'm not going to sit here and listen to this. I've done nothing but try to help you. I'm telling you that Bryan's death is tied in to all this. Because you haven't discovered the connection yet doesn't mean it isn't true." I gathered my purse and shot out of my seat. "Am I under arrest?"

The sheriff sat back, amused, one hand on the table primed to write, the other balancing a cup of coffee on his knee. "Now, Miss Campbell, there's no need to get upset. We're having a conversation."

"Am I under arrest?"

Jimmy said, "No. You're free to go."

I stormed out of the room.

Jimmy followed behind me. "Rook, wait."

I didn't stop until we got out in the parking lot. I spun on him. "What's wrong with you? How could you believe I'd have anything to do with those crimes?"

"I don't. But the sheriff wanted me to call because he figured you wouldn't come in if he asked you. He's my boss. I can't disobey his orders."

That tamped down my anger a bit. I sighed. "But you know me."

"Yes, I do. I don't think for a minute you did anything wrong." He squinted at the sun. "I followed you out here because I wanted to tell you that Bryan's toxicological screening came back. You may be right. There was definitely poison in his system. I told them to look for English Yew. We should know something soon."

"Why did Goodman act like there isn't a connection? Why's he treating me like a criminal?"

"He's working you, digging for any additional information he can use. That's it. It's not personal. It's only an investigation technique. We're interviewing everyone."

"No. You're not. You're interviewing persons of interest."

"It's a formality. That's all."

"I guess you'll be saying that when you slap the cuffs on me, too. Huh?"

"I'm not the enemy here."

"Neither am I. You'd better remember that."

Chapter Thirty-Seven

I arrived at work an hour late, still mad as a wet hen. Storming into the main building, I headed straight for the break room in search of chocolate. I had some heavy feelings to eat.

Holly and Len were gathered at the coffee machine, whispering and pouring their respective cups of coffee. It seemed like an intense conversation. They stopped talking when they realized I entered the room.

I tried to ignore them as I searched for my credit card.

Len approached me and ran his hand over my back. "Good morning. I tried calling you last night."

My stomach knotted under his touch and bile rose in my throat. I stepped away from him under the pretense of searching the vending machine in the corner. I wasn't in the mood to play his game this morning. "I know. I was busy." I slipped my credit card into the reader on the machine.

Holly sniped under a veil of humor, "You must've been really busy. Because we all started work an hour ago."

I selected a Hershey bar with almonds and fished it out of the vending machine. I definitely wasn't in the mood for Holly. I wanted them to know that I'd been talking to the sheriff to see if I could get a read on their reactions. But I also wanted to say it in vague enough terms to put them on edge while also trying to protect myself in case they got any ideas about retaliation. "I guess you'll have to discuss that with the sheriff's office."

Holly and Len exchanged a serious look.

Len said, "Why were you there?"

"I had to go in for questioning."

"Why?" Len frowned.

I put on an air of nonchalance. "They're interviewing people since there've been too many deaths surrounding this place." I opened the candy bar.

Len and Holly exchanged a glance loaded with fear and concern. *Bingo!*

Holly flipped her hair with a toss of her head. "Nonsense. There's no killer at this distillery. We're like a family here."

When I bit into the candy, the creamy chocolate shot serotonin and happy feelings directly into my brain. My body relaxed a little. "Funny, because from everything I've seen, most murderers kill people they know."

She sipped her coffee. "If it is murder, what do they know? Did they tell you anything?"

This might be a good opportunity to draw them out a little further and gauge their responses. "They aren't going to tell me details of the case, Holly. But I wonder who would want Bryan, Dewey, or Randall dead? I wonder how they all connect?"

Holly said, "I don't know."

I took another bite of the candy bar. "Actually, I've heard there are a few people who had problems with Bryan. Everyone had problems with Dewey. Not sure how Randall connects, except he and Dewey fought. Heck, maybe Dewey killed Bryan and Randall and then killed himself when he couldn't live with the guilt."

Holly's eyes lit up. She seemed on the verge of shouting *Eureka!* "That's the best explanation I've heard. I bet that is how it happened. Dewey did act awfully troubled."

Len leaned against the soda machine. "How did Dewey die? Did the sheriff say?"

"Nope." I bit into the chocolate. "But logic dictates it wasn't natural circumstances if they're interviewing people." I spun on my heel and left the room, but stopped to linger outside the door.

Holly hissed, "You need to take care of *that* immediately."

They were definitely talking about me.

"Okay. Okay. I will."

"And another thing. Did you talk to Keith about...you know?"

I pretended to be texting so passersby wouldn't know I was eavesdropping.

Holly said, "He screwed up. None of this was supposed to happen. He shouldn't have—"

"Hush. Do you want someone to hear?"

"Don't tell me to hush. That idiot Keith almost..."

Dang it. Lucia was coming toward me and would likely draw attention to my presence, so I moved quickly away from my spot toward Lucia and greeted her first as I passed her and moved toward the marketing pit.

Sitting at my desk, I stared at my computer's sign-on screen, thinking about what I'd heard between Holly and Len. What had Keith done? He must've been involved with Randall's murder. Maybe even Dewey's. Recalling the thin, quiet guy I'd met at the barbeque, I could well imagine him stealing bourbon. But he didn't seem like the murdering sort. He seemed too laid back to exert the effort it would take to be a killer. However, it seemed Len and Holly were involved in whatever Keith had done, but to what extent?

Chapter Thirty-Eight

I dropped some papers by Holly's office. She wasn't at her desk, so I placed the papers in the box at the corner of her desk. The picture frame on her desk caught my attention. It was a rustic wood folding frame. One side was her as a U of B cheerleader. The other was her husband standing by a gold SUV parked in front of a Tudor-style home. He was wearing a Hornets uniform identical to the one Jimmy had worn to my house several days ago.

I recognized the house from the pictures I'd seen on her Facebook page. The gold SUV looked a great deal like the one that had tried to run me off the road—the same one that drove by the abandoned gas station where Keith had dropped the bourbon. However, I couldn't see if there was a hornet sticker because of how the SUV was angled. Looking closer at the home behind the SUV, I noticed something else. Shrubs around the house. They looked a great deal like English Yew.

Holly spoke behind me, causing me to jump. "Can I help you?" She sounded vexed.

"Oh, uh, I was dropping off these papers and I saw these pictures." A memory nibbled around the back edges of my mind, just out of reach of recall. "You have a lovely home."

"Thanks." She stepped around her desk, taking her seat. "It cost way more than we could afford, but it was worth it. I love my house. There's also a swimming pool in the backyard and a Jacuzzi tub in the master suite."

"Wow. Sounds opulent." I looked at Holly, struggling to put on a fake smile. "I like this SUV, too. I'm thinking about getting a car like this. What kind is it?"

"Cadillac Escalade." She stared at her computer screen. "It's my husband's pride and joy. He won't hardly let me drive it. Sometimes I sneak out in it on the weekends, though, to go grocery shopping or to Pilates."

Or to run people off the road in an attempt to kill them. I tried to keep my voice steady. "I like it. It's a cool car."

"You know, I'm super busy here. So…if there's nothing else you need…"

"Well, I was curious about something else. I love the landscaping around your house. What kind of shrub is that? That would be perfect for my front yard."

She took the picture from my hand and returned it to her desk. "I don't know. Something my landscaper put in."

"Oh? You have a landscaper? I'd love to know who you use. I have a bunch of work to be done in my yard, and I wasn't blessed with a green thumb."

She glared at me. "I don't know."

She was lying. She must suspect I was on to her. "I need to get my work done. Are we finished here?"

I rushed from Holly's office and out of the building, ducking behind the visitor's center. I texted Jimmy. **Do you know a player on the Hornets team last name Parker? Does his wife work at the distillery?** I waited for a minute, but he didn't respond.

Fine. I opened Facebook. Holly took pictures of everything. I was willing to bet she'd either taken pictures of her landscaper or they were in her friends' list. While I was in there, I copied the pictures of Holly's house that showed the yews and the gold Escalade and sent them to Jimmy, telling him they belonged to Holly Parker at the distillery. Then I searched her friends' list. There it was: Primal Joy Lawn Care. They were a small family-owned business. They wouldn't be too concerned about annoying privacy concerns.

I dialed the number and an older lady answered. I dipped into a deeper country accent because people in these parts tended to trust or at least underestimate a down-home accent. "Hello, I'm a friend of Holly Parker's. She tells me you take care of her yard."

"Yes."

"Well, I was interested in planting shrubs around my house, and I love the ones she has in front of her house. Can you tell me what kind those are?"

"One minute." She put me on hold. I assumed she was consulting a written record or portfolio. Or maybe she was asking one of the workers. She came back on. "Sugar, those are English Yews."

My stomach dropped. That meant Holly had access to the poison that might've killed Bryan.

The lady was still talking. "Would you like to schedule a time for us to come out and have a look at your property? We can provide an estimate onsite."

"I'd better talk to my husband. You know how that is. Then I'll give you a call back."

We wished each other a good day and hung up. With shaking hands, I texted Jimmy the information I'd discovered, along with Primal Joy's phone number.

When I returned to the marketing pit, Marla seemed agitated. "There you are. We have to stay late tonight."

"Why? How long?" Mentally I raced to arrange for Prim's care. Maybe Batrene could stay later.

Marla kneaded her neck. "At least a couple hours, though we may have to go longer."

"What happened?"

"The headlining band backed out. The drummer's leaving the band. So, we have to redo all the fliers, press releases, social media content—everything that has their name on it. We have to find a replacement band. Jeff knows a band. He's calling them now. We're waiting for confirmation, as soon as they confirm, we'll need to replace the social media first."

"Okay. I'll help you." Sitting at my desk, I phoned Batrene to ask if she could stay later with Prim.

"I wish I could, hon, but tonight's my nephew's first football game with the Thoroughbreds. Bonnie and I are going to go watch him play."

Crap. I dialed Millie next. She was working at the massage center. My shoulders tightened. I dialed the only other person I knew—the one I was trying to avoid calling. I blew out a breath. I hit Cam's name on my phone.

When he answered, I said, "Hey, I know you're probably upset with me and I don't deserve your kindness, but I have to work late tonight and I need someone to sit with Prim. For an hour or two at five, when Batrene leaves."

"I'm not upset with you. Why would you think that?"

"Because of the whole thing with Jacie."

"That's on Jacie. She made a dumb choice. Besides, she and I were having problems anyway."

Relief unraveled the twist in my shoulders. "If it helps, I'm sorry for what happened. When things have cooled off, I'll apologize to her too. I never meant to come between you."

"Okay. I can only sit for a couple of hours. I'm short-staffed now with Jacie gone. Can you be home at seven?"

"I'll try my best."

I hung up and jumped into my work.

At about six-fifty, I gathered my things. I spoke to the group, "I hate to leave, y'all, but my grandma needs me."

"That's okay," Len said. "See you tomorrow."

"I'll come in early tomorrow to get caught up. Leave me notes about what needs to be done."

The evening sun cast an amber light across the parking lot. As I walked to my car, I texted Cam to let him know I was on my way. I received a text notification from Jimmy. I put my key in the door and was trying to open Jimmy's text, when there was a scuff behind me like the scrape of a shoe on the asphalt.

The sound had barely registered when a jolt of pain rushed through the back of my head. My vision blurred as something metallic dropped to the asphalt and someone ran away. I fell against my car and slid to the ground. A haze flooded my brain. I couldn't think straight, but I knew I needed help. A high-pitched ringing filled my ears, and nausea rippled through my stomach.

I held my phone close and spoke. "Siri, dial nine-one-one." Then I vomited.

Within fifteen minutes, help arrived.

Jimmy was shouting, "Her car is over here."

The next thing I heard was shoes running and scuffling on the pavement.

Jimmy crouched beside me. "Rook, Rook... You okay?"

His hazel eyes, shiny as marbles, were close to mine.

"I'm sleepy."

He spoke to the people behind him. "I believe she's concussed."

A blurry man knelt in front of me. "Ma'am, I'm going to shine a light in your eyes, okay?"

The light stabbed through to the back of my head, sending a wave of nausea through my body. He spoke to Jimmy and the other man. The men loaded me onto a gurney.

The man kept shaking my shoulder or patting my hands. "We need you to stay awake, okay, ma'am?"

They fed me into the back of an ambulance.

Jimmy shouted, "Rook, I have your stuff. I'll follow you to the ER."

The door slammed.

The hospital was a buzz of confusion and my head was electrified with pain. Everything was intensely bright and loud. A cacophony of voices and noises and lights. I closed my eyes.

Jimmy nudged me. "I need you to stay awake."

"I'm awake."

"It's easier to tell you're awake if you can keep your eyes open. You can't go to sleep."

I groaned. I didn't feel like arguing or fighting. Fatigue weighed on me and my head throbbed. Sleep would make the pain stop.

Jimmy nudged me again. "Hey."

I was put through a battery of tests that included answering questions, reflexes, coordination, balance, and senses, and finally they did a CT scan. I was enough in my head to know this was going to amount to thousands of dollars.

After the CT scan, I was rolled back to the staging area in the ER. I told Jimmy I needed to get out of here. I tried to sit up and climb out of bed. My head swam, dizzy.

Jimmy chuckled and guided me to lay back. "Whoa, hold on there. You're not going anywhere."

"Need to get home to Prim." I tried to sit up again.

He kept a hand on my shoulder. "Nope. Not until the doctor clears you to leave."

"Can you at least call Prim and Cam. Let them know?"

"Already taken care of. Relax."

I lost all concept of time, lying in the emergency room. Maybe I'd been there an hour, maybe five.

The doctor finally came around. "Everything looks normal. There's no swelling or internal bleeding. The concussion is mild. You were very lucky."

"Hardheadedness runs in the family." I smiled at my joke.

The doctor continued. "You need rest, ice, a bland diet for the nausea, and Tylenol or Advil for the pain. Minimize your time on electronics, including watching television, for a day or two. No driving." The doctor looked at Jimmy. "She needs close observation for at least twenty-four hours."

After the orderly rolled me out to Jimmy's car, Jimmy tried to help me in the car, but I pushed his hand away. "I'm not broken."

Jimmy laughed, handing my things to me.

"What happened to me?"

"You don't remember anything?"

"I was at my car. Checking my phone."

"You were cracked in the back of the head with a copper pipe. We found it on the ground by your car. We're going to dust it for prints."

Propping my elbow against the window, I leaned my head into my hand. "I'm not holding out hope you'll find anything. Anyone with half a brain cell would wear gloves."

"True. Do you remember anything at all that might help identify the person?"

"I wish. I remember being on my phone. That's it."

When we arrived at my house, Cam came running out to the car. "You were supposed to be home hours ago." He helped me out of the car. "You okay?"

"Yeah, I'm fine."

Prim met us at the door in her pink gown and robe, holding the door open. "Oh, my heavens. You okay, hon?"

"I'm fine." Irritation needled my skin. Now I knew how Prim felt when we fussed over her. Must be a genetic trait. I wondered if my mom had been that way too.

Cam led me to the couch and sat me down. "Who did this to you?"

Jimmy said, "It's probably best not to ask her questions right now. Those can wait until the morning."

"The hell we can." Cam lifted me forward to push a pillow behind me. "Someone tried to run her off the road a few days ago and now this? I want to know who's trying to hurt her."

Jimmy hooked his thumbs on his utility belt. "She may still be confused and hazy. She needs rest right now."

Cam said, "Man, what she needs is for you to do your job."

Jimmy's voice lowered. "I'm going to pretend you didn't say that to me."

Cam rubbed the back of his head with one hand. "I'm sorry, man. Really. But this is…"

"I know you're worried. You should be. There's something bad going on at the distillery."

"I've been trying to get her to quit. But she won't listen to me."

Prim brought ginger ale, crackers, and chicken noodle soup on a tray and prodded me to eat while she hovered nearby. I drank the ginger ale and nibbled a soda cracker, watching the scene between Jimmy and Cam.

"Are you getting anywhere at all in the investigation?" Cam said.

"We are, but these things take time."

Cam motioned at me with an open palm. "It looks like your time is running out. The next time, which I hope there isn't one, she may not be so lucky."

"I promise you, I'm doing everything I can."

"I'm sleepy," I said.

The room fell silent, except for the late night news playing softly on the television. Everyone looked at me.

"Great," Cam said. "Now what?"

CHAPTER THIRTY-EIGHT

Jimmy said, "We're going to run fingerprints. Right now that's all we can do."

"At least I was attacked on a Friday so I'll have the weekend to recover." I chuckled at my own lame joke.

Cam replied, "You're not going back to that place."

"I can't quit."

"Do you want to end up like Bryan?"

The air left the room. My face flushed.

He raised a hand. "I went too far. I apologize."

My head pounded. "No, I don't want to end up like him. But I'm doing this for him." My voice was rising in volume. "I need to know who killed him. Do you understand that? He was like a brother, and I can't sit idly by. I'll go crazy if I can't help Bryan and Batrene. I owe it to them."

Chapter Thirty-Nine

I wasn't expecting a visitor. I'd just finished my shower and was in the upstairs bathroom still dressed in my flannel robe and plucking my eyebrows in preparation to go to Kim and Keith's house for the Jessie Bell's makeup party.

There was a knock on the kitchen door downstairs. Though I wasn't exactly presentable, I jogged down the stairs to see who the visitor was because I didn't want Prim to be troubled to get up. As I hit the last step, I peeked around the corner and shrunk back as if I'd stepped in ice water. Len. *Dang it!*

The notion of ignoring him passed my mind briefly. But Prim was shouting from living room. "Who's at the door?" She lowered the volume on the television.

When I glimpsed Prim scrambling to get up, I knew I had no choice. "Don't get up," I called out. "I'll get the door. It's Len."

"Who?"

"That guy from work I went to dinner with."

"Oh, hmm." Her voice was flat with disapproval. "He isn't going to stay is he?"

"No. I'll go outside to meet him."

"Good." She turned up the volume again.

I opened the door and he moved to step inside as I stepped outside and closed the door behind me.

He was dressed in mirrored sunglasses and a tan sports jacket over a black T-shirt and dark blue jeans. Apparently *GQ* was missing a model. The corner of his mouth lifted sideways in a smirk and he removed his sunglasses. "Hey there, sunshine...."

"Hey." I didn't smile and stood against the door.

He scanned my robe and red, puffy eyebrows. "Thought I'd come by for a bit. You busy?"

I would not soon forget the way he used me in his game with Holly. I had to work with him, so I'd be civil (even if it gave me acid reflux), but that was going to be the best he'd get from me. "I am, actually. I've been invited to your sister's house for a Jessie Bell makeup party."

"Oh." His brows shot up and he laughed. "I'm sorry. I guess I should've warned you that you'd be targeted for one of her makeup parties."

"I don't mind," I lied. Sort of. I didn't really want to get my face made up or buy over-priced makeup, but I did want to see if I could dig up some information on Keith while I was there.

An awkward tension loomed between us. He shifted from foot to foot unsure of how to handle my lack of hospitality. He scratched behind his ear. "Well, I just, uh, came by because..." He tucked his hands in his pockets and shrugged. "Concerned. I've been trying to call you. I had a good time the other night and I was hoping we might go out again sometime."

My heart sped up. He wanted to be alone with me. When I'd left the break room yesterday Holly had indicated to Len that he needed to 'take care of *that*.' I'd assumed she'd meant me. What I didn't know was how he was planning to do it. He didn't give me a chance to answer and I didn't like his nervous demeanor.

"Can I come in? Maybe we can talk for a bit?"

"I don't think so. I need to take care of Prim before I leave."

"I see." He glanced out at the drive then down at his shiny black loafers before turning puppy-dog eyes on me. "Have I done something to upset you or make you mad?"

Oh, boy that was rich! Again, he didn't give me time to answer.

"I was thinking, what if, maybe, you and I took a little drive right now. Just so we can talk about whatever is bothering you."

It was all I could do to keep from laughing in his face. There was no way on earth I was getting in a car alone with him. He must've been planning to get me alone somehow so he could do to me what was done to Dewey or Randall?

I needed to be careful here. I didn't know exactly what he was involved with or how dangerous he was. But anger shot through me, soon suppressing the fear and throwing my mouth into full gear. "You're a piece of work aren't you? How dare you come here to my home, unannounced, trying to act like nothing happened." My plan was to make him think I knew *only* about the affair and that I had no suspicions regarding the bourbon or the murders.

His eyes darted. "I don't know what you mean."

"Don't you play dumb with me you ol' tick-infested skunk. You've been dating Holly. A married woman with kids. All while trying to get with me." I crossed my arms. "How long has that been going on? And I wonder why you brought me into the picture?"

He lifted his hands. "Wait, no, i-i-it's not what you think."

"Yeah right. You think I'm stupid? I've seen you two together out by the pond. I saw you kiss her."

He closed his eyes and dropped his head back, throwing his hands over his face. "Ahhhh." He rubbed his face then looked at me. "Okay. Busted. How long have you known?"

"Does it really matter? I know now and I don't appreciate you using me in whatever sick little game you've got going on between you and Holly. You're going to leave me out of it."

"I told her it wouldn't work. She was afraid people were going to find out about us and so she wanted me to use you to take attention off of us."

"That's sick."

"Hey, look, if I hurt you or anything, I'm..."

I threw my hands up. "Save it. I don't need or want your useless apologies you trashy jerk. The only thing I want from you is to get off my porch before I go get my rifle."

He lifted his hands again. "Fine. Fine."

The phone rang inside my house.

He paused at the door. "You said you saw us together?"

"Yes."

"Did you hear anything?" His attention was sharp, his dark eyes piercing. He was trying to read my face for the slightest hint of a lie. The phone stopped still ringing.

I drew from every ounce of acting ability and lying gifts out of the deepest recesses within me. I scrunched my face. "No. Of course not. I was too far away." I drove forward with a flash of anger to make my ruse convincing. "But I didn't need to be able to hear when my eyes could see the truth plain as day." I noticed over Len's shoulder, Batrene exited her house and came rushing through her yard toward my house. She had Prim's glass casserole dish. But I could tell by her pace and the way she carried the dish in one hand like a bat that she wasn't coming for a neighborly visit. Bless her, she was coming to my aid.

Silent tension as thick as a humid Kentucky summer hung between Len and me as we studied each other, trying to read each other's lies.

Prim knocked on the window behind me, causing Len to glance in her direction before locking eyes with me again.

Prim opened the window. "Boy, it's time for you to go." When Len didn't move, she added. "Go on. Git. Skeedadle, you old polecat."

Batrene called out. "Hey, girl. Everything okay?"

Len glanced over his shoulder at Batrene, then back at Prim. He said to me. "You didn't hear anything Holly and I talked about?"

"I said I didn't. And between you and me, which of us is more likely telling the truth?" Of course we were both lying at this point, but his lies were way bigger, more hurtful, and more frequent; I felt justified in using the tactic against him, hoping he'd have enough of a guilty conscience to convince him that he was worse and thereby exonerate me in his estimation.

He nodded. "All right then." He opened the door and paused, looking at me through the screen. His voice and eyes filled with a dark threat. "You'd better hope you and I can get along at work." He jogged down the steps, letting the door slam. He swept past Batrene who stood at the corner of the screened porch, clutching the glass dish, ready to weaponize it.

I stepped across the porch to shout at him as he crossed the yard to his car. "You and Holly had better stay out of *my* way then."

Later that Sunday afternoon I pulled up in front of Kim and Keith's house about ten minutes before six. The heat was abating and the sun cast a mellow, honeyed light over the neatly groomed Tilkey yard. Though it had rained recently, the yellowed grass hadn't fully recovered from the brutal summer. The ranch house was simple but well-kept. A few shade trees were perched in the front and back yards and a walkway from the drive to the porch was trimmed in bright marigolds and zinnias among the hostas. A detached garage with a truck backed up to its open door stood at the back of the house.

There were already a few cars in the driveway. I opted to park along the road, straddling the bank of a shallow ditch, so I could leave early. I shouldn't have driven at all. But I'd convinced myself it'd be okay if I drove extra slow and wore my darkest sunglasses. In spite of my precautions though, dizziness swept over me and the sunlight stabbed painfully into my eyes, webbing pain through my brain and all through my head. I lowered my face closer to the A/C. The cool air reduced my nausea and pain, if only temporarily.

Dread weighed heavy and cold as marble in my gut. I was crazy for coming here. I should've listened to Prim and stayed home. I was pretty sure Keith had contributed, somehow, to Randall's death. He might've been involved in Dewey's, too. But I had to do this. It might be my only opportunity to get close to Keith and possibly gather information. I needed to stay cool and stay low. Blowing out a breath, I reminded myself of the promise I'd made to Prim to stay no more than an hour. Already, I was looking forward to being at home in my pajamas with a bowl of popcorn, watching *SVU* or *Cold Case Files*.

Cake carrier in tow, I exited the car and started across the yard. A hot summer wind waved across the yard, sending the wind chimes into a broken song. I heard a noise from the detached garage, like metal dropping on the concrete floor.

A truck with a hitch trailer was backed up to the mouth of the garage.

Only the tail of the trailer was inside the garage. The trailer was loaded with crates, partially covered with a blue tarp. When the breeze lifted the tarp, I noticed a black stamp on the side. I squinted but couldn't make it out. Maybe I could sneak around there to have a peek before Kim knew I was here.

As I neared the garage, music wafted toward me and Keith rose from behind the lawnmower, whistling to himself. He twisted to take a tool from the workbench behind him, pausing to mutter to himself. After a moment, he resumed whistling and ducked behind the machine again.

Fear cut off my breath. I shuddered to think I was within fifty yards of a possible murderer. I veered toward the front door, hoping to avoid being seen. If he was like most men, he'd have no idea who his wife had invited to a makeup party, and I wanted to keep it that way. As I stepped on the porch, a car pulled into the drive. A few women got out, chattering and laughing, and joined me on the porch, choking me in a variety of perfumes.

I held my breath and rang the doorbell. My headache returned with a vengeance.

Kim answered the door. I exhaled a quick hello and ducked inside to put some distance between me and the Perfume Queen. The well-chilled air of the house was filled with the delicious spicy, peppery scent of fajitas and tacos. That was a perfume I certainly appreciated. My stomach growled with a demand for food. Food first. Then I'd figure out a way to investigate what was under that tarp-covered trailer in the garage.

Twelve to fifteen women, ranging in age from thirty to sixty, packed into the living room. They perched on the brown leather couches, red floral armchairs, matching footstools, and cushioned dining chairs brought from the dining room.

A brief glance of the group in smart casual summer wear—neatly pressed linen Bermuda shorts and sleeveless blouses or sundresses of varying lengths—told me I'd fit in well enough in my pin-striped palazzo pants, black cap-sleeved shirt, and black sandals.

Kim held a clear Solo cup filled with a red frozen margarita. I eyed her drink with envy. She greeted me with the happiness of a hostess whose party was going well and who was half-lit on margaritas.

"Rook, come on in," she shouted over the loud conversations in the room. "Oh, I see you brought cake. Is this the apple-bourbon cake you told me about?"

"Sure is." My wide smile went with my too-peppy voice I used for uncomfortable social situations. "Apple spice cake infused with bourbon and topped with a caramel-bourbon frosting." I leaned in. "Good thing this isn't the church group."

She laughed loudly and nudged me. "You crack me up." Her eyes were little slits, as if they were too heavy to hold open. "But I promise at least half of them drink on the sly." She snorted a laugh.

Kim was definitely deep in her cups, as Jane Austen and Georgette Heyer might say. I sure pitied the woman who sat for a makeover tonight.

Kim turned to the group at large. "Hey, y'all, this here is Rook and she brought us an apple spice cake spiked with bourbon."

Greetings and whoops went up among the ladies. They fell into a more animated chatter among themselves.

Kim lightly tapped my arm. "C'mon, I'll show you to the kitchen." She scooted unevenly across the floor in her bare feet and spoke over her shoulder. "The food's almost done."

We passed through the arched doorway into the kitchen.

"There are tortilla chips and sausage queso there. Help yourself. Let's get you started on a margarita. Woo-hoo!"

The kitchen was best described as cozy. Her appliances were stainless steel and black and complemented the terracotta floors, cherry-stained cabinets, and black marble countertops. The theme wasn't readily apparent. She had a few signs on the walls that said "Blessings" or "This house serves the Lord" or "Family" and the obligatory "Live, Laugh, Love." Several of the knickknacks and pictures had sunflowers and watering cans.

She slid bowls around on the island to make space. "Put your cake here. Let me get a look at that."

I lifted the lid on the bundt cake with bourbon glaze.

"Mm-mm mercy. That looks good. I'm half-tempted to take a piece now."

There was never a shortage of desserts at any gathering in the South. There was a Derby pie, a peanut butter pie, and a plate of cookies and brownies.

"Go for it. I'm pretty sure there will be some left. We have plenty of sweets." My stomach growled.

She snorted and sniggered as she cut out a large chunk of cake. She plopped it onto a paper plate and wrapped it in plastic wrap. "I'm going to hide it right in here." She put the slice in the pantry and replaced the lid.

Kim moved to the back counter while I filled a small plate with tortilla chips and sausage queso. I stepped over to the window, peeking out to try to catch a glimpse of the tarp-covered trailer, but it was tucked away in the garage behind the truck, so I couldn't see it. But it didn't matter. As long as Keith was out there, I wouldn't be able to sneak around.

Kim introduced me to the margarita machines. "There's regular and strawberry. You won't need much. I made them strong. Salt and sugar for your cup right here." She shook a container in each hand. "If you don't want that..." She opened the fridge door and pointed. "There's iced tea there, water, Coke, and juice." She closed the door and opened a small cabinet near the fridge. "If you want to make yourself a cocktail, here's vodka, bourbon, and rum. You make yourself at home."

She scooted to the stove and stirred the fajita and taco meats while I begrudgingly filled a cup with iced tea.

"These are ready..." Kim switched off the burners. She dumped the meats into their respective bowls then refilled her glass with a little of each margarita flavor. "I like mixing them." She swayed in place. Kim shouted, "Hey, girls, supper's on!"

I moved away to a corner of the kitchen to eat my nachos while the herd pushed into the kitchen and began filling paper plates with chips, shells, meats, cheeses, and all the tomato, lettuce, peppers, salsa, sour cream, and guacamole fixings. The chatter hadn't stopped. The doorbell rang, and Kim left the kitchen to answer the door.

As quickly as they'd entered the kitchen, the group left, taking their chatter with them. I jumped in at the end of the dwindling line and filled my plate. As I stood in the entryway, searching for a seat, Holly stepped through the doorway in a blue sleeveless sundress. She smiled and exchanged a few words with Kim.

Someone across the room shouted, "It's Holly! Hey, girl." She skipped over to hug Holly and talk enthusiastically with her.

I sat on a footstool by an armchair near the window. It was a less crowded area—comfortable enough for now. At events like this, people played musical chairs, so I'd land a prime spot in an armchair soon and plant myself there for the rest of my visit.

Making small talk with strangers was an art I'd never mastered. I tortured myself and the women beside me with awkward conversation centered on weather, work, and food.

Holly passed through to the kitchen, waving and fake smiling at people. She hadn't stopped talking since she entered the room. I couldn't help but admire her ability to work a room. Holly looked directly at me, no, through me, and turned away without acknowledging my existence.

Fine by me. I preferred genuine people. Besides, not only was she a married woman catting around outside of her marriage, she was angry at me for unwittingly dating her illicit possibly criminal boyfriend. That took some kind of nerve.

Soon after everyone ate, Kim carried a box into the living room. "Okay, ladies. I wanted to show you a few of the latest products, then we'll eat dessert. And I have lots of samples." She set the box on the table and began pulling out a wide range of makeup and perfume samples and a few full-sized testers. The women flocked to the box and began digging through everything, spraying perfumes and smelling their wrists, and rubbing lotions and foundation into the backs of their hands.

Kim shouted over the voices, "I'm putting a basket right here. Put your name in the basket for a chance to win a free facial or a makeover. Whoever wins those will also take home a little goodie bag." She lifted two pink gift bags with white spiral bows and tufts of white tissue mushrooming from the top.

The women hooted.

"There will be one winner for each prize tonight. I'll draw names after dessert."

I didn't want to deal with the hassle of a facial, and I certainly didn't want a margarita-fueled makeover, so I let the other women crowd around to scramble for their chance to win. Besides, even sober, Kim put her makeup on with a spatula. Hating the feel of thick makeup, I preferred a natural look, thank you very much.

After the women had picked the samples pile clean and entered the drawing, they returned to their seats to compare and discuss each other's findings. I, along with a few other women, retreated to the kitchen to get our desserts before the kitchen was overtaken.

The scent of coffee filled the air. Kim had this hostess thing nailed down; she'd thought of everything. I loved a cup of coffee with dessert.

A lady was sitting at the small kitchen table. She was about fifty, square-jawed, with mid-length brown hair, layered and flipped up at the ends, with bangs cut across her forehead. She wore a white linen button-down tank with khaki shorts and white sandals. "This cake is one of the best cakes I've ever eaten."

"Thanks." I sliced the cake. "I made it."

"Oh, mercy." A lump of cake bulged in her cheek like a chipmunk. "You have to give me the recipe." She emanated kindness. She was an attractive, down-to-earth lady.

"Sure..."

"My husband loves bourbon. Especially that Devil's Kiss stuff. He's going to put us in the poor house going around buying all of it he can find."

"Ooooh. I wish I could afford to use Devil's Kiss in this cake. The spices in that bourbon would be a perfect complement."

She screwed up her face. "Yeeees. That'd be delicious." She crammed another bite into her mouth. She chewed with obvious delight. "How'd you get this cake so moist?"

"Sour cream."

"You know, I've heard that, but I've been too afraid to try it. It doesn't sound right." She swallowed her food. "Oh, I'm so rude..." She offered her hand. "I didn't introduce myself. I'm Linda Anderson."

Chapter Forty

I nearly choked on my cake. This was Burt's wife; the wife of the man who'd made a purchase at the garage the night of the barbeque. Fortunately, at that moment, the other women crowded into the room, which gave me a moment to collect myself. A few women came over to speak to Linda. Linda praised my cake and introduced me. "You have to try this cake. Seriously. It's one of the best things I've ever put in my mouth."

If I was careful and asked my questions in the right way, I might be able to find out exactly what Len, Keith, and Randall had been doing the night of the barbeque and what Burt had purchased. I had my suspicions, but I wanted them confirmed. I answered a few polite inquiries about the cake.

Soon the room cleared out again and I was left alone with Linda. We ate quietly for a moment while I grasped for the right way to broach the subject. I poked at a bite of cake. "You said your husband loves Devil's Kiss bourbon?"

"Oh, yeah. Adores it. He comes home every night after work and has two fingers of Devil's Kiss, warmed slightly."

"Kind of like a hot toddy." I smiled.

"He goes through a bottle in about a month. Sometimes he'll give a bottle to a special client." She chuckled, lifting her cup to her lips, and swallowed "Whew! I put too much rum in my Coke. I should probably get coffee, like you." She blinked slowly but didn't move.

"I'll get you a cup." I hoped to keep her talking. "How do you take it?"

"Three sugar, three creams."

I moved to the counter to fix her coffee.

"Anyway, I told him if he keeps up his pace, he'll put us in the poor house with all that bourbon."

"Sounds like he buys a lot of it."

She snorted and took a deep draw of margarita. "You know those safes which are a little bigger than a mini-fridge?"

"Yeah." I set the coffee in front of her.

"Thank you, sweetie." She plucked off a piece of cake, the fork hovering near her lips as she spoke. "He has one of those filled completely with nothing but Devil's Kiss bourbon." She pushed the fork into her mouth.

"Are you kidding me?" I gasped. "That's a lot of bourbon."

She chewed, "Right? And he's trying to figure out a way to store more."

"Wow. His liver might die before he drinks all that."

She shook her head. "It's not all for him. He says he knows a guy who can get him a good deal so he doesn't have to pay full sticker price."

A jolt shot through me as pieces began to fall into place. Burt knew three guys, in fact: Randall, Keith, and Len. I was willing to bet my eyeteeth that Burt purchased Devil's Kiss the night of the barbeque. Burt had asked for a much larger order and Randall hadn't seemed excited about the prospect. Keith seemed eager to fill it. Len played the middle and said they needed to talk about it more before dismissing the idea completely. They must've been behind the recent Devil's Kiss heist. They must've had it all planned out, only something went terribly wrong and Randall ended up dead. What happened there?

But I wanted to confirm I was on the track. "I'd love to get my hands on some discounted bourbon. Who can I speak to?"

She shrugged. "I don't know. Burt never told me. I asked once and he told me to mind my business. I know better than to press that issue."

Dang it! So close. I remembered the crates sitting on the trailer outside. I bet those crates were from the distillery and were full (or were once full) of Devil's Kiss bourbon. If I could sneak out there and take a picture, that surely should be enough proof for Jimmy to make an arrest.

"Rook! Rook!" Kim shouted from the living room. "Get in here, girl. You won the drawing for the makeover."

247

"That's impossible," I said to Linda. "I didn't enter the drawing."

"Who cares? Go get your makeover. It'll be fun."

Standing in the doorway of the kitchen, I scanned the living room, confused. "I didn't enter the makeover. I don't know how my name..."

Holly sat on the couch, smirking. "I entered your name, silly goose. I thought you might enjoy a makeover. A bit of a treat."

I pinched out a smile, but I looked daggers at Holly. I balled my fists. "I do appreciate the thought, but I don't wear much makeup. You might enjoy it more, Holly, since you wear more makeup than I do."

Holly flashed her dead-eyed grin. "No, I insist you get the makeover, Rook. Maybe you'll learn to apply it correctly. Then you'll enjoy wearing it more."

The other women didn't miss the barb. A few looked uncomfortable and others bit their lips to keep from smiling. Others sniggered behind their hands.

Kim grabbed me. "Oh, c'mon. Don't be shy." She led me to a chair. "This is my favorite part, y'all."

She seemed so genuinely happy that I stopped fighting it. But the worst part was strangers gawking at me while I received a makeover. If I'd been friends with these women, I could've borne it all with more humor. Grit layered my throat. I didn't like being the center of attention in this way. I burned with humiliation. I endured by feeling a sort of kinship with the lady next to me who had a slimy pink clay mask on her face.

Kim had a rough touch and pounded the foundation onto my skin with a sponge. "Your skin is pretty. You don't need much makeup. What do you use on your face?"

"I wash it in the morning and use Olay lotion."

"It's clear and smooth." She dipped her face close to mine as she doused my face with the third layer of foundation. Her breath reeked of onions and tequila. "I have some products..." She launched into a sales pitch about blah-blah rose toner and a serum with SPF whatever.

I responded with polite "Uh-huhs" and "Oh, I sees," but I had no intention of buying anything. I could only think of getting outside to peek under the tarp and snap a picture of it.

Squinting and tipsy, Kim brushed a darker shade in the hollow of my cheeks and around my forehead. Her face was too close.

She powdered my face, brushed on bright pink blusher, and powdered me again.

Holly was whispering with a friend, eyeing me, and giggling. The other women talked among themselves, a few chuckled. This was like a sorority hazing nightmare—or at least what I thought what a sorority hazing might be like since I could never afford to be in a sorority. Holly looked at her phone and was texting.

Kim selected a palette of blue eyeshadows. "Now, close your eyes." Kim dabbed my lids with a brush. "You need more color. Especially for your nighttime makeup."

When she paused, I dared to open my eyes.

She put her face near mine again. "Now, do this." She rolled her eyes upward as her mouth dropped open in the classic eyeliner/mascara application pose.

I sat very still while she applied the eyeliner and topped it off with heavy layers of mascara.

She stepped back and admired her work. "There. You look like you're ready for a night out." She handed me a mirror.

Yeah, as a hooker. I smiled at her. She seemed proud of her work, so I didn't want to hurt her feelings, though everyone appeared to be struggling not to burst out laughing at me. Let them laugh. I liked Kim. She was a warm, genuine person. I pulled on my brightest smile. "Thank you. I wish I could apply makeup as well as you can." I stood with a little stiffness. "I appreciate the makeover. That's sweet of you."

Holly lifted her phone. "Smile!" She snapped a picture of me before I'd realized what was happening. Then her thumbs tippity-tapped over her phone. Likely, she was sending the picture to Len so they could share a chuckle over it.

Kim beamed. "My pleasure. I wish I could've gone to cosmetology school. I love doing makeup."

My soft spot for her expanded.

"Don't forget your little goodie bag." She handed me one of the pink gift bags.

Holly walked out of the room, staring at her phone.

I heard a light bang, like a door closing in the kitchen. "What was that noise?"

Kim leaned over and looked in the kitchen. "We're still in here. You've got to go downstairs."

There was a mumble of a male voice.

She waved a manicured hand. "That's only Keith. He's grabbing a plate of food. He'll go in the basement to watch the football game. The Thoroughbreds are playing tonight."

That was good news. Now I could try to find out what was on the trailer.

Chapter Forty-One

Kim focused on the lady with the pink mask on. "Darlene, let's take off that mask. Ladies, her face is going to shine like a pearl. Hey, after this, y'all, we're going to play a game because I have a few more goodies to give away."

Several of the ladies hooted and clapped.

The makeup weighed like cake batter on my skin. I couldn't wait to get home and wash my face. I eased, unnoticed, into the kitchen and toward the back door. Across from the back door was the basement.

Watching the kitchen entryway, I grabbed the knob behind my back and slowly rotated it until it stalled, indicating it was locked. I fumbled with the lock. Boots clomped up the basement stairs.

I reached over, locked the basement door with one hand while unlocking the back door with my other. The basement knob jiggled as I opened the back door and slipped out. I shut the door, hearing Keith knock on the basement door.

I skittered diagonally across the yard to the garage, hoping no one saw me leave the house. I raced full speed to the garage, ducking inside. The garage smelled of oil and old grass. I was once again sneaking around in a garage. Maybe my life wasn't on the right track.

The tarp on the hitch trailer was pulled off and tossed in the corner, exposing the crates. Several of the crates had been stacked along the opposite wall. There was a black stamp on the boxes with four horses surrounded by a ring of laurel branches. The Four Wild Horses logo.

I tried to lift one of the crate lids on the stacked crates, but it was nailed down. I looked around the workbench for something to pop off the lid. The bench was a mess: tools, nuts, bolts, dirty rags, wrappers, empty cans. Finding a hammer, I wedged the claw under the lid and pulled. The nails gave a little and the wood cracked. I shifted the hammer claw and pulled again. It cracked open enough to peek inside. There it was, the embossed gold devil on the lid. There were several lids. My heart sank. "Oh, Keith," I muttered. "Poor Kim."

I pulled my phone out of my pocket and snapped pics of the crates. I sent them to Jimmy then tried to call. No answer. I grumbled and switched to text: **911. Found stolen bourbon. 3451 Green Grove, Miltonville. Hurry!** I needed to get the lid open wide enough to take a picture of the evidence.

A door closed and I heard a whistle. I peeked around the truck: Keith! Crap! I shoved my phone into my pocket, and threw myself in the dark corner behind a pile of boxes covered in oilcloth. Only a second after I settled, he stepped into the garage and began unloading the crates, stacking them around where I was hiding. He sang "Simple Man" by Lynyrd Skynyrd under his breath, humming over the words he didn't know.

I heard faint steps on gravel outside the garage. "What are you doing?" a female asked.

That wasn't Kim. That sounded like...I peeped around the edge of the oilcloth. *Holly?!*

"What does it look like?" He stacked a box near my hiding spot. I drew myself tighter.

"Why are these here? You should've moved them already."

"Well, I've been thinking." Keith pulled off his ball cap, scratched his head, and clapped the cap on. "It's stupid for us to sell all this to Burt really cheap when he'll sell it for way more."

That rubbed against what Linda told me. She'd said Burt gave the bottles away as gifts. I was beginning to question how well Linda knew her husband. I doubted she was involved in whatever he was doing. If she had been, she wouldn't have been so free with her information earlier. Burt was probably selling the bottles and pocketing the money without her knowledge. I eased my cell phone from my pocket, opened the voice recorder, and hit the red button.

"With the police sniffing around, we need to unload this stuff as fast as possible. We'll lay low for a while until things settle down."

"The way I figure, I put a lot on the line when I took care of Randall—"

"You did no such thing. You made it worse. Way worse. Because, now if we get caught, they'll charge us with murder instead of theft or fraud or whatever."

He killed Randall. Keith had killed Randall! I wanted to run, shouting it out across the neighborhood. Instead, I coiled my fear and anxiety inside myself and hid, wound as tight as a jack-in-the-box.

"It had to be done. He wanted us to stop everything after that Bryan guy died. Anyway, I've found us another buyer who'll pay a lot more than Burt. We'll cut Burt out. Imagine the money we'll make."

She hissed. "The money won't do us a bit of good if we're all in jail."

"I saw on the news that Dewey's been found."

"Yes. Sooner than I anticipated."

"How?"

"I don't know. I was careful."

"As long as you cleaned up anything that'd connect you, you'll be fine."

"Probably has something to do with that stupid Rook. I told Len to get rid of her, but he's weak."

"What does she know about any of this? She just started at the distillery."

"I don't know, but her friend is a deputy. Which is why we need to get rid of this and anything else connected to us." Holly paused. "She's here tonight. I don't want to take any chances. I thought for sure I'd finished her when I whacked her in the head. She's like a dang cat."

"Well…" He was silent for a moment. "I could arrange an accident for her tonight."

"Fine by me. But it'd better not even hint at a connection to the bourbon or our business."

"Which car is hers?"

"The green Fiesta."

"Eh. A little snip snip to the brake line and she's a memory. Or I could arrange a home invasion gone wrong."

Terror trickled like ice water down my spine. They were planning to kill me. This had to end now. If he went the home invasion route, that would put Prim in harm's way, too, and I couldn't allow that.

"Whatever," Holly said. "My biggest concern right now is getting this bourbon out to the barn. Tonight. The sheriff and his deputies are interviewing me and Len again tomorrow. You can't be far behind."

"No problem." Keith paused for a moment. "What I figure is Len is dead weight. What do you say you and I cut him out and keep the money for ourselves?"

Holly hesitated. "Let me think about it. For now, we're going to move the product and lay low."

"Alright."

"What time are you going out there?"

"About midnight. Kim's so liquored up she'll be passed out by then." Another pause. "The pre-game special is coming on."

He walked away, but Holly lingered. "Hey, it's me. We've got a job to do tonight out at the barn. Around one in the morning. Keith is taking all the crates out there around midnight." She listened then laughed. "Yeah. Right out from under his nose then we'll cancel him, too."

Chapter Forty-Two

My phone buzzed. Screaming internally, I moved carefully to silence the noise.

I was sure she heard it, but I hoped she couldn't locate it. I heard her leave the garage. I hoped she thought she was hearing things and was going back to the house.

After a few minutes, I eased out of my hiding spot like a snake shedding its skin. I flapped my shirt to dry the sweat that had formed on my back and under my arms during my time under the oilcloth. I was getting out of this place before Keith cut my brake lines. I tried to call Jimmy again, but he wasn't answering. I texted **911!!!!!**

Out of nowhere, Holly tackled me. Her powdery perfume signaled her identity before I recognized her face. I fell back against a crate, knocking the breath out of me, pain shooting through my ribs. I toppled to the ground, landing on my wrist. Pain electrified my arm. I cried out. My phone flew out of my other hand and slid across the floor. I rolled over and she jumped on top of me, grabbing my hair.

"You nosy... You've messed with the wrong woman..." She pounded my head against the concrete once.

That hurt. My head was still tender after being whacked in the head a couple days ago. I definitely didn't want any more knocks to the head. But she was strong.

Holly had hold of my ears and was about to pound my head again.

I grunted and pushed her face to the side with one hand, digging my nails into her skin. With the other hand, and guided by an intense survival instinct, I grabbed her boob and delivered a monstrous purple nurple.

She howled. "Let go! Let go!" She released her hold on me, and I pushed her away.

My head was swimming, and pain seared through my brain. My vision blurred and nausea rippled in my throat. I scrambled to get away, but she grabbed my foot and pulled me. My knee slammed against the concrete on top of a piece of gravel. A shard of pain stabbed into my knee. I cried out. She had a hold on my foot while she kicked, quite literally, my butt. I grabbed a broom lying by the lawnmower and half-turning, whacked and poked at her arm, face, hands, anything I could hit. She released her hold.

My phone buzzed as it lay about ten feet away. Praying it was Jimmy, I inched toward the phone while trying to fight off Holly.

She stood and charged me. I instinctively lifted my legs, catching her in the stomach. She stumbled and fell on her bottom. She righted herself and crawled toward me, her hazel eyes bright with rage. I kicked at her, knocking her in the chin. She took the shot, sneered, and flew at me. Man, she was tough. She should've made a career path in cage fighting instead of administration. She might've had a better outlet for her violent psychotic bent.

We tumbled backward and around together, landing on our sides.

"I hate you! Die! Die!" She clawed at me.

Her nails caught my right cheek, leaving a stinging line across my face. I pulled my head away from her reach. Grabbing her mass of curled hair, I jerked it forward then caught one of her hands in my mouth, biting down hard.

She wailed, releasing a slew of expletives to make the devil blush.

The phone fell silent. Still holding her hair and biting her, I worked my knees between us and pushed against her belly with all my strength. As I kneed her in the gut, I released her and rolled away. I had to forget the phone for now. Survival was most important. Pushing to my feet and swiping strands of Holly's hair off my hands, I backed away to run, knocking over a shovel propped against the workbench. Grabbing it, pain shot into my hand and arm, but I pushed through the pain. As Holly rolled around to her hands and knees to stand, I whacked her in the back of the head with the flat side. The metal spade rang out when it contacted her skull. She swayed and toppled to the ground, holding the wound, and groaning.

"How do you like them apples, missy?" I whacked her again for good measure. She fell forward on her face.

I needed something to tie her with because she'd be madder than a wet hen when she came around, and I didn't like my odds if we had to go another round. I also didn't want her getting away.

Grabbing a roll of duct tape from the workbench, I straddled Holly and pulled her arms behind her. Sirens wailed in the distance. Thank the heavens. My numb fingers had swollen thick, causing me to fumble with the tape edge at first. But I managed at last to tape her arms together at the wrists, making sure to include some of the forearms so the tiny hairs would be pulled out when the tape came off. She started cussing me again, so I taped her mouth, too, wrapping it all around her head to include her hair. It wasn't necessary, but she deserved it.

The sirens closed in then stopped. I stood, swaying as if drunk. Everything hurt: my head, my face, my knee, and my hand. My left hand and wrist throbbed and had begun to swell. Great. My fingers tingled when I wiggled them, but when I moved my thumb, pain darted through my fingers and arm. Sucking air through my teeth, I coddled my arm and used my foot to roll Holly over. She kicked and bucked and growled against the tape over her mouth. Her ferocious glare said everything I needed to know. She really did want me dead.

I stepped over her and picked up my phone. "Go ahead, hate me, you nasty jackal. When you're in jail for being a horrible human, I want you to remember I'm the one who put you there. And I'll be out here, free as a bird."

She wriggled and kicked at me, the force of her movement rolling her to her back like an overturned beetle.

Ignoring her, I shuffled out of the garage to a whirl of flashing blue and red lights. I squinted and blinked, shielding my eyes from the swirling lights. My stomach lurched and nausea gripped my throat. I was still dizzy.

Jimmy jumped out of the car, his gun drawn. When he recognized me, he lowered his weapon and hastened to me. "Rook, you all right?"

One hand on the side of the garage, I nodded. Then I vomited.

Chapter Forty-Three

"She's in there." I pointed at the garage with my good arm. "I've duct taped her."

A muffled squeal issued from the garage and a faint glimmer of humor lit Jimmy's eyes.

"I'm not at all surprised." His professional mask dropped back into place. "I'll see to her. You stand near my car."

He mumbled into the radio on his shoulder as he eased toward the garage, his gun aimed and ready. The neighbors began coming out of their houses to lean on their porch rails and watch the unfolding drama. Holly yowled inside the garage. Jimmy must've taken the tape off her mouth.

A faint creak like a storm door sounded to my left. I glimpsed Keith, peeking around the corner. He was looking at the garage, but he must not have noticed me. Maybe the lights blinded him, too. He started to sneak across the drive toward the neighbor's house. "Hey! Keith, you stop right there. Citizen's arrest!" I loped toward him, limping and holding my arm against my ribs, the adrenaline numbing my pain. I shouted, "Jimmy, Jimmy! He's getting away!"

I launched myself to jump on his back, but he zagged and I missed full contact. Instead, I grabbed his shirt as I slid down his right side. My death grip on his shirt pulled him off balance, and we both tumbled to the ground.

"Get off me, you stupid cow." He rolled and sat up.

I wrapped myself around his leg and held on like a monkey on a tree branch.

"Get off me!" He lifted his fist to hit me, but I ducked.

259

Wheels skidded to a halt in the gravel drive and a man and woman shouted in unison, "Freeze! Police!"

I dared to peek at them. It was Sheriff Goodman and Deputy Ladonna. Thank heavens!

I relaxed as Keith threw both hands in the air. He sighed heavily and muttered curses.

Deputy Ladonna approached with her gun pointed at me. Her round face pinched in concentration.

"It's me, Rook Campbell. Don't shoot."

"Oh." She looked closer and lowered her gun. "I didn't recognize you."

I stood and brushed off. "I'm going to be sick." No sooner than I'd stepped to the side, I spewed a pile of vomit. A heavy, dull ache, like rocks, filled my head.

"Are you okay?" Deputy Ladonna asked.

"I'm not sure."

An ambulance pulled in behind the sheriff's SUV, sirens off, lights flashing. "We'll have the paramedics take a look at you, okay?"

I let her escort me back to the ambulance. I looked around for Jimmy. He had removed the tape from Holly's arms and mouth and handcuffed her arms behind her back. As he walked her to his car, she was cursing and shouting, "Wait until my lawyer hears…" and "You're going to be in so much trouble…" and "You're making a big mistake, buddy…"

Her makeup was smudged, and her lips were raw and swollen, surrounded by a red rectangle of inflammation where the tape had been removed. Her hair stood out like big, bad hair from a 1980s yearbook.

The paramedic examined me. "Ma'am, looks like you might have a concussion and a broken wrist. You're going to need to go to the hospital and get checked out. Let's get you on a gurney."

The first thing to hit me was the idea of the bill. Ambulance rides and ER visits were expensive. "I can't."

The paramedic's mouth dropped open. "Ma'am, you could have serious injuries. You need to be checked out."

Sheriff Goodman approached, his voice booming. "Rook Campbell. Why am I not surprised you're tangled up in this? What kind of problems are you causing now?"

I was in no mood. "I'm not causing problems. In fact, y'all wouldn't have caught these meatheads if it hadn't been for me."

He glared at me, disbelieving, scratching his nose. "Now why don't you tell me all about what a clever little armchair detective you are?"

I told him everything, and he still wore a smug, unconvinced, smirk. "I'm going to look into this, and if you're lying…"

"Why would I lie?"

"I figure it runs in the family."

Relief washed through me when Jimmy arrived. "Let's get you to the hospital."

"Jimmy…" I gave him a pointed look. "I can't."

He brushed a strand of hair out of my face. His touch was electric. A warm tingle spread through my core. "No need to worry about any of that. It'll all work out."

Chapter Forty-Four

Cam set a glass of ginger ale on the table by my chair with a painkiller. "Take this."

I lowered my book about the Black Dahlia and did as I was told. "Thank you."

Cam gave Prim her medicine, too. He leaned on the back of her recliner, as the two of them shouted out answers to *Family Feud*. Prim's voice seemed a little weaker.

The front door was propped open, and the screen on the storm door lowered to allow the cool air in. The heatwave had lifted temporarily and a cool front was rolling in ahead of the storm darkening the horizon.

"It'll be storming soon," I said.

Cam looked over his shoulder at the door. "Yep. I should probably get going. Mom and Dad might need help getting the horses in before the storm hits." He sighed, stood straight, and stretched. "I've also got to get to the bar."

Prim was beginning to nod off in her recliner. Cam pulled an afghan from the couch and spread it over her tiny frame.

He whispered, "I guess you haven't had any luck convincing her to take chemo?"

I shook my head, biting the inside of my mouth to keep from crying. "Not yet."

Wriggling off the couch, I stood, my toes gripping the plush carpet for balance. The pain meds were kicking in, making my head swim. "I'll walk you out."

He smiled. "If you say so…"

The chimes in the corner of the back porch tinkled in the rising wind.

"You look like crap." Cam sniggered. "That woman did a number on you."

"You should see her."

He laughed. "Rook, if you need anything at all. I'm serious…anything."

I almost said, "Thanks, but no thanks." I changed my mind. Even without treatment, Prim's care would be expensive. Especially once hospice was required. But I continued to hope I might convince her to undergo chemo. If I was successful in persuading her, we'd need the money. Further, with all the trips to the doctor and the ER recently, we were quickly going to deplete our savings. I still had my job at the distillery, but I needed more money. "Well, once I'm healed, I might take you up on the offer to let me work at the bar part-time, if it still stands."

He raised a hand. "You do whatever you can, when you can. We'll figure it out as we go." He squeezed my arm and kissed my cheek.

It was delightfully familiar and struck a chord of yearning in my gut. Part of me wanted him back. A teeny mustard seed part. But too much had happened, and I wasn't sure I wanted him back for the right reasons. Did I want him because I still loved him and wanted to be with him or was I only wanting the safety and comfort of something familiar? I wanted to be sure we truly loved each other and that we'd both learned how to be good partners. Otherwise, I couldn't go through it all with him again. With such uncertainty, friendship proved the safest route to happiness.

Prim slept through supper and a raging thunderstorm while I ate a quiet no-prep meal of a ham and cheese sandwich and Cheetos in front of the television. A strong afternoon sun splashed across the living room floor, sparkling in water drops on the leaves. I'd opened the door again after the storm, letting the rain-freshened air into the room.

A black Silverado pulled into the drive. Jimmy. I didn't want to wake Prim, so I tiptoed into the kitchen and out the back door, quietly closing the door behind me. I stepped off the porch and met Jimmy in the rain-drenched, plush bluegrass.

He filled out a distressed gray T-shirt and faded jeans nicely. "Hey there."

He removed his sunglasses and hooked them on the neck of his shirt. "I came by to check on you. Make sure you're okay." He looked me over. "You look kind of rough."

"Thanks. I'm good. Aching in a few places, but I'll be back to normal soon. I'd invite you in, but..." I motioned toward the house with my bandaged arm. "Prim's sleeping."

"We can sit on the porch, if you don't mind."

"Nah, I don't mind at all. It's a nice evening."

I offered him tea, but he refused with an assurance he wasn't going to keep me long. We sat in the rocking chairs. The chimes jingled a welcome and the wind offered up a heady mélange of hay, wet grass, and honeysuckle.

He said, "I wanted to check on you, first off. But I also wanted to let you know you were right."

"About what?"

"About all of it. We got Holly Parker and Keith Tilkey to confess to everything."

"Is that so?" I draped a leg over the arm of the rocker and rocked my chair with one foot. "Turns out Keith killed Randall because he wouldn't help out with stealing the bourbon and reselling it behind Len's back. Keith, Randall, and Len were all in on it together. They'd been stealing a few bottles at a time here and there and selling to Burt for two, three times the cost. Burt kept some and sold some for a profit."

"And Holly?"

"You were right about her, too. She helped to steal bottles and to fudge the inventory numbers. However, she didn't realize Bryan had receipts and records that weren't balancing with the inventory numbers. When he began to get suspicious about the books, Holly killed him."

"Did you determine the poison she used?"

"Yeah. It was English Yew. She boiled it down, made a tincture out of it, and put it in his tumbler."

I beamed at Jimmy. "Maybe I should call Sheriff Goodman and tell him 'I told you so'?"

He laughed, dimples in his cheeks. "I wouldn't recommend it. He doesn't like to be wrong."

"He'd better get used to it. Because, one of these days, I'm going to prove him wrong about my mother's murderer, too."

"Well, if the wrong man truly was convicted, I hope you do."

Silence dipped between us.

Looking out across the gold-tinted yard, I sighed. "I guess you arrested Len, too?"

"Definitely. It was his idea from the beginning. But Holly and Keith got greedy, as often happens when large amounts of money are involved, and they started making plans of their own. But Len and Keith were fools. They didn't realize Holly was double-dealing both of them. In the end, she was making preparations to be a very free and wealthy woman. She was laying plans to rid herself of Keith, Len, and her husband."

"Wow. She's a piece of work."

"You've got that right."

I realized I'd forgotten someone. "What about Dewey? Who killed him?"

"Keith. Dewey had been helping them steal and hide the bourbon. He began to insist they include him in the profits, but they felt he couldn't be trusted. So, he threatened to expose them."

"I bet that's why he and Randall were fighting not long before Dewey's body was found."

He shrugged. "Probably."

"What about Burt Anderson? Did you get him? He was buying a bunch of the bourbon."

"Yeah. We got him and four other people buying stolen bourbon."

"Did Holly admit to trying to run me off the road?"

"Yep." He leveled a steady gaze at me; his hazel eyes turned down slightly at the corners, like a puppy's. "She actually wanted you dead."

I lay my head against the back of the rocker and stared at the ceiling fan. Spiderwebs floated around the blades. I still had one question left unanswered. "What about Clarence? What's going to happen to him?"

Jimmy shook his head. "He's a crook, but he's not connected to this case." He stretched his muscular legs out in front of him and crossed his dusty cowboy boots at the ankles. "I guess I'll arrest him tomorrow. I like to do it early in the morning around five or six, right as the sun is rising and the air is fresh. Let the criminals sleep through the night, thinking they're safe." Slowly, he cut his hand through the air. "I swoop in on them and grab them. They never see me coming."

I thought about Saturday morning, around dawn. The early risers would be getting their coffee, scanning the newspaper for yard sales. Or sitting in their pajamas, watching the news, eating breakfast. Fishermen would be out already, boats quietly drifting on the lake. I imagined Clarence would be sitting at the kitchen table in a tank top and boxers, sipping coffee, reading the newspaper. Maybe his wife would be frying some eggs and bacon. The knock would sound on the door...

"You okay?" Jimmy asked. "You look annoyed or something."

I laughed. "Oh, I'm fine. That's my thinking face. I always look like that."

He laughed. "Are you healing okay?"

"Yeah." I displayed my bandaged arm. "This thing itches like the devil. But..." I sighed.

"At least it's only a sprain. It could've been worse."

"Oh, I know. They were planning on killing me." I rubbed the tender spots on the back of my head.

"All the way to the station, Holly insisted she was going to kill you first chance she got."

I blinked. "Better keep her in jail, then." I tried to smile. "Make sure she gets a hefty sentence."

He clapped a hand on my knee. "I'll do my best." He paused and leaned forward. His gaze locked on mine with intense focus. "I've got your back, Rook." His gaze lingered for a moment and drifted to my lips. Then he stood. "I'd better go. I'm sure you'll be called at some point to give testimony."

"I figured as much." I walked with him back to his truck. "Thanks for coming by."

His gaze lingered over my face. "So what are you going to do now, Nancy Drew?"

"Ha. Ha." I playfully slapped his bicep. It was hard as a brick. "You're soooo funny."

Humor lit his eyes. "Seriously."

I shrugged. "Work at Four Wild Horses Distillery. Learn everything I can about the bourbon business. Start trying to pay off a mountain of school loans. Help Prim. Maybe start trying to find out who killed my mom."

He tipped his head, intrigued. "Oh? After all this time?"

"Yeah. This thing with Bryan's murder kind of called up some stuff for me. Memories. Unanswered questions. And with Prim being sick, it'd be nice if I could give her some truth about mom's death, some closure."

"All noble things." His eyes scanned the yard. "But it sounds like all you're going to do is various forms of work. Don't you want to have any kind of fun?"

"Like what?"

His tongue darted over his lips as he tucked his hands in his back pockets and rocked back and forth on his heels. "Like maybe you'd want to go out with me sometime?"

The painkillers clouded my mind. Jimmy was good-looking and exactly my type, but his friendship with Cam had closed off any romantic feelings I might've entertained about him. "Where do you want to go?"

Confusion flitted over his face as a slow smile bloomed on his lips. "I mean, on a date. With me."

I blinked. "Oh, uh…" I had to put Cam behind me at some point. I couldn't go my whole life lingering in limbo between an attachment to Cam and the rest of my life. That was no way to live. I needed to see if there was happiness on the other side.

He put up his hands. "I'm sorry. I understand. I shouldn't've—"

"Hold on. What about Cam?"

"I'll talk to him. I'm sure he'll understand. I figured I'd ask you first. Otherwise, it was pointless to speak with him. But, I mean, you guys have been divorced for a year."

"A year and six months."

A corner of his mouth ticked upward. "I was thinking dinner at Bolton's and maybe a movie?"

I lifted a brow. "Depends. What movie?"

His answer to that question was of the utmost importance.

He said, "Not sure. You decide."

I smiled at him. It was the perfect answer.

Acknowledgements

Thank you, God, for the gift. (Proverbs 3:6)

There are so many people a writer meets on her journey who are essential to the creation of a single work. I want to thank my agent Dawn Dowdle with Blueridge Literary Agency and my editor, Shawn Simmons, and the talented team at Level Best who helped bring this book to life. To the Cops & Writers Facebook group, you've been an invaluable resource.

Thank you also to readers of the early drafts who provided important feedback: Brack Benningfield, Shannon Powers, Erin Scoggins, and Joe Bursinkas. And an extra special thank you to Carmen Erickson. I'm so thankful God brought our paths together.

My deepest gratitude always belongs with friends and family. This isn't an exhaustive list of the people important to my writing journey, but it's a start:

To my mom and best friend, Mildred Pierce, who provided me with my first books, thereby opening many worlds and igniting my imagination.

My dad, Don Smith, for telling me I could do anything I set my mind to. It's the greatest gift you've given me.

My brother, Chadd Smith, for showing me what's possible. I'm so proud of you.

Anthony Pierce, I'm a better person for having you in my life.

Richard Benningfield, I miss you and wish you were here.

Betty Benningfield your enthusiasm has been uplifting and encouraging.

Also love and gratitude to Hatice and Aden Smith; The Miller family, with a special mention of Bonnie Miller who encouraged my writing early on; Meg, John, Anne, and Ben Blevins; John, Jackie, Drew, and Emily Benningfield. Shannon Powers, Carmen Erickson, Freddie Smith, Bill Ekhardt, Eran

Bosley, Melissa Holt, Amorina Stone, Chris McCabe, Bonnie Coy, Sharon Brown, Charlotte Downs, and Sylvia Meinlschmidt.

To everyone here, and anyone I might've neglected to mention, the gift of your love, friendship, encouragement, and support have been more valuable and precious than rubies. I'm grateful to have you all in my life.

About the Author

Michelle Bennington was born and raised among the rolling hills and lush bluegrass of Kentucky. Her early and avid love of books inspired her desire to write, and has developed into a mild book-hoarding situation and an ever-expanding To Be Read pile. She currently resides in central Kentucky where she spins tales of mystery and intrigue in contemporary and historical settings. Aside from reading and writing, she enjoys a wide range of arts and crafts, touring old homes, attending ghost tours, baking with various degrees of success, and spending time with her family and friends.

SOCIAL MEDIA HANDLES:
   Facebook: https://www.facebook.com/michellebenningtonauthor
   Twitter: @MichelleAuthor
   Instagram: https://www.instagram.com/michelle.bennington.author/
   Pinterest: https://www.pinterest.com/michellebenningtonauthor/_saved/
   Goodreads: https://www.goodreads.com/user/show/4055592-michelle-bennington

AUTHOR WEBSITE:
   https://www.michellebennington.com/